USHER

MATTHEW CONDON

USHER

University of Queensland Press

First published 1991 by University of Queensland Press
Box 42, St Lucia, Queensland 4067 Australia

Typeset by University of Queensland Press
Printed in Australia by The Book Printer, Victoria

This is a work of fiction and all characters depicted are fictitious.

Cataloguing in Publication Data
National Library of Australia

Condon, Matthew, 1962-
  Usher.

  I. Title.

A823.3

ISBN 0 7022 2401 4

For Marsha Pope
my twin sister
with love and admiration

. . . the greatest and the most bitter mystery in my life was my father. It was he who invited an abortionist for dinner. It was he who was discovered drunken, debauched and naked but for a string of champagne corks. He was the drunken old man in the roller coaster when I thought he had drowned himself and he was the old man reading Shakespeare sonnets to the cat. I was determined not to lose that sense of locus that I would have lost if I dismissed him as a tragic clown. I persevered, I may have done no more, but it is all part of a chain of being and when you have sons, as you will, it will be easier to comprehend.

John Cheever

Acknowledgments

I am grateful to my family and friends, particularly to my parents, Karen and Ron Condon, for incalculable support; and to Georgia Savage, Rosie Fitzgibbons and Judy MacDonald.

The prologue to "Usher" was first published in *Harper's Bazaar* Australia, summer 1989. A portion has also appeared in *Australian Short Stories*.

The epigraph is taken from one of John Cheever's letters, reproduced in part in *Home before Dark* by Susan Cheever (Boston: Houghton Mifflin, 1984).

Extensive use was made of Ross Fitzgerald's excellent two-volume work, *A History of Queensland: From the Dreaming to 1915* and *From 1915 to the 1980s* (St Lucia: University of Queensland Press, 1982 and 1984).

My thanks to the Literature Board of the Australia Council, the Australian government's arts funding and advisory body, for grants given to assist the writing of this novel.

PROLOGUE

After my father disappeared into the ocean I arranged for an ice sculpture of his head to be made for his wake.

He had made me promise about the head years before, after he saw carved angels with trumpets on a smorgasbord table at an automobile convention. Often he would recall the beauty of the angels, their wings rosy with the reflection of crab meat.

Even as the sculptor went to work on his unusually thick eyebrows, his bulging eyes, broad forehead and thinning hair, I expected my father to return from the sea. For him to stand, shivering, before my mother, as she separated the damp and tangled fringes of his usher's epaulettes. For him to brush fragments of seaweed from his coat, flick a seahorse off his lapel, and go back to work.

"What time is it anyway?" he would ask, shaking his wristwatch. "Have I missed the evening session?"

My father, T. Nelson Downs, JP, amateur magician, botanist, and owner and head usher of the Universe-Cine-by-the-Sea, had vanished that day during the matinee screening of *Twenty Thousand Leagues Under the Sea*. As Kirk Douglas descended to confront the evil Captain Nemo, my father was skipping across a cluster of basalt boulders at the end of Burleigh Heads beach.

To those who knew the usher, this was not unusual. Whenever he saw Spencer Tracy battling the great marlin he would go home and clean his rod, reel and creel. The boxing classic *Body and Soul* was responsible for the Everlast punching bag hanging in his orchid hothouse. He even took up smoking a pipe during a Sherlock Holmes festival.

Knowing he was not due back until *The Great Gatsby*, he hopped from rock to rock with his hands in his pockets, noting his reflection in the pools of coloured stone, shell, transparent

1

fish, and miniature lawns of vivid green moss, and simply slipped into the ocean.

Two elderly bathers, forced from the waves by a herd of jellyfish, found his upturned silk pillbox hat on the sand, and inside it some torn orange matinee tickets and a small black torch. They reported their suspicious find to a lifesaver. He, in turn, waited until dusk, watching the hat from his elevated booth. Then he called the police, and within the hour a thin yellow crime scene tape encircled my father's belongings. Some people stopped to look inside the circle.

I know of this tape and how ordinary things — bread and butter knives, bricks, wood, underwear, shoelaces, even food scraps — become something else in crime. They suddenly develop a peculiar glow, a preciousness.

The yellow tape had transformed my father's moth-nibbled cap into the evidence of tragedy.

I remember I was sitting at the rear upstairs window of my rented townhouse waiting for my neighbour to take her evening spa. The bath was embedded in the centre of her small backyard, surrounded by paving stones and plants. I had seen her twice the week before, naked and alone in the bubbling water, gazing into the bird's nest ferns and staghorns, or upward, through the wire of her clothesline to the sky. Sometimes, she would rest her head on the lip of the bath, and close her eyes.

My Uncle Sidney, who had not spoken to our family for nine years, telephoned to tell me that my father was missing and presumed drowned.

"Trust me, son, it must have been quick," he said. "If you could see the king tides at the moment, you'd understand. For sure. Hey, long time no see. How is it, big reporter in the big city, hey?"

I didn't even recognise his voice. All I could remember of him was his dyed mustard hair, and the trays of cheap silver echidnas, koalas and kangaroos of his mail-order jewellery business, their stomachs heavy with fragments of opal.

I still have an old book of postcards he once gave me — *Souve-*

2

nir de Toulon — filled with painted boulevards, docks, theatres, large-wheeled prams, umbrellas, and men and women, all in bright pastels. The shirts, trousers and dresses of the holidaymakers are slightly removed from the black outlines of their bodies, as if they are strolling with their souls as companions.

"And I'll tell you something else," said Sid, above the sigh of the surf. "The police say his torch had been left on."

"His usher's torch?"

"Yep. They said they detected a faint glow from the filament. Isn't that just like your old man? Eh?"

"You don't know that he's dead yet."

"Honestly, if you could see the sea, son. It's rough out there."

I wondered if my neighbour had come out yet and chased away the cats that occasionally drank her spa water.

"Your mother's down on the beach. She's okay, really. Upset, obviously."

She was sitting next to the circle of tape, he told me. They had taken away the usher's belongings and sealed them in plastic bags. Crying, my mother had asked them to leave the tape for a while. She touched shoe craters in the sand, still warm from the police arc light on a tripod.

"I'm standing in the foyer and I can see her. She's all right. Maybe you should think of coming up, son."

He was silent for a moment, and then said: "Hey, love to catch up with you soon. You married yet? Plenty of women, eh? You don't have to tell me.

"Oh, we had to cancel *Gatsby*."

It was late and the woman had still not appeared. Looking into her yard I thought of the stories my father often told me of the Oceanic Baths at Burleigh, where he used to swim when he was a boy on holidays, and the mermaids there.

"If the sea was rough the whole pool would be choppy and sway along with it," he would recall. "It was right there, just beyond the fence, crashing in over the rocks. You could feel those big currents hitting the concrete, really. Swear to God.''

When the developers destroyed the old baths with explosives, my father closed the Universe for three days. For a long time he did not speak about it, but later, during our rare evenings of port and panatellas, he described the fall of the pavilion's columns and the dislodging of the pool's shell from the earth. How men drilled holes in the mermaid-shaped pylons at the front of the baths, and filled them with gelignite.

''It was rape,'' my father said, whispering the last word. ''They drilled into their vaginas, for a joke I guess. Put explosives into those beautiful women. Blew them to smithereens.''

Fragments of sandstone mermaid flew out into the face of waves — locks of hair, scales, a breast, ears, fingers and small fins.

''I hate this age of explosives,'' he always added solemnly at the end of his story.

Charlie, the delicatessen man on the corner, told me of my neighbour.

''Such a beautiful woman, eh, but always alone in the spa,'' he said one evening, preparing his meatloaf for the next day's trade. ''So many people have been in there, hundreds, maybe thousands. But she, always alone. She has a light in her too, that spa. I put it in. She looks like that Liza Minnelli, yes?''

Charlie would invite me behind the counter for coffee, and tell me of his family, and the old lady proprietor before him who electrocuted herself when her new food warmer had been incorrectly wired, and the history of my house.

''You know yours and her place were both brothels?''

''I wondered about the wall of mirrors,'' I said.

''Under the stairs? That was the office. Yours and hers was the one big brothel.''

And there had been the man who had come to my screen door, months after I had moved in.

''This it?'' he said, speaking through the flywire.

''Pardon?''

4

"Is this it?"

"I'm sorry? Is this what?"

"Come on, you know."

"What?"

"Come on. Let me in."

Charlie told me that I once had a red spa also.

"Where your kitchen is," he said. "That's funny, eh, you walking all over that floor where the hundreds had been, thousands. I put the tiles in there when we took her out. Over the hole."

Charlie lived above his delicatessen. He had a small bedroom at the rear, and a front room full of pinball machines. Sometimes, when he entertained his male friends, he would switch on all the machines in the dark, illuminating Vikings, naked women brandishing swords, space travellers and reptiles, and their bells would keep me awake.

"And in your bedroom," Charlie said. "That's where the doorway was, into your Liza's house. I filled that in.

"Some nights the madam would let me look through the peephole. I drilled that. I seen my bank manager there. True. Wrapped in plastic, eh, like the stuff I wrap the cheeses in. Eh, you want some meatloaf?"

The spa light was on, but there was still no sign of her.

I wondered how Sid had come to be in the foyer of the Universe so quickly, the cap still roped off on the sand. The last I heard was that he had married on Fraser Island. Just Sid, his bride — a sixteen-year-old factory worker from Thailand whose job, I had been told down the line, was to sweep up fragments of silver bevelled or buffed off the bodies of my uncle's animals — and a celebrant. The wedding had taken place on the rusted bow of a stranded container ship.

Sid had always avoided family occasions — the engagements, the births, illnesses — but now had appeared in his usual cream suit, a baby orchid in his buttonhole, and wearing, on the little finger of his left hand, a ring made of a penny fashioned into the shape of a military slouch hat.

"It is like that," Charlie told me before I headed north. "My father, he too drowned in Malta. A flood knocked a wall out from

5

under him, eh. Came from nowhere. Bang, he's gone. I fly home to my mother and brothers and everybody is there, the cousins, the children, the dogs, everybody, sleeping everywhere. On the stairs. In the garden. Some I never met before.

"With the wedding or the baby there is nothing for them. With the death there is the money."

At midnight, with my father somewhere out to sea, still dressed in his maroon usher's suit with its thick gold buttons and black cummerbund, she walked to the spa in a towel. She put a wine glass on the paving and flinched in the cold. Steam lifted from the heated spa water.

My neighbour removed her towel but I could not see her clearly through the tattooed rain stains of my window, and my tears.

Her white body wavered amongst the hands of her ferns. Gently, she eased herself into the water.

Since taking over the old cinema, thoughts of death had come to the usher. Aged exactly a half-century, he had even chosen how he wanted to die: sitting on one of the refurbished red leather seats in the centre of the Universe-Cine-by-the-Sea, a Wee Willem cigar in his right hand, his feet up on the seat in front of him, and his head back, looking into the galaxies of pinpoint lights in the ceiling.

He would prefer his heart to explode suddenly, for there to be a buzz, undetectable to the human ear, and for him to be blacked out like a filament popping in one of his precious roof bulbs.

The first thing he noticed on leasing the cinema was the disrepair of the concave roof and its huge, flaking prewar ribs. Without considering feasibility or cost he ordered more than twelve hundred light bulbs and employed a team of electricians to install them.

"You want a what?" the head electrician said on the telephone.

"Galaxies," my father said, as if he was purchasing a cake or a floral arrangement. "A universe, in the roof."

6

"Are you kidding me?"

"No, no, not at all. There used to be one in Brisbane, when I was a kid. Like hundreds of stars."

They began work, and my father shouted instructions to them from the cinema's central aisle. Several men dangled from the main roof beam in specially made canvas harnesses.

"You up there, yes you!" he yelled. "Make it swirl a bit on the end. Swirrrl!

"And you! Put a tail on that bunch. The smaller bulbs. Use the smaller ones for the tail, do you hear me?"

The electricians only picked up fragments of his dialogue in their fear, having never installed star formations, distant planets, moons. They carried bulbs in belts, as shooters carry bullets, and occasionally dropped a spanner or screwdriver into the empty seating.

It took ten days to put my father's artificial universe in place. As planned, it gave off just enough light for patrons to find their way amongst the seats.

"You should see it," he told me. "You can make out anything you like in it. Animals, objects, anything. Better than the real thing, I tell you, because it's always there, clear as a bell. Just seeing it come together and actually work. It's magic. Magic. Your old man knows how God must have felt, no joke."

He told me the lights had been placed randomly, some clustered and others in the far corners of the great curved roof, built without respect for the charts of scholars or centuries of work. My father's theory was that if the bulbs were of varying size and wattage, it would create, for the seated patron, the illusion of distance. The hundred-watt stars would come out at you they were so close, while the forty-watt specks twinkled, light years away.

The usher knew it had been a success when, walking through the aisles before a main feature, trailing the beam of his torch, he saw a child point to the roof and say: "There's the Saucepan!" or heard an older patron muse: "That has got to be Orion."

As head usher of the Universe-Cine-by-the-Sea, he knew he only had a moment to work the magic of the roof. When the projectors started rolling, his chance had gone. He would flick the universe switch, already filthy with ticket ink from his fingers,

7

and the roof would fade into blackness. He noted that moths swooping between the imitation stars dropped instantly to the blue movie beam and weaved through its gangsters, cowboys, travellers, swimmers, gladiators, spies, horses, skyscrapers, bridges and trucks, and later, a nipple or bare limb. Even with the roof switched on, he knew, the projector light was too dense to see through to the stars.

My father was at times fastidious about many aspects of his life, and careless with others. He was what I called an atmosphere person. His usher's suit was genuine 1950s, rescued from the wardrobes of the West End Mecca in Brisbane. At Christmas he played Bing Crosby on the stereo. He only played bocce on the front lawn if he had chianti in the house.

"Am I really like that?" he said when I presented my theory. "Do you think? I don't know. When I drink my chianti and play my bocce I'm in Italy, aren't I? Quick as that. Across the other side of the world."

He applied this logic to the Universe cinema but on a much larger scale. Later, I realised he had come to understand a form of pattern in his life, as meandering and disjointed as this graph might have been. He told my mother he wanted to get back to the source of errors: in judgment, in his behaviour, even towards me. Back to the road's forks, he would have said.

"The cinema," he said, "means a lot to me. I want to give people a bit of wonder again. If they want to go to Paris, or to the casino in Monte Carlo, or the Austrian Alps, or someone else's house, whatever, they come and see me. I can take them there.

"I courted your mother in one of these things. It was the only place we could be alone, even when it was packed to the rafters, you understand? Bit of wonder. Wonder — do you really know what I mean by that?"

At times, however, the usher's enthusiasm eroded his purpose. He decorated the foyer of the Universe with the junk of several eras. It was crowded with enough memorabilia to fit out a dozen movie houses. The chandeliers were so large that their refracted light stretched through the front glass doors and onto the beach, revealing a trace of surf. It was said that even the trawlermen could see the burning foyer as they headed out to sea, and

8

used it as a navigational aid, and a marker for the best prawn sweeps. He covered the floor and stairs in swirling burgundy and mustard carpet, and the walls with angled art deco mirrors.

"You don't like them?" he asked me. "I'll tell you something. Gentleman was in here the other night at the candy bar and saw the back of a woman in one of the mirrors. Thought she was gorgeous. Look at that, he said. Winked. Found out it was his own wife. What do you think of that then?"

He painted gold every bannister, door edge and runner board. He fitted old pink and blue powder room signs above the toilet doors. Behind the snack bar was a brass cash register and advertisements for chocolates and cigarettes that had not been manufactured for decades.

He, the head usher, stood at the foot of the giant twin staircase that embraced the ticket office like the gold-plated claws of a crab. He always wore his maroon suit and, at his side, attached by a short chain to his belt loop, was a torch. In his left vest pocket he carried spare bulbs, and in his right, batteries.

To enhance the atmosphere he wore his hair heavily oiled and parted just off-centre. Those he escorted to the upper stalls would perhaps recognise his scent, once synonymous with the daily wearing of hats, or antimacassar coverlets, and notice the dated trim of his moustache.

"A good evening to you both," he would say to the upstairs patrons, taking their tickets with his left hand, the right kept behind his back.

"It's a pleasure to see you again. Haven't seen either of you since, when was it, *The Beast with a Million Eyes*? I trust you'll enjoy this evening's feature."

He never tore the more expensive upper stall tickets. It was his sign of trust in those who had paid more for the cloth seats with springs, to be closer to his magnificent universe. From the stalls, built on a downward angle towards the screen, it was possible to see the full arc of the bulbs.

I have stood there, at the rear curtain, and heard them play my father's game.

"Good clear night tonight, Mr Downs," one would say. "You could see for miles on a good clear night like tonight."

9

"Indeed."

And another: "There has to be life out there somewhere, don't you think, Mr Downs? I'll never forget those bright lights, violet coloured they were, I'd have to say they were violet, hovering over Samford. All together, they were, like a squadron. Do you suppose they have squadrons like us, Mr Downs?"

"Highly possible."

Sometimes, when he turned off the universe after a session, a bulb would pop. He said he could always instinctively feel if one of his stars was missing, and would go to the centre seat after closing time and scour the constellations with his horse racing binoculars.

"Got it," he would say to himself, red rings circling his eyes. "Another one. Damn."

He mentioned the problem to my mother.

"How in God's name are you going to replace those things?" she asked.

He agreed it would be ridiculous to hire a man to replace them one by one, to have someone rigged, like a mountaineer with ropes and safety lines, clawing across the face of the universe in search of a broken filament. At the same time, my father theorised, such a man would have to carry the fragile new bulb on his journey, keep it intact and even protect it as one would an irreplaceable object of history.

"Ludicrous," he said. "It's a worry, certainly. A genuine worry."

"Then what are you going to do about it?" my mother asked again. "You can't have them popping all over the place."

"I don't know. I'd hate black holes to appear. That'd be a disaster. It would frighten the kiddies. Maybe their parents."

He went away with the problem, contacted experts at the light bulb company, consulted electricians, powerhouse workers and even the engineering faculty at the university in Brisbane. Then he made some calculations.

"We have nothing to fear," he declared to my mother some weeks, and another bulb, later. "With a total replacement every five years we stand to lose eleven bulbs per year, maximum, for the next thirty years.

"You see? The universe could not possibly disappear in our lifetime."

My father couldn't be dead because I didn't really know him yet. I studied photographs of him, and traced every rollercoaster loop of his handwriting.

I imagined him being pulled out to sea by a current threaded with swiftly moving seaweed, jellyfish bulbs, strengthless fish and the occasional matches, bottles and sandshoes of fishermen.

I called to him: Do not panic, Father! Tread water, like you taught me years ago. I know you've been rowing in the lounge room back home on that strange machine of springs and rollers, but you aren't fit, not nearly, you know that. Don't panic! Form a star with your body. Spread your arms and legs wide to conserve energy.

By nightfall I presumed he had lost his fear of sharks, and of stingrays, and was smiling, with hope, at the distant helicopter and its thick blue searchlight probing the troughs and crowns of the waves. He would be comforted by the beam, and maybe wonder, for an instant, if someone had turned off his usher's torch back in the hat.

Of course, yes, my father is fine now. This sort of thing does not happen to people like us. Without realising it, he has been picked up by another current running parallel to the one that claimed him. At some stage the star-shaped usher has entered the focal point of the currents, been turned around and shunted back to shore.

His star is a little closed now, but the usher is breathing comfortably, floating beneath the nylon lines of several rock fishermen. Inching up Tallebudgera Creek they see him, an epauletted man in the glow of their kerosene lanterns. They bring him in with a hand net.

He could not be missing. I don't know you yet, Father. I never even considered death.

"Come and help us down here, will you?" I can hear someone yelling. "We've caught ourselves a frigging admiral."

1

I will tell you everything that I know.

Only the facts. The fragments of information exactly as I receive them, or as they occur to me. Precise. Verbatim. They say in my profession that if you go through life and get just one big story, one so monumental that it is always remembered, then you are lucky. This is mine.

I have no time to waste. If the trail goes cold, and I do not begin while there is still light coming off objects and places and people, then it will be lost. Memories can be short.

I neglected many opportunities, I can tell you. I had him there, alive, breathing (albeit in short puffs), going about his daily routines, able to be tapped on the shoulder, faced over a thimble of port and spoken to at any time. I could have observed him working, that dumpish shadow trailing a thin beam of light, guiding strangers safely down stairs, or across legs and chair arms, to their seats. Illuminating troublemakers and romantics in the back rows.

Let's start. Let's take careful notes, and listen, and get it right. Let's speak to as many people as we can, and reveal what actually happened, and not just what we are told.

There is one thing you will not get me to admit — that he is dead. If and when you produce a body — or even a foot, hand, or ear — then, perhaps, I will concede that he won't be coming back. But without that evidence, he will always be alive for me.

I prefer to think of him sailing around the world, abreast a lost shipping container full of exquisite Italian furniture, or a tonne of coconuts lashed together with rope, or, even better, as captain of a teak vessel that quietly slipped its moorings in Madras. At worst, hitching a ride on dolphins, whales, or driftwood, and travelling as nature dictates.

It is travel, he told me, cut free from the tiny pyramid of your family, your own people, your country, that reveals to you your place in the world.

Listen to him. This, from a man who never left this island of ours. Not once. A man who sold motor cars but could not drive those with manual gears. Who rode a bicycle three times in his life, and crashed it twice.

He almost got the quote right. I have sourced it and, as Michel de Certeau said, not of coconuts and containers of lampshades but window and rail, this cutting off from the world not only produces unknown landscapes but the strange fables of our private stories.

But this is what he was like. The man's vocabulary was an ingenious amalgam of movie scripts, snatches of lyrics, newspaper gossip snippets, advertising jingles and old jokes. He could pull out a line, a ditty, an obscure fact, to match any circumstance. I'll give that to him. He had perfect, totally perfect, timing.

I'll tell you what happened. The great reporter, upholder of truth and champion of the code of ethics, witness to murder, to slashed throats, headless drivers, political rhetoric, lies, deceit and corruption, took a flight north when the usher of the Universe disappeared. A journey homeward to share grief and stare at the horizon from the beach as one would at a killer.

He picked up his bags off the snaking conveyor belt, stepped out into the humid, tropical evening of his place of birth, untroubled by small tornadoes of bug and mosquito, almost gladdened by the distant television towers of his childhood window, and ran away. Left the country. Vanished.

Like father, like son, you might say. But could you have faced it? I doubt it. Not with a father somewhere out to sea, and a mother wailing louder than the crash of waves on basalt. Not with a government in crisis, the one that had shaped you, that you had worked under, that had fooled you and destroyed your family, being dissected in a small courtroom only a clock chime away from the City Hall.

No, no. I would like to have seen you in that predicament. You may not agree with the way I handled it all, but that's how it happened. It's not out of character. We have always been a family of extremes. My missing father, for Christ's sake, spent a

13

good deal of his early years trying to carve farm animals out of ice cubes. I kid you not. My mother too, you may not be aware, was a stripper in the days when they still called them exotic dancers. I have black and white postcards bearing her image — a blowzy Cleopatra with a cheap jewel in her bellybutton — if you don't believe me. Then there is my uncle, who still earns his living selling grotesque, Taiwanese-made symbols of our nation; flora and fauna crudely fashioned into cheap jewellery. You may have one of his brooches or tiepins yourself.

So, equipped with two changes of underclothes, a spare pair of trousers, three T-shirts and a pair of socks, as well as notebook, biro and credit card, I circumnavigated the world.

Exactly twenty-eight minutes after take-off, at roughly nine thousand metres above the Tasman Sea, I began taking notes for what would become the obituary of my father. I did not know it then, of course, and this was not me conceding death. In newspaper offices around the world most notable people's obituaries are written in advance and filed while they are very much alive, awaiting the moment of death.

There is always a chance with my father. For example, many years after he disappeared I thought I saw him on the television, sitting in the third row, below the scoreboard at the Wimbledon tennis championships. He looked in great shape: a charcoal grey suit, immaculate white shirt buttoned to the top and fashionable sunglasses. I would have pointed him out to my mother, but he had an attractive young woman seated to his right, putting the straw of her drink to his mouth.

Technically, then, my work was not a bona fide obituary, but the word suits my purpose. It is an attractive one, irresistible. That much I learned from my craft as a daily witness to history.

It was he, actually, who first suggested the word to me, over and over near the end.

"Every life," he said, in that high-pitched voice of his, "each and every one, deserves an obituary."

It was a strange thing to say, for sure, but that was him. He was a sensitive old bastard, if nothing else.

Father, do you remember when I was a child I tried to write a

14

history of the world? It was only twenty-three pages long, with diagrams of explorers, generals, slaves, galleons, clay gourds, lizards and maps in black ink.

I still have it, and wonder why a boy of ten years would try and write the history of man. If you remember, I simply copied it from other works and crudely pieced it together. I didn't do too badly, summarising our progress to the turn of the century in so few pages.

It came to me again as I placed the hot airline towel to my face. I could see in the darkness the gladiator with his oblong shield, his spiked ball and chain poised to strike the string binding of that little book. I watched the movie in this tiny cinema in the air, and saw you beside the velvet curtain, swinging your torch.

I was so tired that the hour in Auckland was like a dream. The main thing I remembered about the stopover was a glass cabinet at the end of the corridor. I walked to the cabinet to stretch my legs, and inside were jars of honey sealed with gauze lids. Behind the jars were fragments of honeycomb, the hexagonal networks crumbling with age.

At the back of the cabinet was a giant cardboard bee, standing arrogantly with its hands on its hips, or where its hips should have been. It was poised on frayed feet, bantering like a young boxer, in the stale air of the cabinet.

I leant down and saw, at the very front near the glass, a pile of real bees, but dead. Someone had made a cairn of the insects. They formed an awkward pyramid, like a group of child acrobats. A couple had fallen from their positions and rested hopelessly on their stiff wings.

This, I know, would have appealed to you. Like myself, you would have wondered why anybody would have taken the time to construct the pyramid, and how it stayed virtually intact, rising to a point of upturned legs. I would have taken a photograph of it for you, but I had left my camera on the aircraft.

"Marvellous insects," a man said to me. He had suddenly appeared, sucking on a crackling pipe. "So ordered. So exact. But good to see them dead all the same, eh?"

He, too, stooped down to look more closely at the pyramid.

15

"My nephew died from a bee sting."

"Is that so?" I said.

"Yep. Asthmatic. Couldn't get the oxygen to him on time, poor beggar." He shook his head slowly. "Make all that beautiful honey and still got the power to kill a person."

There were other cabinets of Maori jade war clubs, their handles etched with swirling patterns, placed in metal hoiders like my mother's Wedgwood plate of the Queen back home. Behind them were photographs of warriors, their faces tattooed with the same spinning currents, dots and circles as the handles of their weapons. I looked closely at these, at the real pores forming their own patterns beneath the Indian ink, and whiskers firing off in opposite directions. Even the faces were a friction, I thought, and at war.

I could see my reflection in the glass, superimposed over the faces of these whale killers and murderers. That is how tired I was, aligning my face with that of a chief.

"Jade is harder than steel," one card read beneath the duckbilled ends of the war clubs.

Further down was a photograph of a whale gutted on a beach. A group of men stood near its head, waving the same jade clubs in celebration.

I went to the gift shop counter and said: "Can I buy the club that killed the whale in the photograph?"

The woman stared at me for a moment. "I beg your pardon?"

"Is that club in the cabinet the one that killed the whale, and can I buy it?"

"The clubs are replicas, I'm afraid, but they're certified jade."

"Do you know what the markings mean?" I asked, looking over at the cabinet.

"I'm sorry, no. We have some books here on Maori culture if you wish to buy one."

"Are you a native of this country?"

"Yes, of course," she said briskly, serving a jar of local honey to an American in a stetson.

Our connecting passengers had arrived, and smelled of a

16

thousand hotel soaps and perfumes. Some wore jade tikis around their necks, the familiar angry faces resting on powdered chest bones, between breasts.

A noisy group of American girls took photographs of the war clubs and the solemn tattooed warriors. Some days later, I imagined as I walked back into the waiting lounge, the face I had placed my own over would emerge from a processing machine in Dallas, or New Orleans, or Richmond, Virginia.

"Your aircraft is now ready for boarding."

With my seat belt clipped, I looked at my watch and realised I had not changed the time. I was confused, and for a moment did not know if it was night or day back home. If my mother had gone back to the empty house and attempted sleep. If my father's missing brothers and sister had come together for the first time in two decades, and were making her a meal, or applying hot towels to her forehead.

I looked out the window for some time, thinking I might spot you despite the blackness. I drank five bourbons so I could stay awake and keep watch.

"Hey," I nudged the elderly lady beside me, "my dad's down there."

"That's nice, dear," she said, and turned her head away.

"For some reason," my father said, "my brothers and sister and I collided like atoms."

That's how he put it. Atoms.

"It happens with some families, and it doesn't with others. Let's hope it never happens to us," he always added, over dinner, or in front of the television.

Atoms or not, my uncles Sidney and Mitchell, and Aunty Tabitha may as well not have existed.

Tabby, as we called her, had not spoken to the usher in over fifteen years. Her photograph had once graced all the major billboards of Brisbane. He remembered the advertisements vividly: a young Tabby in a tight black cocktail dress, not a day over seventeen, wearing a pearl necklace and white gloves, sipping a

17

glass of champagne. Giant bubbles fizzed all around her. She was six metres high.

When my father drove all over Brisbane selling home fire extinguishers from the boot of his massive Ford, he saw his giant sister several times daily. From the lights at Red Hill, looking down over the railway yards. Across the river from Auchenflower, her body, on a still day, sliced by young rowers at practice. Even on the side of the Valley pool.

There were smaller versions of her, on the sides of buses or the green-seated trams that glided down through the city. Standing at intersections, he found himself at times staring straight at his sophisticated sister. She disintegrated into dots the closer he put his face to hers.

''That's my kid sister,'' he said to anyone within earshot.

Following her champagne billboard success she had caught the train to Sydney to become a model. She had gone as far as she could in her home town, my grandfather told her. She loomed at every street corner, off every highway. You can't get bigger than that, he told her. Go south. Make millions. Make us proud.

At the Roma Street railway station, my father presented her with a bunch of white roses. They kissed goodbye but it was awkward for them, as both could not remember the last time they had kissed. There, on the platform, he wondered where the years had gone, and how he could have missed his sister's childhood. He told no one, but it had been a shock to see her shapely form all over the city.

After a few months he imagined his sister's face as one of the most recognised in Sydney, possibly Melbourne. He could see her, unfurled on canvas above the entrances to the great department stores, illuminated along Broadway. She would be unable to walk along Pitt Street without being stared at. People in her block of flats would not go a single day without mentioning to somebody that they lived above, below, next door to the Tooth's Face or the Goanna Oil Beauty.

My father had planned a trip south, to take her out for a meal or a drink at the Marble Bar and tell her how many of her billboards lined the track between Brisbane and Sydney, but he never made it.

18

He learned that his sister had not become a celebrity, but was engaged to be married to a spectacles salesman. She had included, in the letter to her mother, a small smudged newspaper advertisement from a page of the Sydney *Sun*, of herself, almost featureless on the grubby newsprint, holding a new General Electric juicer.

"There goes the millions," my grandfather repeated on and off for years. "At least we'll be able to get cheap frames."

When my father began his wanderings in search of antiquities, he visited them in their home in the Blue Mountains, and purchased from his brother-in-law a pine box of glass eyes, dated pre-World War II.

"They were my father's," Howard, the spectacles man, said. "He was an optometrist you know. He fitted the returned servicemen with glass eyes. He did extremely well out of it, I might tell you. That and the First World War, when you think of it, have probably been the only great boom times for glass eye specialists."

"Good point," my father said.

"That's the secret, isn't it, Nelson? You stay a step ahead of events, then stock yourself up, prepare yourself for when it happens."

"You're right, Howard. Absolutely."

The eyes were of an infinite variety of green, brown and blue, and sat neatly in foam sockets within the box. T. Nelson did not really have any need for a box of eyes, but he wished to show some family affection to this thin, balding man who had captured the six-metre champagne girl.

"I tried optometry for a while," Howard went on, "but found out I was colour blind. An optometrist, colour blind!"

They laughed. Tabby sat on the arm of his chair and stroked his forehead.

"They want me for Vietnam, you know," he continued.

"Is that right?"

"Absolutely. They did tests which showed I could pick out any shade of green, no matter how similar they were. I was buggered on all the other colours but green."

"You don't say."

19

"They want me up in the choppers," he said, squeezing his wife's knee. "To spot the camouflage. I could pick them as easy as buttering a piece of toast.

"They really want me up there. They're still calling me, aren't they, dear? Will you come up, Howie, and spring us a few VC up here in the jungle?

"No way, Nelson. It's not that I'm scared or anything, not at all. But it's that Agent Orange stuff, she burns the eyes I'm told. They're going to want glasses when they get back. I'm stocking up, Nelson, stocking up like a bear for winter."

At Christmas, when they both had families of their own, they would send small gifts to each other through the post. Each year the presents became smaller.

"Shortbread again," my mother would say. Or: "Deck of cards. Wattles on the back."

After a while they only received cards, and then nothing.

Lola reciprocated with nothing, and the intermittent phone calls stopped.

At times my father could not decide if his childhood had been a dream or reality. He remembered the films he had seen, at what time of year he had seen them, his favourite lines, the exact details of the characters' faces at moments in the drama, but had only the palest recollection of his brothers and sister as children.

Eventually, the pine box of eyes came into my possession, and I used them for years as marbles. My mother would find them under the couch, my bed, in the front garden or in the soil underneath the house, and every time it would alarm her.

I took the pine case to school, and at lunch recess went through the ritual of flicking open its brass latch as I sat in the dirt outside the hand-drawn ring, revealing the almost perfect grid of eyes to my exasperated colleagues.

I fired the eyes from the thumbnail of my right hand, the retinas spinning crazily and cracking against my opposition's marbles. I would place them in pairs in the dust to scare the girls. Sometimes an eye chipped, and I collected the fragments and glued them back in at home. For a while I wanted to become an eye doctor.

The eyes, however, distressed my father. One day, without

warning, he took the box down to the concrete pathway that led to our clothesline, and smashed each one individually with a hammer. He swept the shattered eyes into a dustpan and threw them, as he did all junk, into the incinerator.

"I'll buy you some proper marbles," he said to me, picking a fragment of blue iris from his bleeding thumb. That was all he ever said about it.

Only months later, I was diagnosed as having a "lazy eye", and would have to wear a patch, sit before a candle and look at the flame, from side to side through red and green cellophane, to strengthen the muscles. My father, acting in accordance with his own peculiar logic, blamed himself and the way he had violently disposed of the box of eyes, intended for the sockets of the airmen, sailors and soldiers of Australia.

At the Royal Hawaiian Hotel, I walked into its pinkness, this old seashell not far from Diamond Head, with my eyes swollen and watering.

It was difficult to see anything, and only after I bumped into a potted fern did they enquire about my well-being. I was led to my hotel room, seven storeys above Waikiki beach, and told to lie down while they fetched the house physician.

I could hear the waves, and the shrieks of children and hot dog vendors, and went to the balcony for my first real view of America. Dozens of canoes, powered by bare-breasted men, were racing to shore, and in the glare, I hoped to see you, Father, at the bow, coxing the local natives, guiding the rhythm of their muscles and brilliantly festooned paddles.

The doctor arrived, probed both eyeballs with a pen-sized torch, then disappeared.

Fifteen minutes later, a small opaque bottle of eyedrops was delivered to my room on an engraved silver tray.

The house doctor telephoned me later, to see if the drops had had any effect. He told me my eyes had probably reacted to the lei of pink hibiscus flowers draped around my neck at the airport.

I took the lei immediately, I must tell you, and holding it at arm's length, went to the balcony and tossed it down to the people of America.

He always remembered the carcass of the starfish that had somehow slipped into the folds of the family tent, and tattooed its own shape into the canvas by virtue of its moist and leaky death.

The family had, as they did each year, stacked the tapered tent poles into the back of the trailer, along with cardboard boxes of kitchen implements, two kerosene lanterns, a collapsible kitchen sink with tea towel holder, candles, matches, fishing rods and ice chest, and headed down to the Oceanic Baths Caravan Park. They invariably arrived at dusk, after pies on the side of the road at Yatala, and their father's two beers and a quick bet at Southport, and had to erect their holiday home in the twin beams of their old Ford.

It was not unusual to find salt and sand in the tent, even fragments of oyster shell or a child's grainy footprint, locked in the tight folds from the previous year. On this occasion, the fossilised Asteroidea, defiantly clinging to the front flap, revealed itself.

"What the hell is this?" said Urban Downs, touching the body lightly with his thick forefinger. "Nelson, get the torch."

Gathering around their father, the four children — Nelson, Sidney, Mitchell and Tabitha — stared with interest at the shrivelled arms of the dead creature, illuminated by the torch beam. Urban prised it off with a butter knife.

"Which one of you damn brats did this, hmm?"

"Urban, please," their mother Betty said. "It's their holiday."

"I'll give them holiday," he said, but before he could turn around they had scampered into the shadows beyond the headlights, and remained there, watching their giant father pull the tent into shape, pounding steel pegs into the earth and drawing the slack on ropes.

It was like this every year. They placed everything in the same position. They knew the park manager, most of the occupants, the exact number of paces to the kiosk or the Lucky Wheel on the driveway of the ambulance station, the soft, hard or squeaky

22

seats of the cinema, the best fishing spots around the base of the Burleigh headland and the point in the Oceanic Baths where one could feel the maximum pull of its surging tidal waters. (T. Nelson had decided one year, submerged just below the surface of the baths, his tiny frame buffeted by the collision of currents, that he wanted to fly space rockets.)

The Downs family felt safe at the Oceanic. They were familiar with the contours of their plot of earth — Lot 39, Third Avenue. It had a dip on the western side that collected rain. A small patch at the rear always miraculously absorbed sink water, pan oil and scraps. T. Nelson believed that it fell all the way through to the jungles of Peru. He once left his sandshoes at its edge and, when they had disappeared by morning, silently thrilled at the thought of them on the feet of a child hunter.

The family's routine was always the same. At 7 a.m. they ate bacon and eggs. The boys were then free to fish, play in the dunes or swim in the baths. By mid-morning, Urban had taken his usual place in his red and white striped canvas deckchair, to read detective novels with pictures of scantily clad women brandishing weapons, or pinned down by the black-gloved hands of gangsters, on their covers. At midday the family gathered for lunch, then walked together around the bluff or to the tip of North Burleigh. On alternate evenings they went to the cinema or the Lucky Wheel, then back to the tent.

Urban was so powerful, his arms strengthened by a lifetime of carpentry, that he spun the wheel with a force that rocked it on its tripod and sent specks of blue and red glitter over spectators. The only thing he ever won, after several years of spinning, was a deck of cards. Each card bore a picture of a capital city of the world, or famous sights such as London Bridge, the Eiffel Tower, the Forum, the Empire State Building, the Taj Mahal, all beneath a thin coating of plastic.

They played with the same deck year after year, singeing the Taj's brilliant marble with a cigarette end, polluting the Rhine with spilt claret.

"Urban says we may get over there next year," Betty repeated during their poker games with Oceanic neighbours, brushing Diamond Head and Mount Fuji with her fingertips, passing Pompeii back to the dealer.

"Is that right, Bet? How marvellous."

"I say that, do I, old girl?"

"It's a good time now, with the kids getting older."

"After Saturday then, my love. I've got a good tip."

For T. Nelson, quiet on the top bunk, listening to the chatter of his parents, the Oceanic meant life turned upside down. They walked to the stucco shower blocks with their towels and underpants and fresh clothes bundled under their arms, in full view of everyone. Inside, the cubicles had chipped soap holders and brown doors etched with pictures of copulating couples and giant genitals. Other people's suds, urine and slivers of soap passed by in the communal gutter that ran through the showers. Men whistled, and T. Nelson could see hairy feet on each side of him.

Not only that, women washed dishes in the open air, and set up tables, chairs, napkins, knives and forks and ate outside, just off the edge of the park's dirt lanes, as if overhead flocks of rosellas or the nod of strolling couples were usual at dinnertime.

Only a thin stretch of canvas separated T. Nelson from the night. When it rained it was like being inside a drum, and on quiet nights he could hear people cough, or fart, or argue, and the tangled tunes of their radios. He knew it took only the silent peeling back of a flap and he was outside, free to skitter amongst the dark canvas shapes held to the earth by flimsy rope, and that anything was possible.

Amongst my father's notes for what appears to have been a brief history of Burleigh Heads and its environs are dozens of newspaper clippings on caravan park life: murders, rapes, fires, damage by cyclone, real estate wrangles and so on. There are two here that even carry my by-line.

My father writes of the Oceanic: "This, for me, is the real Australia. The volcanic plug. The beach. The baths. Everyone knows everyone in their tents and vans, just as it all started in this country. Little settlements thrown up like the gold mining boom towns. Each dependent on each other for this and that. Nothing to hide. All of us in it together.''

He goes on with his theories about permanent dwellers and holiday transients, oceanfront and industrial sector sites, mobile homes and tents.

He rang to congratulate me on one story about Dodge City, a van park not far from the Oceanic. He went to visit it himself, and got the manager to take his photograph, standing under its hand-painted red sign, bracketed by two wagon wheels.

Dodge City is built on reclaimed swamp land, a pad of dirt surrounded on three sides by bullrushes. Because of its distance from the coast, and its lack of public transport, it is self-contained, an island, with its own mini-supermarket, itself delivered on the tray of a front-end loader, and pool hall. Its residents are mainly employees of the Hinterland motorcar manufacturing plant, or mechanics, or drivers, and its lanes are dotted with wrecks or stock cars under repair.

My father noted, with some perception, that a community so reliant on the wheel had taken extraordinary lengths to disguise the fact. There were gardens in front of most vans, and pathways of rubber matting. Some dwellers had enticed choko vines up their television antennas, and he could not avoid a quip about all the soap operas, the religious services, the news items from around the world absorbed by those vegetables.

A large percentage had also covered their van tyres with lattice or skirts of canvas, concealing the wheels which, he wrote, were the central support, the point of balance, the reason for that feeling of flotation underfoot. Some had even attempted to disguise their tow balls.

Ropes, too, he went on, were an illusion. To the outsider, to one who lived within brick or wood, they appeared to anchor the van and its annexe as if it were a balloon. The holiday camper is constantly tightening them, afraid a storm will lift a dwelling off the ground and dump it into the ocean or bushland. And to children they are a danger, melding into the landscape and becoming invisible, able to bring down a runner of any size with a deep twang.

To the permanent residents, however, the ropes are what

beams are to a house. Their homes have external support structures, making them infinitely more vulnerable and precious. They are open, even, to sabotage, which my father concluded could cause anxiety. To boot, he added, one's life is silhouetted against the canvas.

Dodge City was a refuse tip for years before it became a caravan park. The children who play amongst the bullrushes told me that objects periodically appeared: refrigerators, door handles, chairs, billiard balls, insect screening, toothbrushes and bottles.

Because of the housing shortage, Father, the park has now been classified by the government as a housing estate. Some have placed street numbers on the outside of their vans, as strange as the nebulus of our dead starfish.

The families that came to the Oceanic every year made up a strange, fragmented neighbourhood, apart most of the time, going about their lives, growing older, but reacquainted for those two weeks in summer. They picked up and carried on as if no time had elapsed ; as if they had woken, tied back the flaps of their annexes, and emerged from a sound sleep, resuming conversations and incomplete arguments.

Sometimes a neighbour did not reappear at the Oceanic. The others would discuss the possibilities: a birth, wedding, tragic accident or death.

"She said she had a lump under her arm, remember?"

"No, no, no. She had a mole on her back. Rubbed against her bra strap."

"That's right. You're right, Mal. Could've been cancerous. You've got to get them checked regular, you know. Dear oh dear. What a shame."

They had to wait for the following year, if ever, to learn of the circumstances of disappearance. Those who vanished completely were replaced by new families.

Because they only saw each other at long intervals, they particularly noticed each other grow older. They shook hands or kissed as slight strangers. Girls reappeared as young women. A stroke may have dropped the side of a face. Some returned with

26

one arm or leg, glasses or different coloured hair. A year was long enough to make some of them cynical, or frivolous, or addicted to drink. They never got to know each other intimately, though they pretended as much. They invented their own versions of the missing year.

"He played up on her, right, and she hit him with an axe, that's what happened. Couldn't save the arm." Or: "Isn't he the machinist? Probably ripped it straight off. Wouldn't have felt a thing because of the shock, you know. Christ, poor bastard." Or even: "Are you sure that's her? She seems bigger, you know, up top."

"You'd notice that, wouldn't you, of all things?"

"No, honestly, does she have a sister?"

"Shut your mouth."

T. Nelson and his brothers and sister were never permitted to go swimming in the open sea.

"You know the story of your grandfather and it should be a lesson to you about the power of the ocean, do you hear?" Urban said every year. "He was a captain in the first war. Risked his life to save others and was swept overboard."

"Where?" T. Nelson asked.

"I don't know, exactly. Somewhere off France, or below the Middle East. Somewhere around there, it's not important."

"What was the name of the ship?"

"Listen, all I know is he went down. Never seen again. He was a big man, remember, bigger than me. The sea even got a big man like him. Listen to your father. If it can take a big sea captain like that, quick as a flash, it can eat up you squirts in the blink of an eye."

T. Nelson later discovered that his grandfather had actually been a vegetable peeler in the stomach of an old trading steamer, and had died of consumption. He was wrapped in a sheet and dumped overboard with bags of cabbage spines and potato eyes.

"You kids have got to understand this place, and respect it," Urban went on, sipping a lager. "We're an island, see. Water everywhere."

"Not in the middle there isn't."

"Pipe down. Anything could happen to us. Big storms, tidal waves, anything. It's the old saying. You don't fool around with the sea when you live on an island, now do you? You listening to your father?"

The children were, however, allowed to swim in the Oceanic Baths under supervision. It had its own small pavilion, with stone columns nipped in at the centre like giant hourglasses, cedar roof beams and a skylight.

The columns fascinated T. Nelson, and he ran his hands across the smooth stone. He imagined one of the columns had breasts and would stare into it so long, his chin on his hands at the edge of the pool, that the caramel swirls of the sandstone moved. At the eastern end of the baths was a small wooden grandstand for parents, towels and bags.

Back then most swimmers wore bathing caps, and adults could identify their children by their coloured domes, like party bulbs, bobbing in the salt water. Some women had caps covered in giant plastic daisies, roses, or limp poinsettia flowers, and T. Nelson enjoyed paddling up close to these exotic headdresses.

During the king tides, the sea boiled up around the basalt boulders and spilled into the baths, surging around the three exposed sides to the screams of the swimmers. T. Nelson would cling to a corner, his small body tossed about by the currents and the wash, and collect the pieces of seaweed that were dumped onto the wire fence and into the pool.

His mother had never swum in her life. She simply sat in the grandstand knitting, or sleeping upright with her arms folded. She always wore long-sleeved shirts or cardigans, even in summer, because of the accident in the Brisbane linen factory, years before T. Nelson was born. Her cuff had caught in a press and pulled her arm into the machine. Her face remained jammed against steel for nearly two hours, her fine brown hair caught in cogs and rollers. She said nothing. Did not even scream or cry, so Urban recounted, but remained terrified of machines from that day. She avoided open car bonnets, electric tools, bicycles, even her husband's vices and their new refrigerator. They were

28

one of the last families in Brisbane to buy ice regularly by the block, and in summer fanned themselves with newspapers.

But they did have a radio, shaped like the entrance to a cathedral, with a small map of the world on its dial which lit up when switched on.

My father always remembered that piece.

"It brought us together, you know, like the Oceanic. It's those little things, isn't it, that bring people together?"

T. Nelson was accident prone as a child. His feet always found glass, oyster shell fragments, fish hooks. They had a joke in the family that whenever their mother lost a pin while sewing, she would call T. Nelson to find it. At four he too was diagnosed as having a turned eye, and wore a black patch in his first year at school. He relished the attention. In school dramas he played the pirate, the gangster, the bad guy.

The Oceanic gave him the opportunity to develop his extraordinary selling talents. Each morning he went down to the dog-legged beach and collected the overnight debris. He displayed them at school on his return, and claimed he had prised the objects from the walls of an underwater city, or the furry cannons of wrecks. His classmates gave him coins and marbles for his artefacts.

He was the child remembered for his bulging eyes, his hyperactivity (according to school reports), his head and the margins of his schoolbooks filled with expeditions, ancient civilisations, rockets and moons. He often drew the Oceanic Baths, and himself in the centre of it.

At the Oceanic he believed he grew closer to his father. He noticed things, like how loudly he sipped his coffee. The length of time it took the big man to groom himself, even for the seventy-metre stroll to the shower block. The way his father ran a comb back through his hair with such exactness, holding his free hand before his forehead, as if protecting his eyes from the sun, though not quite touching his eyebrows. He even watched him shave: a ritual like many others considered personal in the Downs household.

Cyclones hit the Oceanic three times. T. Nelson remained un-afraid of the gusts, thinking of the shells the storm might bring, possibly from Tahiti, or at least Fiji. He hoped to go outside when the winds and rain had died and find them on the beach, in the baths, on the roofs of bus shelters or cars, or lodged high up in the pines. During the cyclones the Downs family huddled around the central pole of their tent, their arms around each other, gripping the wood, the swirling isobars felt through the timber.

"I could smell those bread and butter pickles on my father's breath," he told me. "And my mother's ear. The shape I mean. One stuck out more than the other. You never notice those things, you know, then bang, you see it, and can't believe it's been there all along."

I have verified this and it is correct. One Saturday I arrive un-expectedly at the nursing home to check on my grandmother's ear. It is thirty-nine degrees Celsius and she is there, asleep in the usual chair at the front door, her arms crossed, wearing a lilac cardigan, head tilted to the left, towards the kitchen. Her mouth is slightly open and her breaths barely detectable. She has two nylon poinsettia flowers, side by side, on her slippers. I lift her dead hair and note the contours of her ear with its large lobe hanging, loose, but relatively close to the scalp. I wait a long time for her to shift her head to the other side, then check the suspect ear. There it is, the cartilage flatter at the top, ridgeless at one point, but definitely the ear of another person.

She stirs.

"Hello, sweetheart," she says, taking my hand. I kiss her on the cheek, the odd ear in full vision. "Have you been here long?"

It was at the Oceanic that Urban Downs chose to impart his les-sons in life to his sons.

"When you shake a man's hand, always have a strong grip," he said on the way to the showers one evening. The boys practised on each other. "You can tell the substance of a man by his handshake."

And later: "All adults are just big kids. When you're in a spot of bother, or someone's trying to get one up on you, thinking they're pretty good, just imagine them sitting on the lavatory with their pants around their ankles. You'll have nothing to be afraid of, you listening to me?"

On the crop of basalt boulders at the end of Burleigh beach, Urban explained sex. The four of them sat facing the ocean, holding their rods.

"You know, boys," he said, threading a segment of worm onto his hook, "you know that you have a penis, right? That's what you have."

"Yes."

"A woman, a girl, is different, you understand?"

They did not take their eyes off the curving rods, staring straight out at the trawlers heading for the horizon like a thread of fireflies.

"The woman, she has a vagina, right? She doesn't have a penis. Listening?"

"Yes."

"The man, that's you, us, puts his penis into the woman's vagina. That's how it's done, got me?"

"He puts..." T. Nelson said, turning, taking his forefinger off the line.

"Into, into, boy."

Beneath their lantern the worms were struggling from their pile of sand on the newspaper, lashing against news of a cricket series between England and Australia. T. Nelson looked at the photograph on the page and a worm, full of blood, slithering across a tilted cap, down two arms and a bat, and into the darkness.

"And don't play with yourselves either."

"Yes, Father."

"Not good for you."

At some stage during their vacation, Urban Downs also repeated his story of the lighthouse at the urging of T. Nelson.

31

"Yes, yes, correct, it was made of beautiful sandstone," he said, "and they dragged the blocks all the way to the headland."

"By cart."

"By cart."

"To Burleigh?"

"No, I don't think so. Further south, I think. I don't know exactly where. That's not the point."

He sipped his beer. At the base of the lighthouse was a wonderful home for the keeper and his family. It had fireplaces, cedar mantelpieces and wide windows that looked out to sea.

"And you could see all the way to South America?"

"Slow down, boy. Perhaps, from the top of the lighthouse, perhaps. But that's not the point, boy."

It was discovered months later, he went on, when the builders, surveyors and government officials had returned to Brisbane, that it had been built on the wrong headland. A simple incorrect turn in the scrub, one degree left or right, had caused the blunder that later became a scandal.

"An honest little mistake, you might think, on a coast with many headlands," Urban said, slowing now for greater effect. "Were they lazy, these lighthouse builders? Tired, perhaps, after dragging those sandstone blocks all the way, hmm?"

It operated for a short time before the error was realised, but it was long enough for several ships to be guided onto the rocks. A shipload of horses had reared onto boulders in the blackness.

"Those horses' screams, well," Urban said, leaning forward, almost whispering, "they could be heard in Coolangatta. Swear to God. High-pitched, bloodcurdling screams, like those of a woman."

"Urban, please," their mother said, preparing the bunks.

The lighthouse, he said, was abandoned, and later used as a target for bombing practice by the Air Force. One pilot had perished during the practice swoops, his wing clipping the ancient stone turret, the fighter spiralling down to the beach and exploding on impact.

"An unlucky light, hey boys? All it took was that one wrong turn, easy as pie to do, and look what happened."

T. Nelson imagined the lighthouse's giant bulb, blown hundreds of metres out to sea by a young pilot, home now to travelling sunfish and curious whiting.

Indeed the remains of the lighthouse are still there, coloured with graffiti. And yes, I did go down to the beach of wrecks and dead horses.

I was hoping to find, what? Horseshoes perhaps, lead plates and cups from the old ships, even skeletons.

What I did find I have here in a plastic garbage bag. Five milk cartons from Taiwan, a fruit juice bottle from the United States, two Japanese detergent containers featuring a flying boy wearing a cape, and the one-armed frame of a pair of glassless spectacles.

Mother told me she was scrubbing the crazed face of a girl on the mirror behind the candy bar when she heard you yell "Bury the eyes!" from inside the Universe. You shouted it several times from your central seat, and as you were dusting the menagerie of relics you had placed near the stage — kingfishers with outstretched wings, a small stuffed horse, a wagon wheel and cabinets of monocles, spurs and rotting corsets. Your little museum.

She paused, and a speck of rose cheek came off beneath her cloth. She put it in the pocket of her pinafore and went to the rear curtain.

"Are you okay in there?" she said.

"Something's been getting at the cockatoos."

"What are you yelling about?"

"Half the tail of the black cockatoo has been eaten, Lola," T. Nelson said. "Did you place those traps like I told you? Did you? Damn it, Lola, this is a valuable collection if you didn't realise. I told you to place those damn traps."

She did not respond and went back to her cleaning. An hour before the evening session she went up to him. He was dressed in his usher's uniform, sitting again in his favourite seat. He had already switched on the stars.

"Do you want me to call the hospital again, Nelson?" she said, putting her hand on his stiff epaulettes.

33

He said nothing and continued to look into the white screen.

Urban Downs had collapsed outside a betting shop one Wednesday afternoon. When T. Nelson received the call he was underneath the Universe, inspecting the rear foundations after noticing the subsidence of a tin-capped stump. Although the stumps were made of cedar, he was concerned, remembering the sink hole at the Oceanic, and feared that the whole Universe was built, at worst, on sand, or impacted garbage.

He arrived at his father's bedside where two men in dark suits were already seated.

"I'm sorry? You're from where?"

"The tax department, Mr Downs."

"Tax?"

"If we could just ask a few questions."

"Can't you see he's gravely ill? My father? Get out, please. Give us some time alone."

"We're just doing our job, sir," one said, clicking the end of his pen.

So Urban Downs was interrogated about his life, stretching back fifty years. He spoke in a confessional tone, to T. Nelson's surprise, at times weeping, gesticulating with his hands as if the tubes running into his nose did not exist. As if the truth travelled through his drip, bubbly and exposed to everyone in the room. A nurse was called to watch the cardiograph machine, the thin blue line responding, so T. Nelson imagined, to dates and events through the first half of the century.

T. Nelson heard later that a joke had circulated through the hospital. That the old man had offered his body to the government as compensation for a working life of unpaid taxes, and that Urban had stipulated: "Just don't take the eyes. Bury the eyes!"

During one visit, the nurse took T. Nelson into a corner. "Mr Downs," she said, "excuse me if this sounds insensitive, but do you have any children studying medical science?"

"No, no I don't."

"Good, I just had to ask," she said.

34

"Why do you ask?"

"Your father, I believe, has consented to donating his body to science."

"That is what I heard from the cleaner at the lift," T. Nelson said sternly, "but I doubt it very much. I think he wants to be buried. He's terrified of fire, a family thing, so I know he would not be cremated."

"I see."

"What if he did?"

"I just wanted to assure you that if he did donate, it is unlikely his relatives would recognise him."

"I don't understand."

"It's just that if he did donate his body, well, they take great lengths at the university morgue to disguise the heads."

"Disguise?" T. Nelson said, looking over at his sleeping father.

"In case a student's relative ends up as a specimen."

"Oh."

"They break the nose," she said. "Thoroughly."

"I see," T. Nelson said. "Thank you for that."

T. Nelson feared more that his father would go to prison. He sat there, looking at his heaving chest for some hours, when his mother arrived.

"Mum," he said, standing, "what the hell's been going on all these years?"

"Please, Nelson, don't wake your father."

"Mother," he said, grabbing her thin arm.

It took less than ten minutes for T. Nelson to learn that his parents had invested all their money in a southern horse syndicate. They owned, so it seemed, one-fifteenth of a chestnut gelding called Time and Tide.

"Which fifteenth?" he later asked Urban, after he had strolled around the grounds of the hospital to calm his nerves and watched, for a short while, the gangers erecting the giant ferris wheel inside the Exhibition grounds across the road.

"The bloody tail it seems," Urban said, attempting a smile.

The old man sat up and the three of them locked arms and joined heads and cried together.

"Have I been a father to you, boy?" Urban asked. "Have I been a good one?"

T. Nelson sniffed: "Of course, don't be silly."

"It just goes so quickly, you know? You can't slow it down. One minute you've got all the time in the world and then it's gone."

"I know, Dad."

T. Nelson wondered if Lola was coping with the evening session, a cartoon then *Hang 'Em High*.

"We used to go fishing, remember? Remember everything I taught you about fishing, boy?"

That night T. Nelson returned to the Universe and, with horses' feet thundering above his office and bullets ricocheting beneath his stars, he discovered after a few quick phone calls that there was no record of the chestnut Time and Tide. His parents had invested a lifetime's savings in air.

He made it upstairs in time for the final credits.

Approaching Los Angeles, I thought of the helicopters and search planes looking for you, swooping low at nightfall then resuming again, as they say, at first light. If only your usher's suit had been white, you might have been easier to spot.

I pushed up the perspex curtain of my window so I could see the great United States, and hopefully the tiny Hollywood sign in the hills, but we were still too high, and the early morning sun was dazzling.

Over on the far side of my row I noticed the old woman who had been helped to her seat before dinner the previous night. She had her head crooked into the window, her mouth slightly open, and had not moved. It was cold, and yet she had no blanket.

I noted she did not touch her dinner, and had slept in the same position during the movie. They gave her breakfast, too, and she had not eaten a morsel.

As we disembarked she remained asleep, despite the juggling of luggage and excited chatter.

I discovered later that the woman had died.

"You knew she was dead?" I asked a stewardess, who had

36

kindly given me extra nips of bourbon during the flight, at the taxi rank. (You would have liked her, Father. She looked a bit like Kim Novak.)

"Sure. We just pretend they're still alive so we don't alarm the other passengers."

So this is death, Pop. Not the mutilated bodies I had seen so many of, but being unable to watch a movie, blanketless, with a cooling omelette and those plastic cups of orange juice before you, rocking from side to side and untouched, high up in the heavens.

2

Beth La Valley collected men.

I met her in the dining car of the Amtrak train to San Francisco, and was attracted to her ancient beehive, if the truth be known, like a moth to light. She reminded me of a friend of my mother's, who owned dozens of cheap calypso sculptures, including topless nut holders and straw-hatted cork stoppers. A lampshade with the bulb protruding from the tip of a clay beehive had, I was convinced after a lengthy lunch, been modelled on Beth La Valley.

"See here?" she said, passing a photograph across the table. "This is his grown-up son. And this here, this is him."

She pointed to a man in a peaked cap standing next to a truck loaded with lumber.

"He's very good looking, don't you think?"

She was on her way to Santa Rosa to meet the lumber man for the first time. One of those mail-order bride things, she said.

"I used to go up to Santa Rosa all the time once," she said, looking out the window. She had rabbit teeth and wore a pearl on her wedding ring finger. "I love the wide windows in the dining car, don't you? All I ever ate were club sandwiches. I love club sandwiches. I used to eat six of them."

Today, for some unexplained reason, Beth La Valley dined on chicken. She told me of the previous husband, her sixth, who delivered firewood to the Hollywood stars. He had seven thousand clients now, she said.

We roared through Fresno, past the ice works and four basketball courts where young white men played on one quadrangle, and blacks on another.

"So Beth, now you're moving into the big time," I said, "from firewood to lumber."

She laughed. "I guess you're right. I never thought of that. Yes, I like that."

Beth said Roy, the lumber man, sounded nice on the telephone. "And where are you heading?"

"I don't really know," I said, looking out at the flatlands.

"Let me make a suggestion, then," she said, filing her long nails. "I met three husbands on the Greyhounds across the States. They leave from San Francisco. All sorts of men, I can tell you. German, Dutch, the English. There's women, too, for a young boy like you."

"Do you think so, Beth?"

"Nothing surer."

"I'll think about it," I said, as the waiter brought our bills.

"You know," she said, firing short bursts of hairspray into her beehive from a miniature can she had produced from her handbag, "now that I'm a single girl, I feel they should earn their tips, don't you?"

Sitting in the corner of the Blue Pacific Lounge at King's Cross, my father was entranced by both the rubber cobra headdress snaked around the skull of his future wife, and the fingernails of the magician. T. Nelson sat in the second row from the front of the stage with a miniature horse wrapped in brown paper at his left calf. He had heard of the horse from other dealers of antiquities, and had caught the train south in search of the prize.

He had walked into the lounge on impulse, thrilled over the purchase of a masterpiece of taxidermy, as he described it, and ordered a beer.

The Great Waldo, a short man with a barrel chest and legs like brackets, had chosen T. Nelson to drink with before his performance.

"I was attracted by your donkey there," Waldo said, sipping vodka. "Is it from the time of Christ, my friend? The one that carried Mary, perhaps?"

"It's a horse, actually."

"That donkey of yours, she has small ears."

T. Nelson ignored the man whose cape completely obscured his chair, and continued to watch Little Cleopatra. He thought he could see a tongue dangling from the cobra's mouth.

"If you wish I can sell you an elephant, smaller than that donkey of yours," the magician said, looking left and right. "Alive or dead, as you wish."

Tapping his glass, T. Nelson noticed for the first time the exquisite fingernails of the magician, each a perfect oval surface depicting religious scenes in mauve, maroon and yellow oils. The paintings were so fine that he could make out the crucifixion on his thumb, including rolling clouds heavy with rain behind the crosses.

"You like, hey?" Waldo said. "You get an eyeglass and I'll show you the dice on the blanket. You don't believe me? Get me the eyeglass and I'll prove it."

T. Nelson doubted that the toss would have been revealed, even with an eyeglass, in the dust where the cuticle arched underneath. Only two veils remained, one across Cleopatra's face and the other across her breasts. She had a dumpy figure that greatly appealed to the young antique dealer. He had planned to take his glass-eyed horse back to the hotel room, telephone his sister to say farewell, and catch the first train out of Central Station in the morning.

Despite the sour breath of Waldo, with the final veils removed, he decided to stay another night in Sydney.

"Tomorrow night, my last show here, I will levitate," the magician said. "Then I must see my family in Leningrad."

The forefinger of the right hand, T. Nelson noticed, showed Christ in a cream gown, His arms outstretched, floating above the bottom of Waldo's nail. On the limited canvas of the little finger, he also believed he caught a glimpse of a manger. Only half a star, in brilliant yellow, shone above it, the rest bitten off and ingested, it seemed, by the Great Waldo.

"It's not a good habit for an artist such as myself," the magician said, shaking his head at the new-born scene. "I have others on my feet." Waldo lifted a black velvet boot. "The little toes are difficult, though. Very hard, the little toes."

"Extraordinary," T. Nelson said, applauding Cleopatra with seven others in the bar.

"They are in big demand. I make money this way. I paint

portraits of people's children. On the parents' thumbs. Pets, too.''

"You must have great patience," my father said, still looking at the stage.

"I like the sequences best," Waldo said, describing how he had once painted a life story from birth in the left pinkie finger, across to the strength of the thumbs, to the death in the corresponding little finger.

"That's very interesting," T. Nelson said, reaching down for the horse, "but I must be off." He stood half off his seat.

"But no," Waldo said. "You can't."

"I beg your pardon?"

"There's a reason I chose you to drink with."

"I just came in for a quick beer, that's all. I should be . . ."

"Please," Waldo said, holding up his hand. "Get me another vodka, and quickly, I must perform any minute."

Certainly, it was a far cry from selling fire extinguishers door to door in Brisbane. On his first major expedition in search of relics, my father had been cornered by a lunatic who believed he could fly and who went regularly to Leningrad to visit his parents, long dead I might add, a two-bit trickster who had been instructed by Freud and Einstein, with whom he visited Hiroshima annually. Waldo claimed, my father recalled, that it made the brilliant physicist feel a little happier to view the progress of the city since its razing.

Not ideal circumstances, you might think, for the beginning of a courtship.

Butch, the first person I met on my across-America tour, used to work in an abattoir. He had spent most of his life wearing white rubber boots splashed with blood and fat. In forty-one years, he told me over breakfast, he had gone from slaughterman to quality control inspector. At the hotel in San Francisco he was sampling his first American steak.

He ate like you, Pop. Head down, concentrating solely on the

41

geography of his plate. He made meticulous and identical incisions in the meat, pushing the pieces the same distance through egg yolk. He made quick glances at his wife's meal, and the level of her coffee, and my breadcrumbs.

Two American businessmen were seated behind us.

"Shit, I've got thirty thousand pencil sharpeners just sitting in the warehouse, Frank, and no one's doing a damn thing about them."

"I apologise," his colleague said. "I've tried to get the staff moving on them."

"Well I don't think you've tried damned near hard enough, have you?"

"It's not enough time to shift that many units."

The boss poised a knife and fork over his plate. "The new line comes in Thursday. Move 'em by then or you're out."

"No one wants thirty thousand sharpeners shaped like the Sphinx, Bob. What's a Texan kid want with a Sphinx? They want boots, stetsons, that sort of stuff."

"I see, you're a design expert now." He sipped his coffee. "Shift 'em."

Ah, Americans. You would have loved it here. The whole place in cinemascope.

I studied Butch's cap with a brown steer stitched onto its bulbous crown. Some of the longer threads that crisscrossed its flanks, that gave it form and raised it slightly from the hub of the peak, had come loose. The steer's belly was frayed as if the beast had been savaged from beneath by a sharp-toothed predator. Its entrails shivered in the air-conditioning of the breakfast room.

Being one of the only other Australians on the tour Butch frequently confided in me, sounded out his observations and defended our country loudly when required, as if we were the unique possessors of the Australian soul.

"Been waiting a long time for this," he said as we walked out to the bus with our luggage.

"He has," his wife Dot said, walking behind us.

"You find the steak a bit tough?"

"I just had toast."

42

"Bit sinewy. When you know the business like I do you pick these things up straight off."

"I bet."

"Looking forward to the steak down south, though. Houston should be good for a steak. Heard a lot about it, even back in Perth."

We met our bus driver, Jack, who lined up the luggage on the sidewalk outside the hotel. We stood and waited for the rest of our party.

"They say New York cuts are the best, but I don't know. Best steak feed I ever had was at a pub on the Darling Downs, the Golden Sheaf. Know it?"

"The Sheaf? Sure," I said. I didn't have a clue where it was, to be honest. I was interested in the origin of Jack's slight limp. A car accident, perhaps.

"Have to wait and see about the New York stuff, though."

Dot told me they were going on to Europe after the States, again by bus. I could already see this woman trailing the quality control inspector in and out of the steakhouses of Paris, Munich, Vienna. I could see cattle in the fields outside Salzburg, dotting the steep hillsides of St Anton, or grazing on the summer grasses near Rome, waiting to be slaughtered for Butch.

"Let's move it, folks," Jack said, lighting a cigarette.

Yes, I would say that. I would concede that my father's dalliances with antiquities started off the entire train of events without him realising it. But then, who can see the obituary ahead of the present moment?

Sure, he admitted it all began because of money. No question. He was fascinated at how the common object could transcend its original purpose for existence, and gain in value simply by being. He looked at everyday items and imagined them one hundred, two hundred years ahead in time. He would see a knife and fork on a table and have already erected a glass cabinet around them, before he sat down to eat. That is what he was like then. A young man with his eye on everything. Eager to get ahead. Sharp as a tack.

I have a teaspoon here, salvaged from the kitchen drawer of

my own childhood. Dull with finger oil and caffeine. Unremark-able.

This is what he said about it: "You see the forged roses on the handles? Cheap, nasty-looking roses."

"Yep."

"What will this be worth, then, when the world has no more roses? Hmm? What will the common old spoon be worth then, eh?"

He eyed beer bottles in bins and long grass, crushed bus tickets, loose change, shoes, lamps, a million things that surrounded his and everyone else's lives. To him, everything had potential.

"But you see the problem, don't you?" he said countless times. "The problem with the collector is that he can never out-live the full appreciation of his goods."

It was my generation, he stressed, and the one after that, which would reap the benefits of the teaspoon. I swear to God, he said that.

Capturing the insect-nibbled horse and my mother on the same trip, however, charged him with a new purpose. His sec-ond major piece was a bath plug, that he hung, as a talisman of sorts, from the rear vision mirror of his small truck. The plug had allegedly (my word) come from the bathtub of famous Aus-tralian aviator Bert Hinkler.

"Hinkler's housemaid stole it?" I asked him.

"Took it from the bath as soon as she'd heard he'd gone down."

"What on earth for?"

"Souvenir," he said. "It was handed down through the woman's family."

"A plug?"

"Family heirloom. Family treasure."

"This is a joke, right Dad?"

"You know," he said, leaning forward as he did when he had something important to impart, "the housemaid's great-granddaughter was using it in the kitchen sink when I heard about it. Bert Hinkler's plug, every time she washed the dishes. This is what I'm telling you. People your age are losing respect for our history."

"You really think so?"

"I'm not suggesting it about you, my boy. No, not at all. It's because we've been reinvented, and continue to be, that's my theory. That's why they forget."

"How much did you pay for it?" I asked.

"A steal. Swapped it for half a dozen new plugs, didn't I?"

A safety pin, a false teeth glass, a shoelace excited T. Nelson Downs provided it had been baptised by what he called the "un-explainable glow of legend". I have these words in a rare letter. Such objects were valuable depending on their place in the "sphere of the hero". I liked that one in particular. Personal items relating to hygiene were worth more, he argued, as they were closer to the living body of the historical figure. Undershirts fetched higher prices than shoes, for instance, spectacles more than floor tiles.

"Did you enjoy dealing in dead things?" I asked, long after he had abandoned the trade full-time, when his concern shifted towards dreams of the biggest hothouse in the southern hemi-sphere, moving fig trees and palms with cranes — the fragile but very much alive business of plants.

"Dead things?" he replied, surprised. "Why do you think people love antiques? Why are they willing to pay so much?"

"Why?" I asked, expecting a further theory. "Because they have charm? Because you can't get them any more?"

"Partly right. I think it puts them in touch with death, that's why. They can look at a chair and know, perhaps without realis-ing it, that millions have come and gone since it was made."

"That's how you saw the trade?"

"Absolutely. I liked how it depended on the courage of the buyer. Some just want an old shaving razor or a thimble to touch and hold. That's enough for them. The occasional stroke of a Moroccan pillbox, something like that. Others have houses full of antiques. It makes people less scared, I suppose. Simple as that."

"Bit morbid," I said to stir him up. I enjoyed that.

"Not in the least. I used to bridge the gap for them."

"Bit parasitic."

"I was the recycling man. That was me. Mr Recycle."

T. Nelson Downs called his first and last antique store "The Floating World". It remained open for exactly three months and seven days. Then it was converted by the new owners into an electrical store, and is now a video rental outlet, with dozens of shelf categories like Horror, Romance, Action, Drama and Children's.

When the business failed he often drove past it or stopped, his motor running, to look at the window of Japanese television sets, toasters, waffle irons, juicers and radios. Brisbane had rejected his history, he maintained. In those short months he had secured five sales. A telephone had not even been connected at the time of closure, despite his repeated requests. It was a conspiracy, he decided, though he had no proof. He often looked over to the city, at the cranes above the ridge of trees, and wondered who had it in for him.

At first he thought it might have been other dealers, the big boys down town. No one had brought antiques to the suburbs before. He had been the first, sandwiched between a milk bar and hairdressing salon.

For a time he suspected his neighbours were involved in the plot. They burned their rubbish behind their stores at the same time each day; cardboard, papers and food scraps on the left, and hair and plastic on the right. They knew that the vendor of antiquities had nothing to burn. They knew he could not retaliate. He wondered how much they had been paid to smoke his stuffed eagles, his early edition copies of *Captain Cook's Voyages of Discovery*, or *Epoch Men*.

They were convivial at first.

" 'Floating World'? Sounds like a bathroom shop," said Max the milk bar man, his hands on his hips, looking up at the awning.

"Antiques are passed down, through so many hands," T. Nelson tried to explain. "No one can really ever own them. Do you get it?"

In the beginning he bought his lunch from Max, and even had his hair cut once in Annette's Salon.

"You're starting to lose a bit on top," she said.

"Really?"

"Be gone back to here by forty, back to here by fifty."

"That fast?"

"Maybe sooner."

"Any way to stop it?"

"Nope, unless you want a new scalp," she said, pulling his head back firmly and rinsing it under warm water. "Your sign won't work."

"Pardon?"

"The Floating World. No way people will come in with a sign like that."

"Pardon me?"

T. Nelson, in those quiet moments at the back of his store, reminisced about his mother's habit of hoarding everything. As a child he had played with pencils, cigarette holders, tea strainers, broken fob watches, thimbles, odd cuff links, brooches and belt buckles as other children would with toys, way before he realised their significance, their history put in place by a story, by the description of a moment, only meaningful to his mother and father.

The pencil would be one his father had given his mother when they were courting, on a nondescript day in the Edward Street tea-rooms. She had written her address for him and handing back the pencil and paper he had said: "Keep it." The thimble had been his grandmother's. She had used it to patch his own father's britches, shirts, socks. The tea strainer had been a gift from a friend who had ended up tangled beneath the wheels of a city tram.

These had been his antiques, he thought, their value only relative. They would become meaningless junk when they lost their story, even the pieces that his mother collected of him — the cuttings of hair, pins, exercise books, drawings, marbles, ties, certificates, an empty bottle of hair oil — and other items that orbited his early life.

"Basically it's all detective work," he shouted to Annette, the electric razor squaring the hair at the nape of his neck. "The stuff's out there, I just have to find it."

"No point really, is there?"

"You don't think so?"

"The ultimate waste, really, isn't it? You buy it and it sits there. You dust it and it still sits there." She dusted him now with a powdered brush.

"You're not interested at all in antiques? In the past?"

"Can't afford to be," she said, pulling the pale blue cloth from him. "I have to keep up with what's happening now. If I don't I'm finished."

"Sure," he said, struggling out of the chair. She was already putting on orange lipstick behind the counter.

"Take my advice. Change the name. You'll be pushing it up-hill as it is."

Later, when he leased the Universe-Cine-by-the-Sea, he took my mother and me on one of his frequent nostalgia drives around Brisbane; past his school, the rowing club, bars, his first plant business, and the Floating World, with its cardboard gun-men and kissing lovers in the window. Max's store had burned down some time before. But Annette's salon was still there with the same venetians at the front, the same three chairs, hairdrying cones on stands and mirrors.

He went inside and she was there, reading a magazine behind the counter. She had greyed.

"Good afternoon," she said.

"Annette, how are you?" he said, standing with the front door half open against his boot.

She put on her glasses, still holding the magazine open with one hand, and leaned slightly forward.

"I'm sorry. I didn't catch the name."

Jack had a crewcut and a forged steel belt buckle that depicted a war scene: a helicopter above, near the lowest white button of his shirt, two infantrymen holding rifles at their waists, stalking, as if they had crawled out of his zipper, and a thicket of bamboo on each side.

When we made our first stop for coffee we stood near the bus together and talked.

"You seen this?" he said, taking a small blue travel bag from the luggage compartment. He snorted, holding it up with his forefinger.

"That skinny German kid," he said. "This is all he brought for twenty-one days across the States. Just take a look at that." He dropped the bag. "I can tell a lot about people by their luggage. I've seen it all."

Passengers started moving back into the bus, and I could see their silhouettes through the smoky glass of our Americruiser.

"Had a busload of French folk couple of trips back," he said, drawing hard on his cigarette. "Had to hand them over to another driver just two days into it. Couldn't stand the smell."

Most of the tour group was seated now. There was no sign of Butch. Suddenly there was laughter in the bus, and people moving about, getting out of their seats and looking out the starboard windows.

I squatted and saw Butch's white canvas shoes on the other side.

"What the fuck's going on?" Jack said, crushing his butt.

Butch was there, on the balls of his feet, with a pot of white shoe cleaner in one hand and a sponge-headed applicator in the other.

"Hey," Jack shouted, "what the fuck you think you're doing?" Our tour guide, Gunter, leaned out of the driver's window.

With a few crude strokes Butch had painted a map of Australia on the ribbed aluminium coach. His continent extended from just below window level and down across the luggage hatches. A bit of coastline had splashed on the rear tyres and the greyhound symbol was encased by the map. Brisbane, Father, our humble home, was the bulb of the dog's nose, Sydney the tip of its extended paw. Its ribs, though not visible, arced over the red centre like a canopy. I imagined Ayers Rock as the canine's stomach sack. Next to his skew-whiff nation he had written: WARNING — Australians on Board.

"There you go, mate," Butch said, waving to the cameras inside the bus.

Jack, standing incredulous, knocked back the peak of his cap. We later learned that he had more than thirty hats in a small bag

49

behind his seat. This one depicted dense jungle stitched in brilliant green and gold. A dragon with red eyes writhed through the foliage. In vivid orange the cap read VIETNAM VETERAN.

He said nothing as Butch got back on board.

"Does this shit come off?" he asked me.

"Should do with a bit of water."

"Some of these fuckers," he said, erasing Perth with saliva on his forefinger, "they think they're the first ones to fucking travel. They're all fucking Christopher Columbuses, you know? Shit, look at this. I could lose my fucking job over this."

On the way to Monterey the whole bus learned of Butch's graffiti. At progressive stops they borrowed his shoe polish pot and painted in their own countries. A reduced United States swung across the front door and onto the grille. Europe floated over the rear wheel and embraced the corner that housed the internal toilet. South Africa nestled near the exhaust. Jack, realising the whole day had got out of control, simply waited for the white paint pot to run out. It did, with the United Kindom dribbling onto the brake lights. Beth La Valley would have loved the diverse nationalities.

That night, in the dimness of a remote truckstop and motel with the bus still creaking from the long drive, I helped Jack, the driver with a Viet Cong bullet still lodged somewhere in his body, wash away the world with rags and buckets of water.

T. Nelson arrived late for Waldo's act of levitation. He had caught the ferry to Cremorne Point to see a natural rock bath he had heard about many years before. It was a magnificent little pool, he thought, long and slender, with an overhanging wall of lush plants on one side and the harbour on the other.

By the time he got to the Blue Pacific Lounge it was nearing 10 p.m. He caught the final three veils of Cleopatra who, to his surprise, came straight off the stage and sat next to him.

"Waldo, he wants to have a word with you," she said, dabbing her face with a handkerchief.

"Yes, I know," he said. "Would you like a drink?"

They enjoyed gin and tonics before the magician, again in his cape, appeared at their table.

"I forgot to ask you your name," he said, finishing off T. Nelson's drink.

"Downs. T. Nelson Downs."

The magician tapped Christ against the tumbler.

"How extraordinary," he said, turning the glass over, looking into it. "I knew a T. Nelson Downs in London, turn of the century. Still see him now and then."

"I see." He noted Cleopatra rolling her eyes.

"He was the world's foremost coin conjurer when he was a young man. The back and front palm method, that was his. The ten-coin pass from one hand into a glass held in the other at arm's length. Brilliant. He had an affair, you know, with Mademoiselle Patrice, the Queen of the Changing Handkerchiefs."

Waldo got up quickly and went backstage.

"Don't listen to him," Cleopatra said, cracking ice with her teeth. "He needs to be put away."

She wore a large silk robe over her outfit. It had a peacock fanning its feathers on the back. He asked her name, and then if she wanted another drink. She ordered a cocktail with a blue seahorse stirrer.

"I won't let him come near me," she said. "He reckons he worked in a mortuary for some years and had a relationship with a corpse. What do you make of that?"

"How revolting."

"He says the night watchman caught them once."

"Unbelievable."

"Now you know what I have to work with."

The curtains parted and Waldo was there, his arms outstretched, with a turban on his head.

"Tonight," the magician boomed to the small crowd, "will be the final performance of the Great Waldo, as you see him now."

Some drinkers whistled, and a cocktail umbrella glided onto the stage. A moth had found the footlights.

"Tonight, ladies and gentlemen, I will levitate for you. I will float before your eyes."

51

It was warm and T. Nelson could feel the growth of sweat on his back. Lola continued to dab her face. Then the lights dimmed and Waldo was suddenly horizontal, a metre off the stage, his cape brushing the floorboards. The cat-calling stopped along with the drum rolls from two drunks at the bar.

Waldo then started rising smoothly, the cape levering back until he was so high the black velvet was completely suspended as well, wavering gently in the breeze from an overhead ceiling fan.

"Did he tell you about his mate Einstein?" Lola whispered, holding the head of the seahorse between thumb and forefinger. "And how he can fly through space, to other planets?"

It was then that Waldo began to move, at first rocking gently from side to side, his fists clasped tightly.

"Watch the fan," the barman shouted. "Will someone get that fan?"

But Waldo was already jumping in mid-air, his legs and arms twitching uncontrollably. His turban flew off and rolled almost a complete circle on stage before coming to rest.

"Get the bloody fan someone!"

A doorman had reached the controls and twisted the knob, but Waldo moved even faster and the blades were spinning at full speed.

"My God," Lola said, bringing her fingers to her mouth.

The quivering magician was drawn up towards the fan, close enough to induce a scream from the audience, before being flung across the stage and into a side wall. He collapsed unconscious, his face and hands lacerated with fine cuts.

T. Nelson was walking out of his hotel, his bag in one hand and the horse under his other arm, when the manager called him to the desk.

"A package for you, Mr Downs."

The bundle was wrapped tightly in brown paper and lashed with what looked like piano wire. A heavy duty cutter had to be found before he could open the parcel.

Inside was Waldo's cape, folded with the sequined face of the sun facing upward. There was a note.

"By now I am in Leningrad," the magician had written. "I wish you to be Waldo now. Fly, fly."

In the train on the way home, with the horse and the sun-faced cape at his feet, and the promise of Cleopatra, T. Nelson could not help but smile at the thought of the magician with three separate breaks in one leg and a fractured ankle in the other, gliding through the solar system, his rubber-ended crutches spread wide like wings beneath his arms.

Not surprisingly, Waldo the Great, alias Enrico Hippocrates, could not be found for an interview.

The only evidence I have of him is an old insurance claim, for £100,000, for the injuries he sustained in his levitation accident. His antecedents give some details of his family in Leningrad, his life touring with country fairs all over Australia and gypsy troupes in Europe.

There was one quote, from the manager of the Blue Pacific Lounge, near the bottom of the claim, under Comments from Witness. It read: "We were unable to confirm that any wires were used in the performance by Waldo the Great on that night."

You never became another Waldo, did you, Father? The only trick you ever learned was to pull a billiard ball from your throat, and that was boring after a couple of times.

After closing the Floating World, T. Nelson Downs went on the road. He planned intricate runs throughout the country in search of antiques.

Firstly, he laid out a large map, free from the cartography department of the government, and traced his intended journey in pencil, numbering each town where he'd stop. He then divided the trip into segments, and viewed each leg in more detail on smaller maps. This gave him greater focus: the location of rest stops, public parks, churches, hotels, street grids, farms.

He wrote down on palm-sized cards each numbered leg, including specific driving directions, hotel prices, a food allowance, the maximum purchasing budget depending on the area, and sometimes the nature of goods he was interested in. Roma, he had been told, was good for furniture, Mount Gambier for silverware, Orange for books and so on.

At the end of his preparation, T. Nelson collected his cards, shuffled them in order and kept them together with a rubber band on his dashboard. If he happened to misplace a card, or erase its details with spilt coffee or beer, he drove straight through that town to the next.

Sorting his paperwork, I found more than six hundred of these cards, some speckled with fat and thumbprint smudges, or permanently curved, perhaps shaped in a back pocket, or simply by the damp.

For no reason, I sat down one evening with a green pen and joined the dots of all the towns on a cheap atlas. I was unable to find some towns and pushed the pen ahead to the next recognisable one. Hours later I stood up from the kitchen table and looked at the map.

The entire continent appeared smashed into small pieces.

3

My father would say he began his research into the Burleigh Heads area from the beginning, but they were just the scavengings of a boy, fragments of death that gave him little insight. Surely a boy could not have seen beyond the leopard spots of a cracked shell, or the stench of a shoebox full of starfish.

He did not even recognise the piles of broken oyster shells he found littered around the bluff, seeing them only as annoyances that occasionally sliced open his tender schoolboy feet.

He got as far back as Alfred Swain, pioneer of the coast, and could go no further. It frustrated him, agitated him. Normally he could find a way in, a crack in the door, a weak spot.

All the evidence was there, embracing him, but he could not see it.

How I would love to call you a stupid bastard. To your face. Through our cigar smoke.

But they fooled the big-shot reporter too, didn't they? Are you laughing out there? Sure, I can see you, in the warm waters of the Pacific, a dugong under each arm, giggling hysterically.

"That's my boy!" you're shouting with a weak, salt-dry voice.

Gunter, our tour guide, read out loud a history of America from a school textbook, its cover a watercolour montage of Indians and covered wagons behind the peak of the Empire State Building, the San Francisco Bridge arcing around the spine, and rockets and muskets on the back.

"In the 1930s," he croaked in his high-pitched voice over the small bus speakers, "Monterey was a thriving whaling port, but its main business was sardines."

From the window I watched schools of frogmen on this early

55

Sunday morning, their yellow and green tanks bobbing. Wilson Tyler, at the back, had already lit up his first cigar for the day.

"But in 1945 the sardines, once plentiful, suddenly died, and they were washed up on the beach."

It had to be scuba classes, I thought. They joined hands underwater, like a ring of skydivers. Even watching them made me shudder. You know full well, Father, my fear of being underwater. For me, it was against the order of things; risking life, denying natural oxygen, for momentary pleasure. There were probably thousands of scuba divers dropping beneath the surface of the ocean every hour of the day around the world with their exact quantity of air on their backs. We are all like that anyway, you said. We all have a set limit of air that we will never know. It didn't change my mind.

"The death of the — can you hear me all right back there? The death of the sardines caused massive unemployment and Monterey became a ghost town."

The rotting pylons of the old jetty held up souvenir shops and drums of fresh seafood. As we parked, some of the divers left the water and dropped their tanks on the sand. They flicked water from their long, shining flippers. Jack padlocked the bus, a diesel-powered 102, and we walked to the jetty to the bark of seals.

"I swear he's going to die on me, that old guy," Jack said.

"Who, Wilson?" It was cool and I kept my hands in my pockets.

"I can tell. He's on his last trip and he's going to die. Wait until we get into the desert."

"You really think so?"

"You know how I know, Bud?" He called me that on occasion. "He doesn't have a camera. Did you notice that? Reporters are supposed to notice things like that, right? No camera. I've done hundreds of these trips, spent most of my life in hotels. He's the second one I've seen without a camera."

"What happened to the first?"

"Died in Calico. Bottom of the silver heap."

"Dropped dead?"

"One hundred and six degrees in the saloon."

Jack stopped to light a cigarette with a Zippo he had had since Vietnam.

"What if old Wilson dies in the desert, in the middle of nowhere?"

"Have to put him in the luggage compartment."

I laughed. "Bullshit."

"Listen, a woman died on one of these trips and the driver, buddy of mine, waited until everybody had got off the bus then carried her out onto the sidewalk," he said as we walked up onto the jetty. "Too much paperwork if they die on the bus."

"If they die actually inside the Greyhound?"

"You bet," he said. "An inquiry, the works. Could cost the company millions. And who'd want to lose their job over one stiff?"

"Incredible."

"Hell of a lot of people are out there dying stepping onto or off of Greyhounds, let me tell you." He guffawed in some Marlboro smoke then coughed.

The jetty was lined with metal drums filled with ice, crabs and shrimp. Peter, the English plasterer, filmed the seafood through the smoke from the dry ice. He recorded everything on his video camera. He had one entire steel, round-edged suitcase filled with tapes. He even shot traffic on the highways.

"Cecil B's at it again," Jack said.

I had noticed Peter hold his camera in the air with one hand in the bus, above the heads of the other passengers, the lens aimed out the window. This was his America, through the grey eyepiece of his machine. He played it back immediately on its built-in monitor, to check what he had captured. Whenever we said, "Did you get the divers, Pete? Did you see the Old Bathhouse Restaurant? John Steinbeck's head? The seals feeding on the kelp?" and he had missed it, he would always reply, "Shit, don't tell me. I didn't."

The ice made his lens fog over, and I imagined him back home in Battersea, London, near the upturned table of the power station, screening to the audience of his children the crabs of Monterey, their pink and blurred writhing almost pornographic.

Jack and I chatted with a fisherman breaking ice with his

57

short-handled pick. He told us of the seals, the kelp pools, the sea otters and how they used anything they could find on the ocean floor as a tool to open shellfish on the rocks that dotted the shoreline.

He said the pools off Monterey were once full of sealife, not only sardine. He could still not explain the death of the fish, which he remembered when he worked with his father who was also a fisherman.

The smell of them rotting, millions of them, stranded or floating in with the tide, always reminded him of hard times, of hunger, his father's drinking and the break-up of his family.

The old man laughed.

"They've turned the sardine factory into an aquarium," he said, pointing. "They all got a nice safe home in there now. Would've killed my old man if he seen that."

I asked him about Gunter's textbook history of the region.

"I come back from the war, South Pacific, and the whole lot of them damned sardines is dead. My old man said what we gonna do with all those empty sardine cans, boy? He said they must have had their own war too."

The giant sign for Portola Brand Sardines had vanished.

"Used to be right over there, front of the aquarium," he said. "The old bathhouse, she's gone too. Fancy restaurant for you folks now. The old man would've broken up over that."

We had no time to visit the aquarium. Besides, it was Mother's Day in America and there were dozens of children and women with roses waiting outside its doors.

Driving further south, there were more chains of divers, some tightly formed, some broken, floating with their masks down.

All through our bus was the cracking of crab claws.

Alfred Swain's great-grandfather wrote, in his log, an account of a mermaid he saw swimming above the fists of coral on the Great Barrier Reef.

"She was swimming with sweetlip," he noted, "and her hair was blue, as God is my witness."

T. Nelson Downs, antiquarian, had once owned the journal,

and kept it in his bedside table with a packet of fertiliser sticks, headache tablets and other junk. Occasionally he took it out and browsed through its cryptic navigational codes. He wondered if the shakiness of the lettering had been due to a storm at the time, a rolling of the old rig, or hunger.

He sold it to the university in Townsville, so it could be, as he explained to me, closer to the source.

At Burleigh Heads bluff, the constant emergence of broken oyster shells through the soil puzzled Alfred Swain. He knew nothing of the bluff's history, and was unaware it had been a site of lovemaking, murder, feasting. He had simply inherited it on his father's unexpected death.

To him the shells were an aggravation, their frilled and often sharp edges breaking into the salt air. Swain went around picking them off the site where he would build his mansion. It would, in part, be a memorial to his father, Jon, severed through the torso by the teeth of his own giant timber saw. It had happened only a short walk from the pegged-out rectangle of the house plan.

The family cedar business continued despite the tragedy. The saw that had found its way so easily through the old man's ribs was wiped and re-oiled and was soon fashioning exquisite lumber for guesthouses, ballrooms, legal chambers, as it had always done. Those brilliantly polished panels, so often commented on, absorbing candlelight, the flash of silverware, white waxed moustaches, the beehives of women, medals of honour, or a gloved hand on a thigh beneath the table.

The same saw would artfully shape timber for the Swain mansion already, in planning, a monstrosity of steep roofs anticipating snow despite the subtropical climate, portholes, wide verandahs with railings curved to resemble a ship, and at the top, a wheelhouse complete with bell and weathervane. The oyster shells, however, posed a problem.

Before building the foundations, Swain ordered that three feet of topsoil be removed from the entire site. The soil was then sifted by hand, the shells crushed and collected in a midden for later use on the surface of the carriageway.

"Be resourceful, gentlemen," he told his lackeys, hands behind his back, his European riding boots without a trace of dust, striding around the perimeter of his mansion site. "Use what you have to your own advantage. Use it. Let it work for you, gentlemen."

When the house was complete, steel-rimmed carriage wheels would crackle on the shells and alert the bachelor to visitors, allowing for the final sweep of an ivory-handled comb, or the tweak of a moustache tip.

Despite his elegance, the young Swain was an expert axeman; just under six foot, fair, with a solid chest and shoulders. He was as much a contradiction as his mansion, its supporting beams no doubt carrying traces of his father's blood.

More than occasionally he worked with his gangs of timber getters, yet he ran the financial side of the business meticulously, his records written using a gold fountain pen. When felling trees in and around the bluff, he remained in full gentleman's dress — a stiff collar, tie, riding boots, and a gold brooch with an emerald centre. He wiped sweat and woodchip from his face with an initialled handkerchief.

The timber men, in their slab huts at night, talked of their employer. They said he had his eyebrows manicured by naked women. That the same women washed his back with fresh sponges collected from Burleigh beach. One cutter claimed he had seen, during a late night stroll, a topless woman leaning out of the wheelhouse.

Women did come to Swain, from the fashionable guesthouses of Elston and Coolangatta. Dozens, possibly hundreds of them. Governors, surveyors, attorneys, and businessmen also made their way up his ghost white carriageway, through the pine trees at the edge of the beach. They dined on fresh fish caught off the basalt shelf, and imported condiments that made them imagine Europe. To them, Europe was the world, the seat of civilisation, the model for life. Europe was style, and Swain had it.

Even Queensland Governor Lord Lamington came to dinner.

"I have to say, Swain, that we need more people like you in this State," he said over cigars and port. "Yes, indeed."

"Thank you sincerely, sir."

"It is what is wrong here, in this gem of a State of ours. I don't know if you have noted, but there is a distinct lack — distinct — of the middle and upper classes.''

''We are but young.''

''I would differ there,'' the great man said. ''Just look at the Americas, for example, and their degree of progress. No, no, the upper classes that we do have are greater rogues than the working wretches. Drink? I have toured up and down this State of ours, I tell you, and I don't like what I see. Everywhere you look, life is a party.''

''Is that so disastrous?'' Swain asked, momentarily regretting the question.

''We are hurtling towards the twentieth century, Swain, with a cultural mediocrity that is positively dangerous. Ours is a rich land, make no mistake about that, in the hands of children.''

The Governor sipped again from his small Swedish crystal glass, and looked around the drawing room. ''Anyway, Swain, do tell us about these mermaids of yours. You are the talk of Brisbane, you know.''

Swain had been unaware that his obsession with the mythical sea creature had ignited such public interest, and was embarrassed that it had reached offices as high as that of the Governor.

''It is hereditary, I'm afraid,'' he joked, making light of the matter.

''Come now. They say you've seen one. Is it true?''

Swain paused before saying: ''That is not exactly true, sir. My great-grandfather, you are aware, discovered the Swain reefs up north.''

''Of course. Good fishing there, I hear.''

''Yes. He claims he saw one, swimming with a school of sweetlip.''

''How incredible.''

''I have matched his journal entry with the description given by a sailor off Newfoundland in 1610. In both, the hair was blue.''

''You are giving an old man chills, Swain. Was he of sound mind, your grandfather?''

''Absolutely.''

''How extraordinary.''

"Indeed."

"Let us drink then, to the blue-haired maiden."

Swain was relieved Lord Lamington had not inquired about his weathervane, a goldplated mermaid, her outstretched arms for East and West, and an arrow emerging between her breasts and out her back, for North and South.

The Governor had surely noticed the gold mermaid door knocker, hinged at the back of the head and lifted by a fanned tail. The shininess of her fins was a testimony to his popularity.

Trying to change the topic, Swain said: "Coming to this country, Governor, one almost feels like an explorer."

"How do you mean?"

"It is an old and a new place at the same time. It asks to be made something of, this place. It is waiting, still, for a new history."

"There are the native people, of course."

"We still have some here, you know. I have one in my cutting team."

"You have to have some sort of sympathy for the poor wretches," the Governor said, raising his finger and gently lifting a droplet of port from his moustache. "The women carry their dead children's hands around with them, did you know that? In their little baskets. Frightful."

"I wish to make something here," Swain said, standing, hitching his thumbs into his waistcoat pockets. "Something permanent."

"A monument, do you mean?"

"I work with wood, as you know, sir. It doesn't last forever, wood. It's like us. No, no. Something in stone."

"Good for you, Swain. How about a huge mermaid, my boy, at the tip of the bluff here."

"It wasn't what I had in mind."

"I'll get you as much sandstone as you need. I'll officially unveil it for you, how about that?"

"I'll consider it, sir," Swain said. "Would you care for that game of billiards?"

*   *

62

Do not think ill of T. Nelson. He discovered, courtesy of the sandstone mermaids, and a brief incident beneath carnations of fireworks, his sexuality. He became obsessed with the Oceanic Baths, as one becomes addicted to nicotine.

When he was a boy the columns of the Oceanic still had breasts. His favourite was Moira, as he had named her, the column farthest left of the changing house. From a certain angle in the pool, the ochre of her sandstone shapeliness was accentuated by the lush foliage of Burleigh bluff which acted as a backdrop. He could see the rise of her right nipple, the fingernail sharpness of her scales.

T. Nelson put his arms out to each side, floated with the pulse of the water, and imagined what was going on behind Moira in the female changing room. He looked at those heavy sandstone blocks, immovable, interlocked, and saw women showering, pushing their hair back beneath the warm water, their hips swivelling slightly with their eyes closed, the creamy soap flowing down their spines, or hooping around their waists and down between their buttocks. He wondered if they wore rubber thongs, as his mother had instructed him to do in public showers.

He often imagined what breasts felt like. He was unaware that his mother had any, beneath her cardigans, and never touched his sister as other boys tickled or teased theirs. He figured, floating and facing the sky, that if he knew what a woman's vagina looked like, and felt like, he would be privy to a great secret that was being withheld from him. He could look at any woman in the world, and nod or smile to himself, and be part of the club of men.

It was on the basalt boulders one New Year's Eve, where he had fished with his father and brothers, and within sight of the baths, when part of the mystery was revealed to him.

She was fourteen, a girl he had known for years from Sixth Avenue at the caravan park. They had gone to the rocks to watch the lightning out at sea. The horns from the park were already sounding early, warbling and fading with beer breaths.

They said nothing, but he felt dizzy with the screaming and music from the park, and the bellygroan of thunder way out, chasing in trawlers which were dragging their nets home, pushed by a cool bole of air that rolled in on itself.

They were kissing then, he clumsily despite the hundreds of movies he had seen, his eyes closed as he had observed Cary Grant only the night before. Then just as he had his hands inside her underpants, and the tip of his finger at her vagina, the top joint of his finger locked up, as it always did when he scratched in dirt for long periods, or wrote for too long.

He could never have imagined the feeling of the girl, he thought later. So fragile, delicate, its pleasure striking a nerve that conducted through his body. A special circuit for such things, he calculated in his bunk that night.

He always remembered it feeling like sinking into a warm bath up to his chin.

''You wanna go back to the party now?'' she said, and it was over.

When they first started blasting into the columns of basalt, Swain found dozens of dead octopus, fish, and molluscs on his manicured lawn leading down to the beach. He turned them over with the point of his boot, and left them for his hunting dogs.

Each explosion sent rosellas and topknots screeching and wheeling into the air. Several dropped dead from the trees. A worker claimed he saw a small band of wallabies leap into the ocean, disoriented, before clambering back up the rocks. It was the first time gelignite had been used on the coastland.

At night his men worked with sledge-hammers, neatening the rectangular shape in the rock, the sparks showering onto their legs and forearms.

With the help of Lord Lamington, a sculptor was commissioned to make the five pillars of the bath's changing house in the shapes of mermaids. Each had to have her own characteristics, with her arms upraised. After some months, the women travelled by cart from Brisbane, across the Nerang River on the ferry, to Burleigh bluff.

Swain held a small party for his cutters on the lawn to celebrate the arrival of the women.

For many of the men, it was their first taste of champagne.

"Drink up, gentlemen, don't be afraid," Swain boomed at them. "A job well done. You'll find a little extra in your pockets this week. Come, drink."

Later, Swain sat amongst his women at the edge of the incomplete baths, his black boots lost on the basalt, occasionally feeling a patch of scales or a stone dorsal.

"My beauties," he said to himself, raising his glass then resting it on his knees.

The women, including their breasts and nipples, were all unique. The scale patterns of five local species of fish were copied for the tail sections. Some hips were larger, or the ribs more pronounced. The hair appeared of different texture.

"I was out taking a piss," one cutter reported, "and he was sitting at their feet, swear to God. Touching them, you know."

"Half his bloody luck, mate."

"You know, running his hands up and down them."

"Crikey. Someone ought to tell the poor bastard he can get the real thing down at Coolangatta for a quid."

"He's going off, I reckon, like his old man."

At each corner of the baths were carved black marble seahorses, with copper piping running through their tails and out their mouths. And in the centre of the pool Swain, at great expense, had installed a copper mermaid, seated as a lady would be, with her massive tail to one side, bearing the face of his mother as a young woman.

As summer approached Swain lost all interest in his timber business. The area had virtually been exhausted of cedar, and instead of working back into the Hinterland, he let his cutters go and allowed his saws to rust over.

Every morning he would take breakfast in his white robe at the baths, then swim several short laps around the copper mermaid.

His valet, Dirk, stood patiently with a towel.

"You know, Dirk, don't you," he once said, sitting on the edge of the pool, "that I am the last of the line?"

"Yes, sir."

65

"The last Swain in the chain that is my family. You are aware of that?"

"Yes, sir."

"It's a great responsibility, Dirk. One could almost say a burden, if one looked at life that way."

"I agree, sir."

Swain rose and stepped back into the towel.

"Don't break the chain, isn't that what the old man always said?"

"I believe so, sir."

"The old bastard might have been right, for once," Swain said, turning, walking beneath the arms of the stone women and back to the house.

After considerable effort and for what it's worth, I have located Swain's memorial to his mother. It is not a pretty scenario.

You can find it on the besser brick wall of a housing estate at Mudgeeraba, behind Burleigh, beyond the flood-prone dairy paddocks and about a kilometre west of Wallaby Bob's Hotel. It is bolted to the top of a fence, above the sign "Mermaid Canal Estate". She has been taken to by drunken youths with sledgehammers and blowtorches. Black pubic hair has been spraypainted on her delicately scaled groin.

Near the end of the baths, as my father painfully recollected, the five sandstone women had already fallen victim to the onshore gusts, their breasts levelled and faces sanded into anonymity. Only the fifth, at the far right of the pavilion, retained a nipple, though my father suspected a quirk in the stone's texture.

"He wanted to buy that copper thing — revolting it was," my mother told me. "He thought it'd be fun to put it in the foyer of the Universe, in honour of our first world class swimmer, what was her name?

"The developers got her. Wouldn't let him have her. He used to drive out there. Just sit in the car and look at her. That went on for a long time. Then he'd start."

"What about?"

"Oh, the same old thing. The museums and things. Everything was all over the world, he'd say. Everybody's history, in different museums and collections and galleries and things, all over the place.

"He didn't like that. He couldn't understand how it could have happened like that. It was criminal, he said. He just couldn't understand it."

The Chinese rockets for Swain's turn-of-the-century party were launched from the three sides of the baths surrounded by ocean, and along the edge of the changing house roof, above the heads of his women.

On New Year's Eve it was extraordinarily warm, even for the season, and Swain envisaged that many of his five hundred guests would take to the pool after the fireworks.

The party began mid-afternoon, with horseracing on the beach. It was a favoured spot for racing because of the perfect and clear sweep from North Burleigh to Burleigh bluff, and from the baths his guests could watch the entire race. Others stood knee-deep in the surf, the men belting their knees with their hats. After the race the jockeys led their horses into the surf, where they listed like galleons beyond the breakers, amongst a few interested swimmers.

Having requested his guests, who came from as far away as Toowoomba, to wear black tie, Swain stood beneath the giant pines of his estate dressed entirely in white. He greeted everyone personally, leading them to the striped canvas tent on the front lawn for refreshments.

They feasted on giant perch caught off Swain reef, brought down especially from the north and iced at every available town, served on English silver platters. They drank the finest imported spirits and wines and danced to continual Victrola music, attended to all evening by a young man in white gloves.

An hour before the new century Swain, standing in the wheelhouse of his mansion with a tin megaphone to his mouth, asked the women of the party to gather in a circle around the polished cedar dance floor he had had constructed on the lawn. Once they had assembled, bemused and laughing, he ordered them to take down their hair.

"Do not be afraid," he shouted through the mouthpiece. "The twentieth century is upon us. Do not be afraid."

He then paced around the outside of the circle with his hands behind his back.

"What are you doing, Alfred?"

"Is it time?"

"Pick me, Alfie, pick me!"

Selecting one woman with auburn hair that extended over her pink and white frilled buttocks, the applause went up and the couple waltzed alone on the cedar pontoon. Whilst winding, the gramophone boy accidentally tipped over his concealed jar of brandy, his obscenity drowned out by Strauss's "Blue Danube".

Swain swung the young woman around, lifting her off her feet at times, so expert was he on his own timber. After the others had joined them, and the clipping of heels on the wood thundered up into the bluff, Swain and the woman disappeared.

Later, as the heavy gunpowder smoke still hung over the baths, Swain and his partner swam naked in the warm water. They drank from a champagne bottle placed on the fan of the copper mermaid's tail, and showered beneath the water spouting from the mouths of the seahorses.

In the morning a coachman who had fallen drunk amongst the tufts of dune grass went to wash his face in the surf and found a champagne bottle amongst the aqua domes of jellyfish stranded on the sand. One of Swain's white shoes was also discovered on the floor of the pool, along with a surprisingly large number of kelp ribbons. His clothes were left, folded immaculately, beneath the central mermaid column of his changing house.

At the inquest, the woman denied she had gone to the baths with Swain.

"Madame, there are countless witnesses who saw you and the gentleman Swain depart the dance floor and walk to the vicinity of the beach."

The woman's mother alleged that the young woman was unable to swim, and a Brisbane physician corroborated the theory by saying the woman had had a "tragically irreversible" fear of water since the great Brisbane floods of 1893. Evidence was given that the unfortunate girl was even allergic to seafood which, if ingested, resulted in debilitating facial and body rashes.

Swain's presumed death was ruled accidental.

"Considering the proximity of the baths to the ocean," the coroner found, "and the absence of any safety measures at the edge of the said baths, not to mention the context of the evening in question, it could be said that a death was waiting to happen."

It was rumoured, naturally, that the young woman had fallen pregnant to Swain. Considering his mother had died when he was young, and the two halves of his father had been cremated, a child would naturally have been eligible for inheritance.

She did indeed become pregnant, but some months later, to a travelling remedies salesman and gambler, who had since vanished.

In Swain's private papers, attorneys to Lord Lamington and other government officials discovered a handwritten note bequeathing his body to the Brisbane university's science faculty "for the learning and benefit of future generations".

Without a body, the university was granted the mansion for a period deemed appropriate by the Queensland Government, and converted it into a biological and geological research centre for students.

This was justified by officials on the evidence of Swain's passion for mermaids, and several jars of coloured sand found beneath his billiard table.

I can tell you, the Swain institute for further learning did not last long. Education has never been a priority in this State of ours. If there was a choice between a road and a school, the road would win out every time. Children are of a distant electorate. It is the road that caters for the immediate one.

I have photographs of the mansion, occupied by our distinguished horsemen of the First World War, its ragged lawns trampled on by battalions of horses, littered with cannon and even a primitive tank.

There are other shots of bathers stretched out on the sand, watching manoeuvres down the beach, mock battles and men in full uniform with feathered caps falling as if dead. Horses rearing to imaginary bullets. Snipers swinging around at the thud of a pine cone.

It was there, on the beach, that they trained for the deserts of Africa, the Anzac Cove landings, and other skirmishes that they could only have imagined. But they took it seriously, indeed, despite their audiences of carefree holidaymakers and interested groups of girls in swimsuits.

One picture, retrieved from the local library, shows a number of young men sitting on a dune, their horses a short distance away, pulling at the spinifex. By chance, I discovered an almost identical photograph of a similar group of men in Egypt, delirious with joy in front of the great pyramids, men together, and part of the grand adventure.

Now I begin to see your obsession with the place. It all happened here, didn't it? Everything that happened to our country, the way it evolved, occurred right here. This is where the myths started. What happened here, too, would be our future.

Did you really think they'd listen to you?

You would recall, Father, when the nipples of the mermaids had subsided, their figures less exciting and carved into middle age by the on-shore breezes, I nearly lost my life in the baths.

And where were you? On the verandah of some farmhouse in the Hinterland, negotiating, on your holidays mind you, the price of a pewter mermaid-shaped beer tankard, while I splashed in the shallow end of the ratty old pool, supervised by your mother.

You have denied this — the colour of my bathing trunks on that day, the weather, the seriousness of my brush with death — but I clearly remember slipping, bobbing twice, then sinking into the greenness. My grandmother was unravelling the pocket of a new sweater she was knitting.

I was pulled back to the surface by a man who was smoking a cigarette on the edge of the baths. He dived in and emerged with the cigarette still in his mouth.

After that you taught me how to swim. We went together to the Centenary Pool in Brisbane, not far from the museum, and you stood in the shallow end with other parents, holding me up as I stroked and kicked, watching your feet under the water.

When I think back, it was the only time we were ever really alone, doing something together. Father and son, and dozens of others thrashing the pool water at sunrise. The water alive, as if thick with a school of frenzied fish.

4

I have since had words with the young scribe who reported your death for the local newspaper. We nearly came to blows, I don't mind telling, in the Birdwatcher's Bar in Surfers Paradise. I saw myself in that young man, the thread bare on the seat of his trousers, knowledgeable of all things, waiting in the foyer of the Universe for a word or two from the traumatised loved ones. I was a similar marauder of such sanctities, no question. That was my life, once.

Okay, so a bit about me. For two years I worked beside a dead crime reporter's coat. It remained on the wooden stand behind my desk. It was cream with brown checks so bold that if you stared at it long enough it appeared to move. It had wide lapels, three wooden buttons down the front and one on each cuff.

My memory of Albert Urquhart, the owner of the coat, was of a large man, yet his property, suspended for so long on that metal hook, had become that of a thinner, more angular person. The dead man's dimensions often caused debate. Some said he was of medium build, while others confirmed he was solid. It could have been verified by taking down the coat and checking its size label, but nobody touched it. They wouldn't even dust it.

When I was alone on night shift at the back of the enormous newsroom I was often tempted to go through its pockets. I imagined a notebook in there, perhaps, filled with the shorthand records of men and women screaming, notes on the blue feet of a murder victim, blood on grass. But I did not disturb the coat as I, too, expected Albert to come blustering into the newsroom again, his pockets full of pencil shavings.

On the day of his death he had been visiting contacts, listening to his portable police airwaves scanner as other people listen to radios. He knew what police had for lunch, where they urinated, who was having marital problems, through the scanner. He even slept with it beside his pillow, where it fed him codes and addresses through the night.

Albert was thirty minutes from the office when he picked up an emergency call — the unconfirmed death of a Government Minister, crushed beneath farm machinery. He was the first there, at the hobby farm beside the Brisbane River, and parked his caramel Valiant at the gate. He lit a cigarette (Gitane, picked up from his time in Paris working for NATO) and sharpened a pencil.

Before he had time to step out of the vehicle he had dropped dead at the wheel, the cigarette still burning between his fingers. Across a ridge, beneath a red tractor, was the body of one of our State's most respected politicians. His much-photographed face was imprinted in the muddied surface of a freshly planted lettuce patch. The Minister's wife was there also, trying to push the machine off his body.

She heard Albert's car and ran down to the gate, screaming for help as you could understand. We presumed, while having drinks later for our lost reporter, that she had discovered Albert dead as well, the car filled with rank smoke and a scattering of wood shavings, and fainted.

The first police at the scene must have taken stock for some seconds, with two bodies at the gate and the good Minister half-submerged in soil. A second government undertaker's van would have to be called.

That afternoon I was appointed the new police reporter. My first assignment was Albert's obituary.

"Journalists write well about dead journalists," my chief-of-staff said. "Check the files on some of the big stories he covered. Try and get a comment from the commissioner or some of the other cops he drank with. Should be a mug shot of him in the picture library."

For one so young, I had already realised that in death relatives and friends are important to reporters, their words like precious stones.

"What about his wife?" I asked. "Want me to get her for a quote?"

"Wouldn't bother, she's probably out celebrating. One hundred and fifty words should do it, tops."

I cleaned out the drawers of Albert Urquhart's desk. Apart from the pencil shavings, coins and grains of tobacco, I found some interesting souvenirs of his career.

These included: a comb with dark clots at the base of the teeth that once belonged to the Green Comb Killer; a small metal cross from the stomach of bank robber Johnny "the Duck" Reardon; a swirling thumbprint in blood at the bottom of a letter from accountant and paedophile Harry Glass, and the stiletto heel of Shirley Blight, the Miss Queensland entrant who had vanished one day from King George Square. All that was ever found of her was a sandwich bearing the perfect half-moon indent of her teeth, and the heel.

Going through the clippings, I matched the souvenirs with these moments in the criminal history of our city. I turned the objects over in my hands and feared what was expected of me. For one, I had never seen a body. I imagined I saw one at my great-grandmother's funeral. Standing behind the mourners and looking into a grave with a cracked and lifted slab, I thought I could see a blue floral dress, but then I was a boy, unused to the family tears around me.

Perhaps they chose me to replace Albert because I looked like a policeman. I had short hair, cut cleanly around the ears. I favoured mostly navy and pale blue clothes. I had a pair of heavy black boots. In winter I wore a dark jacket. People often came up to me in the street and asked for directions, or assistance in unfolding prams. On the road motorists slowed down, my squarish head in their rear vision mirror. At a party a young constable asked if I had ever boxed down at the Police Club. He said I had the bone structure for it, particularly around the eyes. He later opened a beer bottle with one of his eye sockets.

My first death was not long in coming. It was at the Golden Nugget Caravan Park on the northern outskirts of the city.

"Love triangle," the inspector said to me as we walked to the cordoned off van.

"What do you mean exactly by love triangle?"

He stopped and looked at me. "What the fuck do you think,

74

sonny? Two blokes, got it, knocking off the same woman. Three. Triangle."

We kept walking. "Why the fuck do I have to do this crap anyway? I was just sitting down to a nice baked dinner. Nice wine. Jesus Christ, I don't know."

Neighbours had gathered around the yellow crime scene cord. They described rapid gunfire, and how the park had suddenly lit up. They stood in singlets and nightgowns, and others, with kerosene lanterns, were wandering through the lanes towards the death van.

We could see detectives inside the annexe, the flash of camera bulbs and the glow of a more powerful light that lit up the green canvas like a lampshade. It was a charade of sharp-edged caps, tape and note-taking. And there were police at the back of the van, guarding something in the long grass and occasionally firing a torch beam into it.

"You can see it there, look, a foot," one man whispered.

"God, is that a hand?"

Triangle. The only ones I could see were made of air, created by the tightened annexe ropes, the canvas and the earth. The inspector appeared again with his hands on his hips.

"See that up there?" he said to the reporters, pointing. "Up on the roof? Birds will get that by the morning."

"What sort of weapon was used?"

"The gun? Good question, sonny. It was the same type of gun that was used to assassinate John F. Kennedy."

We filed our stories of the love triangle. Of the jealous estranged husband who had tried to murder his wife and best friend in the van's double bed. He only struck limbs in the dark and, satisfied in his revenge, crouched behind the caravan, put the gun in his mouth and fired.

"The same gun that killed Kennedy?" the copytaker said. "Someone's having you on."

I cannot describe to you, Father, the pleasure I took in seeing that portly inspector, the one with a taste for Yorkshire pudding and woody claret, gripping his prayer beads in the witness stand at the inquiry.

* *

75

One night, dozens of bodies later, a woman in a full-length mink coat walked into the office.

From my desk beside the black police radio her face glowed with make-up that I was sure contained fine specks of quartz, and her lips were dark. As she walked closer I could smell roses, and noticed a triangle of gold and diamonds around her neck. Out in the foyer, which I could see down a long corridor, stood a man in a white suit and black shirt.

She never spoke, or took her eyes from me for that matter, as she lifted the dead crime reporter's coat from its hook. She stuffed it into a black garbage bag, put it under her arm and smiled at me, sympathetically it seemed, then turned and walked away.

For hours I could smell those roses. The aroma was there the next day too, when I hung my blue jacket on the coat stand for the first time.

Yes, they thought they had me for good. They could see me reading poetry to frail and star-eyed young women, fresh in the trade, over a Heineken or brandy balloon in the reporter's hotel. But one fooled cannot remain in the environment of his discovery, can he? Perhaps I developed a conscience after so long. That word long lost — conscience.

"Over there," Gunter said, pointing to a tiny peninsula and a brown wooden house surrounded on three sides by ocean. "That, ladies and gentlemen, is the house of the famous actor Clint Eastwood."

Our group found this most exciting, as you would, Father. You, who wore a white T-shirt beneath that nibbled usher's coat during your Clint festival. Your tight top lip could never capture that scowl though, could it? My fellow tourists surveyed the distant house with binoculars. They had their photographs taken in front of a fence that protected us from a small but sheer cliff, with Clint's dwelling over their left or right shoulders.

"Star of *Dirty Harry*," Gunter read from one of his palm-oiled crib cards, "*Bronco Billy, The Dead Pool* . . ."

I, too, borrowed a pair of binoculars and hoped to see the great man, perhaps pushing a mower around the yard in one of those legendary shirts, or picking off a few empty Budweiser cans with his Magnum, the sea off this mansion littered with empty shells and shards of aluminium.

In our excitement we failed to notice the arrival of a second busload. Their guide, a neat woman in what, I must stress, resembled an usherette's uniform without the trimmings, led the new group to us, and for a moment the two parties fused.

"That's Mister Eastwood's house over there, the white one," she said, pointing to a Cape Cod neighbouring the brown house that we had been scouring with our eyeglasses.

My tour colleagues were confused. They lowered their cameras and looked to Gunter who was checking his cards, shuffling them, searching for the clue that would verify his authority over the clipped new tour guide. When in doubt he seemed to drop his lower lip. He took the rival guide to one side for a private discussion, and then we were instructed to return to the bus.

There was some laughter as we pulled out of the parking lot. The group, becoming more voluble as the days went on and strengthened by the blush of Gunter's bald spot, so evident to us on that entire trip and its radius growing, so it appeared, with each pitstop, yelled out sarcastic comments and threw tissues.

I wondered how many tour groups he had taken to that exact spot, that worn piece of earth by the fence, and pointed out the home of the movie star. How many people, all over the world, had displayed their slides, home videos and photographs of the faded brown house, telling its story, the northern side of the Cape Cod just visible, or a white blur out of focus?

I took shots of each dwelling, I might add. But putting them side by side, Father, they negate each other, and drain each other's interest.

It would be worth checking signs now, I thought. Picking up facts brochures and navigating on my own map, just to make sure we were where Gunter told us we were. That we were looking at the truth, and not the distorted myths that are passed down through a line of hundreds of bored tour guides.

One day T. Nelson saw a photograph of his brother Mitch on the front page of the *Moreton Bay Courier*. The picture showed him standing on a motorised float making its way down the main coast boulevard, with streamers tangled around its axles and shredded paper being dumped from a window outside the shot.

T. Nelson knew immediately that it was his brother, beneath a banner — Ocean World Aquatic Wonderland — and dressed as a starfish. He wore a foam suit, a deep bottle green as the picture would not show, and was waving his arms which were creamy added appendages between four of the starfish's limbs. A Starfish is Born, read a small sandwich board latched over his two upper rays. Mitch's face was visible through an oval hole in the underside of the sea creature. He danced between a dolphin and a killer whale.

Through his business contacts, T. Nelson had heard that his older brother worked hosing out the penguin and seal enclosures at the marine park. And that he lived in a wheelless railway carriage in the Hinterland, not twenty minutes drive from the Universe.

Often, T. Nelson drove up into the mountains, stood beside the bowser outside the Peacock Cafe, and looked across the ravine at his brother's caboose. It was made of oxblood wooden slats, had a concave tin roof and rested on short stumps. He could see washing hanging from a rope tied between the guardsman's railing and a pine tree.

"Hippies," the Peacock owner said, his singlet mottled with sweat patches of varying age. "Drugs, I bet. Grow their own food too, you know. Thought that had gone out these days, hey? Flower power children, whatever they are."

T. Nelson noticed a motorcycle amongst squares of light and dark green vegetable leaves, empty fuel drums, a car body and a wood heap.

"It's you and me, pal, who's paying for those bludgers. You and me and everybody else."

It distressed T. Nelson that yet another of his family had chosen to ignore him. He considered himself likeable, generous, the custodian of good advice on a multitude of subjects, and trusting. He told Lola he could not help but think that Mitch's thirty-five

78

years had, like the decaying caboose, skewed off their tracks, bounced, and come to rest in the centre of an old dairy paddock.

He had a big heart, T. Nelson. He felt sorry for the whole world, beginning with his own immediate life, then radiating outward until his compassion could not be controlled and was grasped by others with less honourable intentions. But more of that later.

The last I saw of Mitch was at his wedding to a Japanese woman in the upstairs room of her father's sushi bar in George Street. The whole place reeked of fish and salt, which was ingrained in the cloth of the decorative oriental flags that wavered from the ceiling like gills. Mitch wore a caftan, and she a red leather dress. Her face and hair, however, were styled kabuki.

The tables had been parted to form an aisle. There was no cake, although a wedding wish to Mitch and Kazumi was spelled out in delicately placed rolls of seaweed-wrapped sushi. The "i" in Mitch's name was dotted with a miniature rose made from the knob of a baby carrot.

"It seemed to happen after this," my father told me, one late evening beneath the white screen of his cinema. "Tabby was gone but Mitch always managed to stay in touch. You know, Christmas cards, visits, a phone call. If he needed some cash, I'd give it to him. Not a worry. That's what it was like.

"He had a good job, too. Well, a regular one, which was good for Mitch. Cleaning out air-conditioning ducts."

"Cleaning ducts?"

"In the same hospital you were born in." T. Nelson laughed. Well, not exactly a laugh, but the seed of one. "He used to crawl through all the ducts, right through, then start at the beginning again."

"Sounds horrible."

"He asked them if he could do it at night, you know, so when he finished for the day he could at least catch some daylight. It would've been dark in those ducts. Awfully dark."

I thought it was fortunate Mitch was a small man, though work as a jockey's apprentice may have been more healthy, free of the viruses, the reek of antiseptic and the screams that were pulled up into those tin canals through which he crawled.

79

"Then there was the accident."

Now this had always caused some rankling between us. My father analysed the accident over and over, physically went and took photographs of the scene, the vehicle wreckage and the extended skid marks on the bitumen, just as the police had done before him. He was convinced that this moment, over so quickly, in a second or less, had been the catalyst for the further disintegration of our family's pyramid. If Mitch had died, as cruel as it sounds, everyone might have knitted together. If he had suffered lesser injuries, the joy of his perfect recovery might have had a similar effect, reminding everyone of the preciousness of life.

But no, it had not turned out that way. Mitch had died, for thirty minutes. Thirty full, hospital clock minutes. His vehicle, travelling at an estimated speed that had shocked even the police at the scene, had sliced a wooden telegraph pole in half. Mitch fell from the wreckage and into the gutter. His passenger, miraculously unhurt except for a forehead bruise from the dash, simply locked his side of the car and walked home.

The crash was within sight of the hospital where Mitch worked. My father always maintained that if it had been another fifty yards down the road, Mitch would not have made it. As it was, he was clinically dead by the time they started operating, and remained that way for thirty minutes. It later became his favourite number.

"God did not want to take him that day," my father said, which is where we differed. My uncle, plainly, was drunk. I have since seen the police report which took a lot of work to locate. His blood alcohol reading was alarming to say the least. But still my father insisted on the generosity of God, whom he saw, I presumed, as a bearded gent who looked over His blueprint of the world as one would flick through a street directory.

Let's leave that. It causes pain. It was a device so magnificently used by this government of ours in a far more sinister way. How seamlessly they defined Good and Evil for us, and stitched it into our daily lives. I think now of the police carrying the guiding light of the saviour, or more realistically heavy torches that dropped from their belts, able to crack a skull with one swing. And how easy it becomes to accept it all when you are part of it, despite a nagging instinct that something is wrong. But even that can be laughed away. Sure. Nothing easier. Laugh at the bible-bashers, the backward northerners. At least we are following the true light.

As for Mitch, he came back to us with double vision which, understandably, unbalanced his place in the world, even for a man so lightfooted. In a very short space of time he went from duct cleaner to starfish.

"But how bad is it?" I asked.

"I'm looking at you now," my father said. "Say I'm Mitch. On the right side I see you again, another you, but a bit blurred."

"Like the ghosts on a television with bad reception."

"Precisely."

The powerlines that Mitch felled had also caressed his lifeless arm in that gutter, and had carved an orange scar the shape of a flame into his flesh. It was a lifelong reminder that he, for a second, carried through his body enough electricity to light a suburb.

"That's when it all started," my father said with what I suspected was a tear in his left eye. "He left his wife and kiddie and went to live in a caboose. Now what sort of man would do that, Samuel? What sort of man?"

"Maybe it was the electricity."

"Who would dress up as a starfish? I'm sorry, I can't talk about it."

He did, though. About fate. How the pole had been waiting for Mitch. How his own grandmother had died shortly after, as if it had all been part of this train of events.

"There is no coincidence," he was fond of saying. "It is all linked. All of it."

Like a movie, carefully spliced. You had control of that, though, didn't you, old man? The story in the can. Perfect. But it is the forces you cannot control, the electricity failure when, say, a car brings down a power pole and snuffs out a suburb, let alone a projector; the bomb scare from a giggling lunatic on a telephone; the cyclone that tiptoes across the surface of the ocean and heads straight for the foyer of the Universe. These can axe

81

the continuum. It happened to you. Bang. Theory out the window. I hope you're listening out there.

For sentimental reasons, I took a photograph of a sprawling Moreton Bay fig in Santa Barbara. Gunter told us it was brought from Queensland, my home despite his odd pronunciation, in 1871. I touched its trunk, the grainy bark and the eerie fall of its tentacled roots and shadow so familiar to me.

Not long ago an old colleague at the *Cairns Post* in the far north of the State sent me a note and a photograph of Mitch.

The story, however brief, stated that Mitchell Downs, formerly of Brisbane, had the most unusual of jobs in Cooktown. In the photograph, he wore a tall foam marlin suit, and was leaning against a Moreton Bay fig, smiling, surrounded by a group of American tourists.

Make of that what you will.

5

T. Nelson Downs, businessman, was seated at table seven and lighting a cigar paid for by his new friend and luncheon companion, Councillor Bartholomew Wilson, when he first saw the car of ice.

Across the parliamentary dining room of politicians, aldermen, developers and party officials, the vehicle was wheeled in by two capped chefs. The car sat on a black velvet cloth. T. Nelson did not notice the dry crackling of his cigar, still bearing the council's gold and red band, and joined in a round of applause for the steaming automobile.

Later, he walked over to the long smorgasbord table where it had been placed between dishes of fresh crab meat, grilled barramundi and coral trout, sauces, coleslaw and fruits. He leant down, taking the stale cigar from his mouth, and inspected the model of the world's first mass-production hydrogen car.

"It couldn't have been more beautiful if it was a cut diamond," he told Lola that evening.

Even the tyres had zigzag ruts, he swore, the door lock knobs no bigger than a grain of rice.

"And the windscreen wipers, well, the wipers," he said. "Finer than an eyelash."

Several robed angels formed a canopy over the sculpted car, their long-stemmed horns joined at the rims.

"Like the rowers' oars at our wedding, remember, Lole? Just like that."

T. Nelson was so entranced by the ice car that he had notions of buying the old Miami Ice Factory, a short drive from the Oceanic Baths. He would hire the best tradesmen in the business, from Florence, or Viareggio, where Michelangelo selected his choice blocks from the mountains of marble. Lifesize statues could be commissioned for ceremonies up and down the coast. A retiring Rotary president, his robe in ice. Football stars gripping clear kernels. Figures of history. Telescopes, map sheets, replica clothing, all of ice.

Under the heat of television lights the car and its angels began to splinter. A wing crazed and dropped onto the the roof of the hydrogen miracle. Its tiny radials went flat.

"Load of shit, really," Councillor Wilson said.

"The car?" asked T. Nelson.

"Another one of the government's crazy ideas. Spent thousands on it already I've been told. Flown back and forth to Sydney, over to the States. Unbelievable."

"Will it work?"

"They want one thing and one thing only. To be the first in the world. Doesn't matter what crazy shit project it is. Hydrogen cars, cancer cures, spaceships. They want to be first."

A fight broke out at the smorgasbord table. Television reporters were pushing and shoving, trying to record their stand-ups on camera before the car vanished.

"Why don't you tell them it stinks?"

"Who, the government?" the Councillor said.

"Yes. Tell them what you think."

"This government? Are you kidding me? I'm a paid up member of the Party, mate. I'm going for mayor."

The argument ceased, to the applause of the audience.

"I'm going for mayor," the Councillor said again, wiping cream from his chin.

He is still in his position as mayor of Burleigh Heads, I can report. A park adjoining a swimming hole in the Hinterland has already been named in his honour. They say he is being groomed for State Parliament, which would mean, I presume, they would have to change the plaque if he was successful.

Only recently I sat in the public gallery of the chamber, just to see this man, to see him operate. The chamber itself is panelled with dark wood. Behind Mayor Wilson is an Australian flag and a picture of the Queen, the same one that hangs in School of Arts buildings, schools, returned servicemen's clubs, and pubs throughout Queensland.

On this day Wilson, in a cream jacket and brown trousers, has his hands in his lap, as does the Queen, but has fallen asleep. On the wall to his right, an alderman is showing a slide display of extensions to the local sewerage plant. Wobbly amoeba fill half the wall of the chamber.

This is what disturbed my father about Wilson. He would fall asleep in the Universe-Cine-by-the-Sea. He would snore, and even fart.

My father said he could never fully trust a man who fell asleep in a cinema. He was right of course, but as usual did not trust his intuition.

I can tell you now, Father, he did not sleep at the inquiry. He tried, but the court usher stood behind his chair, and prodded him with a pencil.

At home, T. Nelson took ice cubes from the refrigerator and attempted to fashion wheels and axles, then farmyard animals, letterboxes, teacups. The cubes popped from his thick fingers. He brought home a large block wrapped in hessian. With a chisel and hammer, he tried to carve a man at the kitchen table. It had melted to the rough knobs of its knees before he had got to the shoulders and head.

"What is it this time?" Lola said, mopping the floor on her hands and knees. "You're taking up sculpting? Hmm? I can't get a damn thing in the freezer. How do you expect me to keep the meat? It's ridiculous."

"We could make a fortune out of this," he said, biting his tongue as he chiselled.

"Like the boxes of potato peelers under the house, eh? Like the pencil sharpeners. The Aboriginal lamps. The automatic plant waterers. Your brother's disgusting jewellery, eh? Opals my foot."

"Come on, Lole."

"I'm sick of this, Nelson, honestly. The place looks like a dump, and the neighbours are talking, don't you worry. Thirty old bathtubs. They're still down the side of the house. Thirty!"

85

T. Nelson experimented with freezing objects in his blocks of ice: keys, playing cards, forks, bottle tops, even an envelope.

"This could be the future of ice sculpture," he wrote to me. "Picture this. Full sized ice statues of a bride and groom for their wedding. If they're Greek, we put money inside. Or the keys to a house. Or plane tickets for their honeymoon. Anything. It's limitless."

His foray into ice sculpture ended before it began with the poker player's head.

Approaching Las Vegas, the flat earth was covered with Joshua trees. I was forced to look twice through the tinted screen of our bus windows. Gunter relayed how the Mormons thought the trees were biblical figures rising from the heat waves of the desert.

I, personally, saw them as exotic American cheerleaders, millions of them, in bristling bottle-green skirts, the promise of a pantyline ever present, though that may have been the heat affecting my viewing.

But can you see it anyway? Way out here in the desert, encircling Vegas and its money cathedrals of neon and air-conditioning — dancing girls in celebration. Leaping to the new god.

For years after he left the Magic Mile of Motors, T. Nelson Downs continued to play poker with his best friends from the lot in the upstairs Locomotive Room of the Stag Bar in town. Every Friday night they met downstairs, drank beer under the row of antlers above the bar, then commenced their game mid-evening.

At the funeral of his poker partner and friend, Mick Flynn, he conceived the idea of the ice head for the wake, the hydrogen car still fresh in his memory. He looked to the plaster saints of the church, perched in small grottoes, their unseparated toes poking over the edge, suspended above the hats and oiled hair of the mourners, and imagined them in ice. He saw light from dozens of tiny prayer candles refracted through their gowns. He saw

Jesus Christ behind the altar, an ox heart, perhaps, frozen in the centre of his chest.

T. Nelson jotted down ideas on the back of a parish news sheet, as well as the tribute he would read later at the wake.

"Mick was more than a salesman. He was an ideas man, able to draw others into his enthusiasm. This is what made him a great salesman, the type our country cannot afford to be without.

"We all remember him in his office at the back of the mechanics bay. We all remember the tattoo of a dragon on his left forearm, a reminder of his own days as a mechanic. He liked to watch the mechanics at work from his office. It was not uncommon for him, on a busy day, to take off his jacket, roll up his sleeves, and hop under a hoist to help out."

He looked at the casket, and remembered the evening they had met for the last time in the Locomotive. They sat down at the circular table, in the same seats: Mick's back to the old steam train disappearing into a tunnel in the Austrian Alps, T. Nelson's to the black passenger train, stationary at Grand Central Station in New York. The old Brisbane to Gold Coast rattler was dissected by the hotel window, the billowing underwear of the Stag's manageress hanging on a line out on the verandah. Someone had painted children in these carriages, pressing their faces against the glass, looking in at the poker players.

"I nearly married her," Mick said, as he always did, licking his thumb and shuffling the deck.

"Who was that, Mick?" they asked, even though they knew the answer.

"The barmaid. At the train station in Bludenz."

"Really?"

"Yep. Lived on a farm up past Schruns. Gorgeous, she was. Fucking gorgeous."

On a still night they could hear the skaters at the Blue Moon rink nearby, the rumble of their wheels seeming, after bourbon and scotch, to set the locomotives into motion.

On the night of Mick Flynn's death, T. Nelson left early. As was his habit, he drove the short distance to the Magic Mile to check the showroom doors and the security lighting. He also had to keep an eye out for the latest antics of old Mr Wolf, whose tim-

87

ber house was surrounded on three sides by the Magic Mile's wrecking yard. The old man had refused to sell out after repeated offers.

"This is my home!" he yelled at the mechanics and spray painters on most days. "Nobody can force me to leave my home!"

At times he hosed workers, or threw rocks at the tow truck drivers. He had recently placed dozens of raw steaks on the freshly polished bonnets of the new vehicles.

With everything secure, T. Nelson went home.

By Monday morning Mick Flynn was still playing poker with the two mechanics. He had ordered a bacon and egg sandwich and was holding it in one hand, a poor deal in the other, when his solitary king became blurred, and he fell back in his seat, dead.

The mechanics downed tools that day for Mick, leaving cars suspended in the blue air of the garage.

The death of Michael Allan Flynn had a profound effect on my father. That week he joined a gymnasium, bought squash and tennis racquets and new white sandshoes. He read diet books and pinned a daily menu to the fridge door as a guide for my mother.

He telephoned a mail-order company and had delivered, by courier, a home rowing machine which he fitted in the lounge room. Its sawn-off oars, seat and foot pedals made it too wide to remove through the door once assembled, so it stayed there, in between the sofa and the television set.

My mother said that for more than a month he rose every morning at exactly 6 a.m., performed brief stretching exercises, and rowed for an hour on the machine.

She could hear the rhythmic bursts of air from his mouth, and the creaking of the oars, from the bedroom.

"Why 6 a.m.?" I asked her.

"Because," she said, "he liked to row while watching repeats of 'Sea Hunt'."

* *

T. Nelson brought the ice sculpture of the head to the wake in a picnic esky. Late, he turned sharply off the William Jolly Bridge and the head rolled to one side, snapping off an ear.

"Damn it," he said, righting the head after he stopped outside the hotel. He hoped it would not be noticed.

They were all there when he arrived. They were sombre. There were traces of bacon fat on the carpet roses.

T. Nelson wheeled the head, covered by a piece of maroon velvet, into the room on a tea trolley.

"A little quiet please, thank you," hc said. "Would you please raise your glasses in a toast?" His left hand was placed on the crown of his old friend. He held a beer in the other.

"To a good and honest salesman," he said, and as the mourners raised their glasses he pinched the cloth and flicked it high, as a magician would produce a bunch of paper flowers, or doves.

"Jesus wept," someone said.

"Good God."

Several turned away while others stared at the head in disbelief. T. Nelson, proudly, wiped moisture from the scalp, unafraid that his hand could produce a mild imprint.

"To old Mick," he said, looking around the room.

He knew instantly that his tribute had failed. A woman began crying, and was taken to the window, between the screaming children of the locomotive, for fresh air. T. Nelson had not counted on this, or on the humidity of the evening and the heat generated by a collection of breaths and overalls and suits in the small room.

Almost instantly, Mick's head began to deteriorate. His solitary ear became as gnarled as an ancient boxer's, and then evaporated. His smile was transformed into the sour line of an old man's mouth. The top of the skull thawed unevenly. It took only minutes for the once thick Rugby neck to splinter and collapse beneath the pronounced Adam's apple, the head falling forward on the silver tray.

"You know what they've been saying?" T. Nelson told Lola later. "They said it was like Mick died there in front of them. That it was like a horror movie."

"Oh, sweetheart. I'm sorry."

"That he died all over again."

T. Nelson was the last at the wake. He sat at the round table, which had been pushed into a corner, looked into the tray and wondered why an eyebrow and the flared edge of a nostril were the last to melt. He popped the eyebrow into the dregs of his lime and soda, then poured the ice water back into the esky.

He walked down into the street and gently, as if watering prize roses, tipped the remains of his best friend into the gutter.

"He never came back to the Stag," the manageress, Edith, told me. "Someone said they last saw him swimming up and down in the baths down on the coast. You know the one? Down at the headland.

"That's right. He was wearing a red bathing cap, they said. Lost a lot of weight, they said. Just swam and swam. Didn't even say hello."

"Who's that?" T. Nelson asked his mother, pointing to the black and white photograph wedged between two clear jars above the kitchen sink.

"You know very well who it is," she said, the scar on her arm deep purple through the suds.

"Fred's Memory."

"Yes, it's Fred's Memory." She kept her head down.

When the flour in the jar was low he could see the powdery greyhound leaning into the turn, its eyes wide as if they were gulping air, and its ears twisted with speed.

"Moments later," T. Nelson said, lowering his voice, mocking his father, "it would be dead."

"There's no need to repeat the story. Have you wiped those knives and forks yet?"

"It would be carried from the track like a Roman warrior."

"That's enough. Don't let your father hear that talk."

Racing into death, T. Nelson imagined, barrelling out of control beyond the edges of the photograph, between the flour and the basil.

90

"It died with our future on its back."

Later, he hid in the foundations of the new houses in the black paddock beside their own home, a welt the shape of a wooden spoon on the back of his leg. He often wondered, if the dog had become such a symbol of misfortune, why his father kept a picture of the beast on the kitchen shelf, where other families kept portraits of Jesus, His compassionate face collecting the animal fat and vegetable steam of evening meals.

For months after the tragedy of Fred's Memory, Urban Downs cried out the dog's name in his sleep, its parallel ribs and bulging brown eyes stalking his dreams, its rank breath his breath in that small front bedroom.

"I expected the spidery thing to come padding through the house on those nights," my father told me. "Then I began to dream about the damned thing. For years. I remember in religion class we were once asked to draw death. Most of the kids drew a ghost or the Devil or the Grim Reaper. Know what I drew? A giant greyhound with blood dripping from its teeth, its eyes as big as saucers."

T. Nelson had never realised the extent of his father's addiction to gambling. He thought later that it may have been part of a larger quirk, peculiarly Australian, where half or possibly more of the enjoyment of the habit stemmed from the gathering of men, the chitchat, the drinking and the surface camaraderie that connected Urban Downs with something at once concrete but also nebulous.

Consequently, the radio was the heart of the household, particularly on race days. Urban Downs would strike his flank with his awesome palms, riding horses home on a metal-legged kitchen chair: a massive singlet-wearing jockey with crumbs in the corners of his mouth, unclipped nose hair and a trace of body odour.

Later, in lean times, he rampaged through the house, upturning mattresses, smashing china pigs and dogs for change, prying coins from between floorboards and raking the soil under the house with a rusted garden trowel for betting money.

But it started well before then, on the evening of T. Nelson's birth. He was delivered on Christmas Eve, seconds before the clock ticked into the holy day. Sitting in the delivery ward waiting room with two other men, Urban Downs tossed a crumpled pound note into his upturned hat. The others similarly complied, betting on whose child would be born first on Christmas Day.

"She's a week over," Urban said after the bets had been placed. "You're done for."

"Bullshit. Mine's been in for twelve hours already. Any tick of the clock," another said.

Thirty-three seconds before midnight the nurse nodded at Urban Downs. He stood, tipped the cash onto the floor and followed her, shaking his head.

"Bad luck, pal."

"Yeah, have a good Christmas."

"Not only had I lost him a pound," my father said, "but the first baby born on Christmas Day in Brisbane, 1930, won a hamper big enough to feed the family for week. I never enjoyed a birthday my whole life. I was always reminded that I had lost the hamper."

Not far from where Elvis was married, from the McDonald's burger sign in gold wavering neon, we were taken to a second-rate Las Vegas show, featuring the stunning, the spectacular, the startling world record breaking stunt — THREE men inside the Globe of Death. Don't forget your cameras, they said. Would people with heart conditions please inform the management?

The leggy dancers, I must tell you, were dressed identically to the horses that accompanied them on stage. Both wore metre-high caps of ostrich feathers, spangling vests and anklets. The only thing the horses did not have were black fishnet stockings, most of which were laddered anyway. This was the type of show it was, Pop, solely for the thousands of bus tourists of America, the big rigs, including Jack's, stacked like fresh loaves outside in the parking lot. I could not help but feel that the *real* shows were going on somewhere further up the strip. Jack was probably out there, yarning with other Greyhound men about the peculiarities of their passengers: the luggage, hairstyles, mannerisms, the halitosis of their world travellers.

Having come straight from the air-conditioning of the hotel to the air-conditioning of this ratty club, I wondered if anybody actually lived in Las Vegas. It was impossible for me to connect with the place, to get a feel of it, as it was all light. It was perpetually day, as opposed to you, Father, spending your latter years in a continual twilight, comforted by the benevolent authority your usher's torch gave you. I honestly don't think you would take to it.

I wondered if the light of the casinos was intended to deflect the existence of evil, or corruption at the very least. I thought of our good Premier, and how the brilliant and radiant face of God was his partner. Was this the same principle?

Jack told me they decorated Las Vegas hotel rooms with such deliberate vulgarity that one was forced to leave luggage unpacked, faces unfreshened, and head straight for the crap tables and fruit machines. My room was aqua, orange, pea-green and yellow — the heatstroke hallucinations of a dehydrated greenkeeper.

And he told me, which of course I wrote down on the back of a beer coaster, that the single biggest cost of running a hotel/casino in this town of light was the air-conditioning. So why build in such inhospitable territory? Where even the Joshua trees took on the allure of young, gymnastic strippers? You can't escape, that's why. You could spend your entire time in the hotel/casinos, they were so enormous, and never venture outside except for getting on and off the bus. There were very few people on the street, except for the spruikers who wore miniskirts of silver dollars and jackets of twenty-dollar bills. I was offered, *offered*, ten dollars to see Nudes on Ice, but our schedule was too tight.

In the auditorium of our second-rate show, we awaited the Globe of Death. We were promised a world record. There were, according to our waitress, officials planted in the audience to witness the event for history. After magicians and fire-eaters, Jew-hating comedians and crooners, the giant globe of steel was

93

wheeled onto the centre of the stage. There were gasps above the drum rolls.

"How are all you good folks out there?" our master of ceremonies shouted, revealing a small white hole in the underarm of his black dinner suit. "Do we have anyone frommmm . . . England out there?" Cheers. "Do we have anyone frommmmm Germany out there?" And so it went on, eventually getting to Australia with Butch standing, still wearing his steer cap, tugging at my arm, trying to pull me up into the spotlight.

"Allllright. Tonight, ladies and gentlemen, boys and girls, you will see a feat that has never, *neeeeever*, been performed in the world. An act so dangerous, and I don't mean to alarm you, *soooo* dangerous, that several men have died attempting its execution."

The crowd murmured here, on cue and to the delight of our moth-eaten master of ceremonies.

"Please. You will see not one, not two, but three, *threeee* motorcycle daredevils inside the Globe of Deathhhhh."

I noticed a trajectory of spittle from our host as he hung onto that last word, but the rest of the group were buzzing, wide-eyed, applauding.

"Please, preparation for the stunt requires complete silence. If you please."

The lights were dimmed except for three spotlights trained on the steel globe. We heard motorcycles backstage, then suddenly the riders, the daredevils, roared out of the curtains, each helmeted and wearing leather suits with padded shoulders, elbows, knees, and white and gold boots.

It was an illusion, and one you would have appreciated, Father, no question, that the globe in fact did not look big enough to hold three record breakers. Two of the men rode up into the cage and immediately began circumnavigating the inside of the sphere. They appeared to chase each other, getting higher and higher, until both were at impossible angles, a mirror image of rider and machine. I noticed the heads of the audience tilt, askew, their balance already lost. The noise of the cycles was deafening.

Finally the star rider, the linchpin, the man with jewels on his coat, Johnny Jumpstart, adjusted his goggles and his gloves, revved a few times for added effect, then fired up into the globe to the screams of several spectators, even Gunter, who had seen it possibly fifty times before. Stagehands closed the trapdoor to the cage and it was just the three men locked inside, the machines screeching. They began to loop each other and became a white and sparkling series of interlocking lines, similar to those they draw in textbooks to illustrate the shape of atoms.

For five full minutes we witnessed this world record, this odd molecule of men shrouded in blue exhaust. My fellow travellers were aghast. Gunter had a satisfied grin on his face. Butch had pushed back the peak of his cap. Peter had not taken his hand off his video camera, his eye from its viewfinder. Wilson Tyler took a butt from his tortoiseshell holder, and inserted another cigarette.

The only detractor at our table was the physics teacher from Kensington. He was chortling gently, his large stomach moving out of time with his open mouth. When the cyclists left and the applause faded, he was giggling hysterically at the ball of smoke that the air-conditioning units were having difficulty in ingesting.

"He'll run all day," the man in the checked jacket told Urban Downs on the front verandah, leaning forward, a small blue and green feather in his hat catching a light breeze. "You have to go out there and stop him, otherwise he'll keep running around and around until he drops, no bull. He just loves running in circles. He's a natural. Believe me."

The man with a feather in his cap was another of a long line of salesmen, dealers, commodity traders, that Urban always permitted onto the verandah. He would put down his detective novel in the middle of murder, or his Western at the point of revenge, and welcome them in, sometimes assisting in lifting their bags of wares, or the construction of the gadgets. At these times his wife escaped down the backstairs and weeded, or took tea with Wilfred in the sardine-silver caravan next door.

T. Nelson enjoyed the men's unusual goods, but particularly

their stories. Invariably Urban Downs was persuaded to buy quantities of their products: pepper grinders shaped like the Brisbane City Hall, with a swivelling clock tower and peppercorn loading hatch through the roof of the main ballroom; ashtrays with mouths and eyebrows; lampshades made of pilfered North Queensland coral; and revolutionary vegetable peelers.

One summer, following heavy rain, hundreds of wooden Aboriginal warriors were washed from cardboard boxes under the house and scattered across the backyard. Months after, they kept emerging, standing upside down in weeds, trapped against the wire of the chicken pen, some with their heads gnawed off by dogs. A few, T. Nelson imagined, must have journeyed through the city's stormwater drainage system and, with twiglike spears in hand, floated out into the waters of Moreton Bay, to be caught in fishing nets with crab and bream.

The feather man, however, was different. He brought nothing onto the verandah. Only, T. Nelson heard him say, a vision of heaven — a greyhound racer, delivered not in a chariot of gold with mother-of-pearl wheels and carved angels with ruby eyes, but the backseat of a Buick from the country.

"It must be in his genes," the feather man said, stretching back in the chair. "He races anything that moves. I saw him beat a Royal Enfield into Dalby. True. Heard you were a keen betting man, had a good eye, not averse to earning some extra quid, and thought you might want to be a part of it."

The dog was outside in the Buick, and from the verandah T. Nelson saw its bug eyes through the dusted rear passenger window.

"Gave 'im a trial run last week, right? Last week. Ran so close to the rails found white paint on his left side. No bull. He was born beside the rail he was."

The feather man produced photographs from his jacket. In one picture the dog had a silk saddle over its back and a tiny jockey's cap at an odd angle on its thin head.

"Did that one for fun. You know, publicity sort of thing. Like it?"

Fred's Memory and T. Nelson continued to stare at each other. The boy knew, seeing the bony head and eyes, that the

96

whole thing was a disaster. But he said nothing, terrified and transfixed by the animal which would carry his parents' entire savings into oblivion. He doubted his father even knew Fred's Memory was only metres away.

The half-ownership deal was sealed with a handshake and the photograph of the dog in the jockey's cap. As T. Nelson and his father waved off the feather man, there was no sign of the dog. For years the boy wondered if he had imagined it, or if it had been trained to duck beneath the window level of the Buick.

"Do greyhounds get dizzy?" he asked Urban Downs over dinner that night.

"Of course not," his father boomed, already an expert on the subject. "They love running around in circles. It's in their genes, I believe."

"You mean they know to run that way when they're born?"

"Sure."

"Right from the first one, the one in the Ark?"

"I suppose so," Urban said, returning to his meal.

"They had racetracks then?"

"Don't think so."

"So how did they know how to run in circles?" the boy persisted.

"They're smart. They learned."

"But they don't know it's not a real rabbit."

"It's not the rabbit they want, boy, no, no, no, they just want the chance to kill. That's what drives them on."

And it went on.

"Why are their eyes so big?"

"So they can watch the rabbits around corners."

"Can they do tricks?"

"Tricks?" Urban said through a mouthful of potato.

"Can they disappear?"

"I bloody well hope not, or we're not going to get rich, are we?"

"Urban, the language, please."

After wiping the dishes T. Nelson played with his City Hall pepper grinder and stuffed a giant spear-carrying Aboriginal

97

warrior into the ballroom, its wooden face level with the hands of the clock.

It was our last night in Las Vegas and I drew my hotel room curtains tight against the red flickering face of a neon cowboy. The next morning, early, we were to make our way to Montezuma's Castle.

Halfway there we stopped in the middle of the desert at the request of the Germans sitting near the front. It was forty degrees outside.

I was told, by Jack, that the Germans had desperately wanted to photograph real American cactus. We stopped and they virtually ran off the bus with their cameras. Others followed, and before long the whole group had scattered, stopping before the green-brown plants and taking snaps.

"Does a worm do this?" one of the German women asked Jack, pointing to a hole in the trunk.

"Yep," Jack said, his body weight resting on his good leg. "Worms everywhere here. Riddled with them. You stand too long they'll get you too."

He walked over to the shade of the bus.

"Stupid bitch," he said to me under his breath. "Wouldn't know a bullet hole if she had one as a second asshole. Come look at this."

He led me around to the back of the Americruiser and looked at the greyhound insignia between the rear brake lights. He fingered a small hole in the dog's neck.

"Don't say anything. Noticed it this morning," Jack said. "Handgun probably."

"Shit," I said. "You're kidding me." I too poked the dog's wound.

"Could've been in the car park at Vegas. On the road, hard to tell. Crazy assholes out here. Hillbilly redneck assholes."

"Someone could've been killed."

"Welcome to the Wild West, buddy. Not a word, eh?"

Jack kept glancing at me in his rear vision mirror, and Gunter again opened his history of America.

He read into the microphone: "Did you know that the cactus . . ."

Fred's Memory consistently came midfield in its first few starts, lost in bobbing numbers and scissoring ribs. In its fifth race it broke perfectly, "as if in flight" Urban recalled sadly, and took the first turn twenty metres in front of the pack.

For a moment Urban was one with the crowd that night at the Gabba Dogs, punching his fist in the air, springy on his feet. The dog had stretched its lead to fifty metres when it cruised into the final turn. For no reason, none, on a night of perfect conditions, not a breath of air, clear sky, and crisp, the dog's rear legs tangled, the left knocking the right from under it. Having lost its balance and out of control at forty or fifty kilometres per hour, its head lunged towards the rail and, in a tenth of a second, the bat of an eyelid, lodged into a gap in the fence. Its momentum carried the torso forward, snapping the neck instantly, and conversely flicked it from the rail, sending Fred's Memory skidding across the dew-covered track in front of the small grandstand. By the time it came to rest, its rear leg twitching in the air, there was silence.

T. Nelson saw nothing, but watched as the men in the crowd removed their hats one by one, holding the rims with both hands. He noticed dozens and dozens of identical multicoloured feathers in their bands.

Two men in white knee-length coats slowly lifted the dog and carried it to the side gate. Press bulbs popped, and the spectators, the great fraternity of punters one and all, applauded the gallant racer.

Urban Downs watched, speechless, as Fred's Memory, its brown eyes still wide open, frozen in that child innocence that dogs possess and watering heavily, disappeared into the dark tunnel under the wooden grandstand.

That was the end of their father-and-son nights every Wednesday.

"Are we seeing Fred's Memory again tonight?" he asked often.

"Not tonight."

"Is he all right?"

"He's training."

"Did he catch the rabbit last time?"

"Sure. He caught that old rabbit."

"I thought so. That's why everybody clapped him."

"That's right, boy," Urban Downs said. "He was the first greyhound in the world to catch the rabbit."

But T. Nelson had heard the gunshot at the back of the track. As they walked to the tram, he knew by the slight dragging of his father's left leg, the look on his face, illuminated by the gas blue showers of sparks off the tram wires, and the hat tilted down further than usual, that Fred's Memory had come to grief.

He knew no one ever caught the rabbit. He knew it went round and round, endlessly, untouched by the fangs of the pack of dogs.

In T. Nelson's drawing of death, which his mother kept, as she did all his things, he put a red dot in between the greyhound's eyes.

"And what is this?" the teacher asked.

"The bullet," he said, still filling in the red hole, nearly breaking through the paper. "The bullet that killed Fred's Memory."

6

I would say with certainty, yes, with great confidence in fact, that this was the beginning of the end for my father. The plants. More specifically, the ferns. The ferns.

The sharks began to move in — a metaphor I am reluctant to use, for obvious reasons, considering his current state. Poor wretch. I mean that honestly.

It, too, was a time when he deliberately broke free of his life to that point, or perceived that he had, and left himself wide open. He cut all the strings, but more importantly, he dived away from what he knew. Just dropped the lot. Finished.

He was the nimble-footed deer who licked the face of the beast. The beast embraced him, ever so gently. But he paid for it, let me tell you. He was eaten alive, my old man.

The neighbours could only tell when T. Nelson Downs was in his hammock, thinking, when they saw the intermittent glow of his cigar end.

"He's there, do you see it?"

"Where?"

"Look. There. See there? There it is again."

"He must be frozen out there."

When T. Nelson bought the house, before he had thoughts of the Universe-Cine-by-the-Sea, he demolished the old hen shed at the back of the yard, removed its rotting wooden beams and scrolls of grey wire, and built a hothouse. Square. Of green mesh. On the bare patch of earth, scribbled for decades by the claws of birds.

He erected the greenhouse so quickly that the soil remained dark and moist. If he had sifted through it, he would have found pieces of bone, feather quills, even beak halves. Eventually, the filtered light hardened the floor. He even rigged up a hammock between two rows of potted ferns. The timber creaked under his weight. Seeds caught in the hair of his arms as he swayed.

For the first few months the amateur botanist could still smell pellets, egg, damp feathers, rising from the floor of the former henhouse. Whole families of fowl, he thought sipping gin, refusing to abandon the soil. When he slept out there, chickens and speckled bantams appeared like balloons in his dreams.

Since retiring from the business of automobiles, he spent more time amongst his greenery, watching a portable television, its screen no bigger than a cigarette packet, from his hammock. He sang, whistled and hummed to *South Pacific, Paint Your Wagon, An American in Paris, Brigadoon.*

"Can you hear that? Quick, ring Helen and tell her to come and have a look."

He had ceased worrying about the neighbours. He knew they gathered at their incinerators and brick barbecues with spherical or pyramidal flues, and burned for the sake of burning, to catch a glimpse of him relaxing, or dancing, or snoring, cocooned in the rope hammock. He saw the crescents of their faces, lit by sparks off milk cartons or juice containers, and white smoke.

He could have told them there was nothing inside his greenhouse but potted plants, beds of seedlings, and dozens of stubbed cigar ends. Nothing but a strange light and moist air in the day, and a block of coldness at night, holding still leaves, spores, fronds, and fungus as if they were embedded in glass. It was a space, and one that he created, that had its own weather patterns.

He wanted to shout through knotholes and venetians that it had its own time too, measured by the invisible growth of shoots, or his cigar smoke that eased to the mesh roof and filtered through to the outside world.

"Fifth burn-off this week, Ray," he yelled at the fence. "Cleaning up, Ray? Moving out perhaps?"

This is how he spoke to people.

Ray Williams told me: "I gather it was something he developed from his days as a car salesman. They say he was one of the

102

best. I never had any trouble with him, tell you the truth, but we all liked to see what he was up to, you know?

"He was just that sort of person. You never knew what might happen next."

T. Nelson had been head salesman at the Magic Mile of Motors, East Brisbane, for more than a decade. It was easy to confirm. You just had to walk through to the back of the showroom and read the sales graph. His red map pins climbed like a worn stairway to the very edge of the corkboard.

While he still dabbled, as an amateur, in antiquities, the car lot provided him with the perfect stage to relay stories, to communicate, to enjoy the camaraderie of life. It was the unpredictability he liked. The strangers who poked their heads into the showroom, or walked, hands behind their backs, around new, polished vehicles.

And T. Nelson was the joker, the funnyman, beneath all that cackling bunting. He could add optional extras to a sale — air-conditioning, power steering, automatic door locks — with a single joke. He kept notebooks in which he jotted down his favourite gags. Every year he went back to the books, anticipating perfectly the point when punchlines were on the edge of memory, and retell them. They always circulated back to him, months later, via other mouths. They travelled for miles, through kitchens and verandahs up the coast, between men sitting high on horses out west, and back to Brisbane, in fruit trucks or buses, carried as easily as light baggage. The locations of the jokes, the vistas, the weather, clothes, sex and tone of the characters' voices changed, but the bones were always his.

Management recognised T. Nelson's appeal, and featured him in their radio and newspaper advertisements. (*C-r-u-i-s-e through T-o-w-n with T. Nelson D-o-w-n-s. Get Downnnn.*) Pedestrians stared at him in the street. Waved. They loved him. It was a small town.

Everything was perfect. He had secured a multi-million dollar contract with young Bart Wilson of the Burleigh Heads council — twenty-five sedans, eleven trucks, five limousines, two tractors and a grader — and they had begun pressing his red pins into the plaster. Then the new models arrived.

It was not the shape that disconcerted him, the pastel colours, or the intricate Japanese motors. Not at all. It was the digital clocks. He hated them. He had won a small one at the Oceanic's Lucky Wheel and had tossed it in the incinerator.

The car clock had been something he greatly admired. He particularly liked the series with the smooth second hand that did not click into each second, like normal clocks, but glided above Roman numerals, smooth, effortless.

With the digitals the clocks, in vehicles fresh off the front-end loader, were always set at midday or midnight, flashing annoyingly until they were readjusted. They burned like toaster filaments and troubled his eyes. He detested the way five became six, sneakily, the extra bar popping in, unexpected. Rudely. He could not look at the digital and instantly know the time, as he could with hands. He felt he had to calculate it, minutes to the hour, minutes away from the half hour. So he decided to leave the car business.

This was not the real reason. I don't believe that for a second, no pun intended. This whole newness overwhelmed him, this progress that just appeared unheralded. This change that would dictate the next few years, be modified, improved, until another revolution came through the back door.

For the first time he noticed the paunch that hung over his belt, the lifelessness of his hair, no matter how industriously washed, the depth of his laughter lines. He took stock, and didn't like what he saw.

At his farewell in the Stag Bar they presented him, after so many years, with an engraved watering can. He grabbed it like a microphone and gave his parting speech. When he started singing ''Greensleeves'' into its freckled nozzle, the crowd had already returned to their drinks.

Suspended above the Grand Canyon in a light aircraft, I thought of the moat you dug around the incinerator in the corner of the yard. Half a metre across and the same deep, I can see you now,

104

filling it with fresh water as you prepare to burn off rubbish, boxes, newspapers, old shoes.

"When does your old man put in the drawbridge?" neighbours teased.

It was more than a novelty, though. I knew, yes I did, though you never once told me what happened, that it went right back to great-grandma's unfortunate death, and back to the fire in the paddock next to your house when you were a kid, and maybe even further, to the faces and animals and objects you saw in that fire that nearly lifted an entire Brisbane suburb into the sky.

"Everybody's talking. It's embarrassing," my mother said of the moat.

"It's for your safety," you said. "If the council would let me I'd put one right around the house."

"There are frogs swimming in it. Mosquitoes breeding."

"One spark and the whole place could go up."

"Children are coming to the door asking to play in it, for heaven's sake."

"One spark, Lole, one." The argument rolled about for hours, days, longer.

Since the fire that he and Sid had started all those years ago, he collected stories about houses being razed, cigarettes that had rolled gently from sleeping fingers and incinerated elderly men and women, of people who walked to their offices in neat suits or dresses, carrying briefcases with lunches packed inside, and self-ignited at street corners waiting for traffic lights, or behind their desks.

"This is a precarious life," he said, shaking his head, "when you can self-combust at any time. Damned scary if you ask me."

This, in short, was his state of mind since leaving the Magic Mile. He checked the fuse box daily. He wandered through the yard. He polished old bathtubs. He showered morning, noon and night. He had lost his grip, was attached to nothing. He feared losing everything — his house, his family. My mother described it as a crisis. He called it streamlining, settling, coming down to earth.

When he used the incinerator he stoked the fire with a poker and held a running hose in his other hand, just in case. Everything alight in that grotto was a threat — small milk cartons, wooden cotton spools, leaves. Once a rooster on the side of a cereal box took flight, deep orange and alive, lofting into the air towards the frame of his new hothouse. He shot it out of the sky with the hose, its beak, fragile body, dead eyes, exploding into carbon fragments that drifted across the fence.

Ironically, he held no fears about his cigars. He could control their tightly knit sparks. He felt the heat of their miniature furnace through the cheap Philippine tobacco and leaf casing. It tickled his lip, which he enjoyed. At any time, a boot heel could extinguish the danger.

But it was that single match, years before, from the chubby hand of brother Sid, witnessed by T. Nelson, that precipitated further events that led to the scission of the family. That was how he perceived it in later years, focusing on moments, on minor catastrophes, as catalysts for decay. It was irrational, I thought, but he was stretched to construct a chart of their lives and clung to anything, anything at all, to justify himself.

That one match contributed to the unravelling of a generation, he said, struck beneath the earth when he was ten years old. That one match which left a street of men without eyebrows and later his grandmother, charred face down on a lawn, the flowers of her nightdress fused into her powdery old white skin.

"Sid killed her," he always maintained.

Suddenly, after his departure from the Magic Mile, there was time to spare. He kept his suits in order in the wardrobe, colour-graded from earth browns through to a yellow pastel. His shoes were similarly arranged, from black to white, but all with anti-moisture pads beneath the tongue. For the first time since he was a boy, he chose bare feet around the house. He could feel the unevenness of the floorboards, the grain of his carpets, the smooth wear of stairs and the lush grass of his garden.

One afternoon he took from beneath the house a long-handled scythe and planned to clear the man-high weeds from along the back fence.

"This is called scything," he shouted, looking around for the triangular parting of a curtain or the crinkle of a blind. He put his portable radio headphones over his ears, extended the aerial to its full length, and tuned in to a symphony.

"Step one!" he yelled over a French horn. "Take the scythe in both hands and rhythmically strike the base of the weeds. Do not over swing. Be steady. Back and forth."

Despite the rust of decades the scythe felled the weeds. He swept in various rhythms, to the dancing of couples in a Vienna ballroom, a storm, a lost love, a suicide, that came down through his aerial. He found the contact with the wooden handle of the tool so novel he did not wish to stop, and eventually had to adapt a motion in tune with the speech patterns of an interview on the Family Law Court.

In the far right corner of the yard, after an hour of labour, he hit an object which rang on contact.

"Only three per cent of fathers end up with custody of . . ."

He dropped the implement and pulled the weeds with his blistered hands. A blade sliced his left thumb.

"Why is that, do you think? Are fathers naturally considered unfit to care for the children? Is it a physical question, or what we have been conditioned to accept? I . . ."

T. Nelson uncovered an old white bathtub, its lion's feet sunk in the soil. In its green stagnant water, he found a family of tree frogs. Stirring the water with a stick, he saw the small skeletons of amphibians through the murkiness.

Later, in his hammock, he wondered about the skeletons.

It would not have surprised me if he had opened a French restaurant after discovering the bath of frogs. Really. He decided on another business.

He never came to any conclusions about the skeletons, I might add. But once, when I nearly drowned in the Oceanic Baths aged three years and seven months, he called me Frog for a long time after that.

"But why plants, Dad? You know nothing about them."

"I can just feel it's the right thing to do," he told me. "You can't question a feeling like that."

"What does Mum think?"

"I think she'll see its merit."

"You haven't told her."

"I have a hunch," he said. "I've already got a nursery lined up to provide the stock. I'll just rent them out, see? To offices, places like that."

"You'll need a truck."

"Got a trade-in lined up with the Magic Mile. Wholesale. No problems."

"What if they die? You lose money every time they die."

"I'll just rent out tough plants," T. Nelson said. "Tell your old man it's a good idea. Go on."

"Too speculative."

"Come on, that's me. It's me all over. You know me."

"You're too trusting, Dad. You'll get burnt."

"Been burnt before."

"I thought you wanted to get away from this wheeling and dealing. I thought you just wanted to potter around the garden."

"How can a plant business go wrong? Already picked a name for the business. Want to hear it?"

"I'm not sure."

"You're ready?"

"Fire away."

"Forest Hire."

From his verandah, T. Nelson could see the white bathtub in the corner of the yard. He had polished it as best he could, lifted its feet from the mud, and placed the tree frogs back into clean tap water.

"Forest Hire. What do you think of *that?*"

Is this really how the downfall of my father began? With a bathtub? Did it start that far back?

"How could you stop him once he started?" my mother asked me. "When he got going, everything had to be done yesterday. I don't think he had any idea what he was getting into. But I don't think he cared either."

* *

108

It said in the brochure that the Grand Canyon was a living, breathing thing, Father, but all I saw was death in its shadows.

We were almost in the canyon, level with the plateau of America, a whale of air beneath us, and it appeared burnt orange at dusk. Still glowing, red hot, a giant coal, after a fire that could be seen from the moon. Our pilot spoke to us over a microphone.

"Now folks, if you look to your left, about five o'clock, you'll see the famous Chinese temple. See it there? All look over to your left, you'll get a good shot of it."

The woman next to me said, "I don't like this." She had her head down, and occasionally snatched glimpses out the window above the wing.

"Coming up on the right, way out there near the ridge, can you guess what that is? Can anyone back there guess? That there is the Empire State Building, New York, New York. You won't see no King Kong in the canyon today, I'm afraid."

Gunter found this particularly funny. Meanwhile the woman beside me was sweating, dabbing her face with a yellow daisy handkerchief.

"I don't like it," she said. "I think it looks evil."

Laugh if you wish, Pop, but below, as the engines droned, I saw two profiles of myself in a bend of the Colorado River, as if I was looking down at my silhouette on the footpath on a sunny day. One was larger than the other, sharp, the nose more pointed, the mouth slightly open but clearly defined, defiant, the head tossed back, my slicked back hair almost resting on a ridge. The other was smaller, the head forward. If there had been a body attached, and not the veined fanning of the river, it would have been stooped. There was no pure black hairline, but a lighter shadow, the sediment layers of rock visible and the mouth wide open, gasping, a cluster of fallen boulders between the lips.

I could hear the woman's laboured breathing, and leaned over her, trying to take a photograph of my faces on the floor of the canyon. Turbulence struck, as if my older self had exhaled and rocked the tiny plane. I waited for the shadow of the Cessna to disappear into the dark young head of myself before I managed a couple of shots. (Much later, having developed the photographs, the pictures show only the dim daisies of the ill woman's

109

handkerchief reflected in the window glass, floating high above the canyon.)

"And can anyone tell me who that little fellow is over there to your right? Having a snooze there?"

Directly down I saw an infantryman stalking, his rounded metal helmet outlined unevenly by ragged shrubs. There was another with broader shoulders and possibly wearing boots, loading a cannon. He could have been from the Napoleonic wars, the Falklands, Afghanistan. It was difficult to determine the nationality of a shadow, but it was all there: Asian temples, castles on the Rhine, the Alamo, rows of chimney pots, a portion of the Taj Mahal, sea captains with telescopes, giant insects, bridges, cathedrals, hands, eyes, teeth. All in the shadows.

It was the world's history in overlapping and interlocking stencils, Father. If you had seen what I saw as a young man, would you have spotted me, your future son, down there, shaped by nature? Formed by the freak joining of rock fault and hardy plants? Me as an old man, my mouth full of ancient boulders, my bald and cracked head dotted with salt shrubs?

"That's right!" the pilot continued. "That there is the world's favourite dog, old Snoopy, having a nice long snooze on his kennel."

I must say I wanted to ask the pilot how this could be so. How the Charles M. Schulz character could have been born millions of years ago in rock, his spoonlike black ears and bulbous nose carved by ice and the river, and yet still been a phenomenon of our century. Had Schulz flown over the canyon as a young man, seen the jutting rock figure, and taken the image that would make him famous back to a drawing board? (This I have been unable to corroborate.)

The woman next to me reached under her seat.

"Are you okay?" I asked.

"Are there any sick bags in here?" she said quietly into my ear, a bead of sweat striking the calf skin of her handbag. We were circling Snoopy, and passengers were craning with their cameras.

I wondered if the future was out there too, dovetailed with the warriors, the skyscrapers, the myths and cartoon characters. If

110

there were the shapes of objects that would not be invented for centuries. Or pictures of my children, and their children, somewhere on the surface of the disintegrating canyon and its breaking rock, as gentle as the snap of sparrow bone.

"I think I'm going to be sick," the woman said, and vomited into her handbag, over photographs, a comb, lipstick, and hair pins.

I once asked you why you leased the cinema. Why you became an usher.

"That's how we learn about the rest of the world," you said confidently, as if you had rehearsed the answer many times. "Pictures. The movies."

"Is that why grandmother always wore her hair like Scarlett O'Hara?"

"Her favourite screen character."

"And grandfather like Jimmy Cagney?"

"His favourite actor."

"Grandfather has no hair now."

"That was a long time ago," you said.

I know you were obsessed with the burning of Atlanta in *Gone with the Wind*. You sat before the video recorder and slowly, almost sinisterly, lit a cigar at the start of the fire scene. You viewed it so many times, backwards, forwards, in slow and fast motion, that that section of tape became worn, jumpy, as if affected by the chaos of the drama it contained.

"I wouldn't say obsessed, really," you defended yourself. "It's technically brilliant, that's all. Do you see that? Brilliant. Masterful.

"Do you see the horses in the flames? There, look at the freeze-frame. Do you see the horse riding into battle?"

"No, for the hundredth time," Mother said.

"Son, look. Do you see the men fighting?" you said, running your finger across the screen.

I studied the scenes to please you. Went right up to the screen, the flames licking in each of my eyes, the buildings crashing in fountains of sparks.

"Anything?"

"A motor car," I said.

You stood then, fired the remote control through me, and an advertisement for soup appeared.

"You're being smart again," you sulked. "They didn't have cars then."

"They should have had a moat," my mother said. "That would have saved good old Atlanta."

You left then, and finished your cigar in the hammock in your hothouse.

T. Nelson Downs found that checking his orchids daily, planting seedlings, steering the passage of bees, was agreeable at his age. He enjoyed sinking his hands into soil, or hosing until his forefinger wrinkled, far more than he expected.

"Since spending more time with the plants," he wrote to me, "I have eaten more fruit and vegetables and even feel lighter. I have already been approached by some of the ladies of the neighbourhood for my orchids, which they say have been favourably commented upon at City Hall functions."

He leased a small shop at the northern end of the city, near the ancient fig trees of Adelaide Street, between the Animal Crackers Pet Shop and the Botanical Gardens Bicycle Hire. The imitation plants he placed in the front window attracted insects from the mudflats beneath the Story Bridge.

As a boy he had seen a man urinating under the figs, returning to sleep on newspaper between the winged buttresses of its roots. Other men slept there too, in the cradles that the roots provided around their bases, and he thought of it as a strange and grubby hotel shaped like a wheel.

The massive fig roots had spread under the roads that bordered the island of trees, tilting traffic lights and rising under footpaths like arms under blankets. One such root had found its way beneath the display window of Forest Hire.

"A good luck omen; too good to pass up," T. Nelson wrote.

It created the impression, he thought, that the source of the

112

root and its strength was, in fact, Forest Hire. Channelled from his shop and out into the dark trees.

"In a strange way," he continued, "it has instantly given my operation an established history."

Despite this, business began slowly. People tripped over the ridged bitumen outside his doorway. His plant supplier, Tom, a pensioner with a string of hothouses in a paddock at Samford, was hard of hearing, and often brought in pallets of the wrong species. T. Nelson would be left to sweep compost and peat that always fell from the old man's boots.

"Thought you said Madonna lilies."

"The leaves are torn, Tom, look here."

"Can't help it. You want to buy me a new ute?"

"Where are the bulbs on these?"

"On Dayboro Road probably."

"Shit, Tom. Really."

The old man is dead now, his hothouses, one tackily connected to the other in a crooked but linear fashion, overgrown, bursting from within like a giant spiked caterpillar at the bottom of his grazing paddock. I can only assume my father's attention was caught, one Sunday afternoon, by the man's collection of bathtubs, hundreds of them dumped around his old homestead just off the main road, some with copper pipes and taps still attached.

A local public park has been named after the man. It was unveiled by the Minister for Agriculture some years before his death. Two years after the man's posterity had been secured, he was arrested and charged with indecent dealings with boys in the lavatory of the very park named after him.

The local council is still seeking to have his name, branded into a log of local cedar, erased.

One long-time resident tells me: "I have never seen a child in that park since."

The strange fables of our private stories.

T. Nelson's business began to accelerate when the yellow bulldozers moved into Brisbane. The transformation of the colonial town was not a gentle one. The bulldozers, graders and earth movers were virtually paraded down main streets, as are astronauts who have returned from the moon, or Olympiads waving from the back seats of limousine convertibles.

Reaction to their arrival was one of dulled surprise. The streets were suddenly littered with fluorescent witches hats, causing traffic jams, collisions, and the death of at least one corner paper seller. It was not uncommon to find construction workers' helmets floating down gutters after a heavy afternoon downfall.

There was little time to organise opposition to the destruction of sandstone office blocks, wrought iron lace, tin awnings, gas lights and stone horse-watering troughs. They seemed to disappear all at once.

Commuters went to work and found fenced blocks of air, unexpected views, breezes full of mangrove and jacaranda, light instead of shadow. It left them disoriented. Footpaths were diverted. Fruit barrows moved on.

On Friday afternoons, the local newspaper alleged, the concrete-dusted workmen who had invaded the city gathered in their giant pits, viewed bawdy striptease acts and drank beer. Citizens, T. Nelson Downs included, stood at the edge of the pits, behind the cyclone fencing, and listened to the roar of men. Some brought binoculars and fold-out stools.

"She wore what?" Lola asked T. Nelson.

"A school uniform. And white socks."

"It's a wonder the police haven't been called."

"And the men," he said, beginning his meal, "the men, they were nothing short of, well, they were animals, really."

"She was naked?"

"They moved in around her, I don't know. All I could see were hats."

An inquiry was called after a glass sheet broke from its chains and crushed a child and an elderly shopper. T. Nelson imagined the victims, looking to the blue sheet, seeing the reflections of their own terror, before the mirror exploded into millions of shards. The deaths were ruled accidental.

Almost all the new structures had mirrored surfaces, and the

114

city began reflecting distorted images of itself: wobbly clocks, church spires, kings drunk on horseback, a segmented Queen Victoria, pigeons in pieces. T. Nelson noted pedestrians checking their hair, their make-up, the shoulders of their suits in the street-level mirrors of skyscrapers.

"It is this vanity," he wrote to me, "that will bring our little town, finally, into the twentieth century."

The mirrors were blamed for an increased incidence of murder, a proliferation of street gangs and muggings. Satanic symbols appeared on footpaths, post boxes, and building hoardings. A man wearing only a bowler hat was arrested in the Botanical Gardens. Police found, in a picnic basket he had been carrying, a prospectus for the new Riverview convention centre.

T. Nelson spoke to pedestrians outside Forest Hire. He observed that seven out of ten people complained that the old town was "becoming more like America every day".

"It's like a new city altogether," the Animal Crackers proprietor said one morning over coffee, the handle of his cup a thin ceramic tuna fish. "We'll need maps to get around."

The office blocks, eventually, reflected infinitely into each other, and from the southern tip of the city, office workers could look down into the buildings and feel, miraculously, that they were now linked to the major human and financial centres of the globe.

T. Nelson knew it would be good for business. There was even talk, now, of the government commissioning the world's tallest skyscraper, across from the old church, near the site of the People's Palace hostel.

"Why do they want to be noticed, this government?" one old man seeking seeds had asked T. Nelson. "You know they took the mangroves, don't you? Up near St Lucia. The river's gone mad. My son fishes there all the time, brought home a beautiful mullet for Mum and me the other day, tender as anything, but anyway, caught one fish, cut her open, and you know what he found inside?"

"What was that?"

"A boot lace, swear to God. Full length. You know as well as I do, you take away the mangroves, the whole place goes mad."

If my chronology is correct, it was at this time that my father and I had another of our arguments.

"Why don't you come back? The place is really going ahead now. Plenty of stories for you to report."

"It sickens me," I said.

"What is that?"

"One minute we look like a little London, now we're Dallas."

"Got to be something," he said.

"And I'm sick of you talking about money. That's all you ever talk about."

"I don't think that's true."

"If it's not how much you can make out of fucking African violets, it's something else."

"Don't talk to your father like that."

He had lied to me, I told him. He said he had given it all away.

He went into his hothouse and was still there at 2 a.m., watching Jeannie Carson in "Mad Little Island", when I went to bed.

I can only presume that Great-uncle Wilfred was wearing his practice tuxedo, dancing with the rake under the house next door, when the great fire broke out. Did you notice him, Father? I guess you wouldn't have, in your hole beneath the earth. Dear old Wilfred, with the cyclone-shaped scuffing on the heels of his shoes from the graceful turns he made on that white pad of concrete. His sun-spotted hand on the neck of the rake. Those endless tunes from the gramophone upstairs, pushed down through the floorboards and heavy with wood and white ant.

I have been told of his infamous "ballroom ledger", a record of 6,137 dances over forty years in church, masonic, bingo and community halls, under canvas in the bush, in drained swimming pools, at Cloudland on the hill.

Here was a man who worked at the General Post Office for decades purely to finance his shoes, polish, white shirts, bow ties, spare buttons and dancing lessons at Arthur Murray's; who practised under the house next door to you, Father, back in the days when families lived in the same street, spied on each other's backyards or front rooms with looking glasses, and shared each other's lives.

You had a theory about bachelor Wilfred. That the sport of ballroom dancing had impressed in him a state of impermanence. That despite the thousands of waists he had clasped, the gloved hands, the glittering jewellery fake or otherwise, and the promise of undergarments, the quest for a fresh partner became second nature to him.

"Where are you going, Uncle Will?" you often called, even when you had your own family. He would turn, that thin hair parted slightly off-centre, and say, "To trip over that light, boy, you know that."

"And which light might that be, Uncle Will?" your routine went.

"The light fantastic!" he would say, gripping the exact tram money wrapped in paper in his pocket.

When he could no longer walk to the tram stop with that peculiar spring in his step, a bus crammed with old dancers pulled up outside, and he would disappear into its warm air of rose and talcum and head off to some polished Brisbane dance floor.

"That was a different generation," you said to me, "when men and women were content with the grasp of a hand or waist, or just watching other couples embracing and moving in time."

"Did he really practise with the rake?"

"It was his life, you must understand. There's nothing funny about it."

"Did he dress it up, with a wig?"

"He dedicated his whole life to dancing. You have to respect that."

I never could resist the story of Uncle Wilfred, could I?

"Did he ever have a woman?"

"He told me he had danced with more than thirty-five thousand women by the time he was seventy years old. He wrote about the special ones in his ledger."

"But did he ever have a serious relationship with a woman?" I asked. "Just one?"

"He probably held more women than any man in history."

"No one special?"

"He said he couldn't understand them," you said, and that was that.

So it was likely that Wilfred was dancing with his rake when Sid, Mitch and T. Nelson were in their dugout, beneath the earth, in the great vacant paddock next to their house. The children of the neighbourhood disappeared into its tall green weeds every afternoon, and traversed its network of tunnels.

They waged a war each day. They mouthed the sounds of machine-gun fire, grenade explosions and ricocheting bullets. In the Downs bunker it was hot and dark. The boys checked their military map of the paddock with matches, stolen from beneath the kitchen sink. Occasionally their maps caught alight, the blue ink sketches of tanks and cannons destroyed. Once, a twisted match, burned to the fingertip, was tossed outside, still alight.

There were real screams that time, and children fled the paddock with snakes, rats and cats. All of them emerged bemused in the street as the summer tinder went up, exposing their secret world, lifting their memories of tears, mock tortures, death and exploratory sex off the face of the suburb.

Urban Downs and Wilfred were the first at the fence with hoses. The paint on one side of the Downs house had already begun to cook under the heat. T. Nelson was sent onto the roof to block downpipes with socks and fill the gutters with water. Urban had read about this in a magazine.

The men of the neighbourhood arrived, beat at the fence with sugar sacks and passed buckets of water. The iceman had abandoned his afternoon round and threw blocks into the fire.

The heat evaporated the eyebrows and whiskers of the fire fighters who, congregated together later, looked like a strange species of fish to T. Nelson.

The Downs house was safe, but no one had noticed shards of carbon, from the pages of a detective magazine, or girlie pictures, or tree bark, float over to Wilfred's gutters choked with leaves and set them alight. Inside was Wilfred and Urban's elderly mother. She reached the back steps and fainted. She was carried in the back of the ice cart to a friend's house up the street, while women rubbed ice chips on her forehead.

118

Completely razed, you said, Father. When you awoke the next morning there was nothing next door. No gramophone music. No shoe shuffling. Just Wilfred's concrete ballroom floor, exposed for the whole world to see, guarded by black stumps like massive burnt matches around its edges.

For T. Nelson, the skyscrapers not only represented acres of barren floor space and the viability of his plant rental trade, but from certain angles, their surfaces were massive screens on which he could track the movements of the city.

From well-chosen hillocks, hotel verandahs and street corners, he could see the reflections of most of the hills outside the city centre. He could even detect the rhythmic blinking of the red lights on the television towers. Facing east, he could see the loops of the William Jolly Bridge, the neon beer sign and the oat factories beside the river.

As a film and television fanatic the images often caught his attention mid-conversation. From one particular upstairs bar he could see the evening trains packed with commuters heading into the quiet suburbs. He could check the state of the weather from his stool, or the peak hour traffic across the Captain Cook Bridge.

"The strangest thing," he told me on the telephone. "For about ten minutes in the afternoons, a bar of sunlight bounces off the new Commission for the Future building and into my front window."

"You'll have to get a shutter."

"For ten minutes only, but boy, the place heats up like a sauna."

The beam travelled over the footpath and a bus seat to the Forest Hire window display of fake elephant ear plants.

T. Nelson concluded that it was fate that had led this second-hand strike of light to enter his business, considering all the intricacies of design, of blueprints and figures, raw materials and human labour that had gone into constructing the Future building.

One degree either way, and the peach-faced parrots in Animal Crackers next door would have glowed like icons.

T. Nelson anticipated the interest in Forest Hire by placing a large advertisement in the yellow pages of the telephone book. For some months a picture of him grinning, wearing his best suit, remained pressed in the P-section, along with crude sketches of crematorium plaques and Greek plaster heads. He was there as the builders finished rooftop helipads, slate foyers and parking bays.

He assumed it would not be long before decorators opened the heavy volume and found, in his own category, T. Nelson Downs from the waist up, his bridgework perfect in ink, his gold tooth — suited more to the metal of the car trade — airbrushed.

He bought a van with a canvas roof and personally carted his wares around town. He filled lifts with pallets of plants and was always enthusiastically greeted by secretaries and office hands, almost hungry for vegetation, he described to his wife, as if they wished to eat the healthy bulbs and stems.

"They fuss over them, caress the leaves," he said, shaking his head. "They have everything worked out, what goes where. Unbelievable."

Wide leaves swivelled away from the wall, perhaps lightly touching the leather arms of couches or drinking fountains; palms between lift doors, their crisscrossing fronds suggesting strength, reinforcement; African violets next to telephones.

One night, over a pheasant dinner with the couple from Animal Crackers, T. Nelson said he was still amazed at the adaptability of his plants.

"I told one woman to be careful of the air-conditioning," he said, sucking on the knob of a leg bone. "If the seeds get sucked up into the ducts, I told her, the plants could grow right through the building, and the roots could come up through the toilets and hand sinks. You should've seen the eyes on her."

After some months T. Nelson decided to write and produce his own plants-for-rooms directory, which he would supply free of charge.

The offices of the executives should be more heavily populated with flora. With the conviviality that plants bring to the indoors, the executive would be wise to place his/her greenery near the conference table or desk, or wherever business is considered or generally debated.

A balance, however, must be acquired. If the vegetation is too dense, the visitor could feel threatened. It must be remembered that plants cast shadows or the appearance of shadows larger than their own physical sphere, that bases can be moist and their regrowth not always decorous.

If, however, the plants are too sparsely placed, the visitor may not feel that intimacy that can be achieved through vegetation.

As with golf courses, which are becoming increasingly popular and necessary in business, there must be that striking off between the toughness of decision, and the openness and unpredictability of nature.

His manifesto stretched to several pages, illustrated with his own drawings of species and round-headed stick figures demonstrating the techniques of watering and soil rejuvenation.

In corridors and reception areas the leaves must be generous, as arms in welcome. In staff meeting rooms the plants must be hardy, with economical water and sun absorption. Bars and coffee lounges are ideal for large, moist flowers. Smaller cup-shaped bulbs would suffice.

And for the locations where official reprimand is executed, possibly retrenchment, Forest Hire recommends cactus.

At the beginning of his booklet, he included a quote from the famous Japanese film director Hiroshi Teshigahara: ''You can change space completely by using plants.''

He has written on a piece of paper a brief record of the call he received from the Premier's Department.

''Premier's aide called re: plants for Parliament House and Ministers' suites. Will call back for estimate.''

This is how my father became acquainted with, as he called them, his ''friends at the Taj Mahal''.

So simple. One telephone call, the chance of a lengthy contract, and he was in the door.

*   *

As his business expanded he acquired more vans and a small staff. The vehicles were like miniature hothouses on wheels, covered with paintings of rainforest. A local artist had arched ferns across the bonnets. The door handles were knotholes in giant cedars. Even the hubcaps contained spinning wildflowers.

He no longer delivered the plants himself, but occasionally oversaw the installation of massive palms in foyers, or the relocation of a fig, removed and replanted by crane. He relied on Tom only for Madonna lilies, and established a supply network with nurseries that ringed the city.

One evening, in his hammock, he hatched his plan to build the biggest hothouse in the southern hemisphere.

He was watching the news on his small television, and saw a report on the glass pyramid at the entrance to the Louvre in Paris. He sat up and moved closer to the screen, eventually squatting before it, the machine cradled in both hands. At that distance, he could see the old palace reflected in the pyramid's outer surfaces.

". . . said it was the only shape suitable, although the new entrance to the world's most famous museum has met with some controversy."

"I think it is disgusting and has ruined the Louvre forever."

"Appalling. It is not French. It is not France."

Inside, a man in white overalls demonstrated how to clean the pyramid's tiles, dangling from the focal point with a sponge on a stick, several coloured rags hanging from his belt like pelts.

"Bigger than the ones in Egypt," he told me. "Can you see it? Rising for miles."

"You'll never get it through council," I said. "It'll be a circus. A tourist attraction."

"Palm trees, boy. That's the future. For resorts, mansions, golf courses. That's where it's happening."

"My neighbour has a fine garden," I said, trying to distract him.

"Down there? In Sydney? Get out."

"Some nights she comes out naked."

T. Nelson was silent for a moment.

"No clothes at all?"

"Not a stitch."

"What sort of plants does she have?"

"Staghorns," I said.

There was further silence.

"Ah," he finally said. "I thought as much."

My mother confirms that around the time of his invitation to Parliament House, my father took to wearing a Cooktown orchid on the lapel of his suit coat. They were expensive then, taken from the forests in the far north of the State, and brought down in air-conditioned trucks to Brisbane.

"Being lavender, he had to rebuild his wardrobe around them," she says. "As you can imagine, the colours that go with lavender are few and far between. He looked so frightful people forgot about the orchid."

Perhaps he wished to show some form of allegiance or patriotism, the flower being our State symbol. That's how he was. He always felt the need to be attached to something: a club, a nationality, even a religion. To a tradition. To anything bigger than himself.

We came in to land, Father, on a narrow strip between towering pine trees. The smell of sick was overpowering, and Butch was fanning the woman with his cap.

When we alighted our little group started hugging each other on the tarmac. Here on the asphalt, my fellow travellers, previously quiet and guarded, almost danced together, held hands and led each other away from the aircraft.

I couldn't explain this remarkable event. I was unsure if they had opened up to each other in relief that the rocky flight was over and they had made it safely back to earth, or whether some had glimpsed their future in the canyon.

After the paddock fire the land was developed into housing lots. Wilfred bought a small aluminium caravan and parked it in the middle of his concrete slab, propping it up at one end with an old lard drum. He never danced again. His suits had gone up in the fire, as well as his ledger of partners. Thousands of descriptions of female hip bones, ankles, breasts, perfumes and lipsticks over five decades. Gone.

His mother was taken away in a white ambulance to a nursing home overlooking a park of ancient fig trees and the railway yards. The corridors and rooms of the building smelled of old urine. People sat motionless at the glass front doors of the home, held handkerchiefs, slept with their chins resting on their collar bones.

Urban, during his many visits, heard that one man was kept permanently on the lower floor, his wife on the first floor. Both were confined to wheelchairs. Three times a year, at Christmas and their respective birthdays, they were wheeled together.

"You should hear the swearing," a nurse told Urban. "Can hear it right across the city."

Another man, always in black pyjamas, spent his time opening and closing the building's windows.

One night an old man, once an expert on logarithms, was awoken by deep thunder over Mount Coot-tha, and lit a Capstan, secreted in the spine of his copy of Leon Cottrell's *The Mountains of Pharaoh*. After a few crackling puffs he fell asleep in his bed and dropped the cigarette into his slippers.

The thirty minutes that followed, I have discovered, are still being studied at local institutions of learning in my home town. A thesis was completed five years ago. There has been talk of a dramatic production, to put the event into perspective, but the idea was cancelled after technical difficulties over matters of combustion in a theatre in the round.

When the old wooden nursing home went up, patients leapt from balconies, described by police reporter Albert S. Urquhart as "human torches", one of the earliest uses of the phrase in Brisbane journalism. Nylon nightdresses evaporated. A pair of teeth were found amongst the jacaranda leaves across the road, over two lanes of traffic. This has never been explained.

The elderly, still burdened with a variety of illnesses, performed physical feats that belied their medical files. They dived off railings, some completely straddling them, leapt through windows, screamed when previously thought mute.

My great-grandmother, a witness alleged, was seen gliding across the black and white checked floor of the empty refectory, her arms embracing the depleting oxygen, spinning and sliding as the kitchen china exploded like gunshot.

According to police and fire department records, she was "immovable, despite attempts by staff to retrieve her from the burning room".

She later dived from a third floor window, completely ablaze, into the soft and well-manicured lawn at the front of the nursing home.

"I'll never forget it," an anonymous nurse told Urquhart. "This woman was balanced on the railing. She spread her arms out. It was like she was diving into a pool. It was horrible." The nurse broke down in tears, the reporter added.

When they lifted her from the lawn, she had scorched a cross, of sorts, in the grass.

She was a good diver, my great-grandmother. It was she who had first taken so passionately to the Oceanic Baths. She, who had so flamboyantly made every lunge into its waters a performance.

Father, do not blame Sid, or anyone, for the death. As usual, you took the burden of it all upon yourself. The weight was too great.

"They could never transplant your father's heart," my mother once said. "It is too big."

I spoke to an Italian girl in the dining room of the lodge, a few kilometres from the canyon. A band in the corner played songs to please every nationality. Only small groups danced at one time.

"Have you anything like this at your country?" the girl asked.

"The canyon?"

"Yes."

"We have Ayers Rock, in the middle, and a giant reef."

"Reef?"

"You know, coral and coloured fish," I said.

"Ah yes," she said, smiling. "How cute."

"Have you been to my country?"

"No," she laughed. "No, I could never go there."

"Why not?"

"It is so far. It is at the bottom end. I can't imagine so long in a plane."

"Only twenty-four hours."

"Really? Oh no, a whole day in a plane, no. To see a rock and some fish? No, never."

I finished my drink and stood, annoyed I might say. "We are the biggest island in the world," I said proudly, and left.

7

"So you want to build, what is it, the biggest hothouse in the southern hemisphere? Is that correct?"

The Minister sat back in his red leather chair, a single ochre boot on the window ledge of his office, watching the silt dredge at the bend of the river. T. Nelson noticed cowshit on the rims of the Minister's sole.

"That's right. My idea is to . . ."

"We have a botanic gardens here, do we not?" The Minister still did not look at T. Nelson Downs, an arc of river mud spray reflected in his eyes, the television towers on Mount Coot-tha splinters on the curve of his retina.

"I intend to grow some plants for profit," T. Nelson said, pointing to his pencil sketches on the cedar desk, the *Adiantum preuvianums* smudged by the sweat of his palms, the *Aglaomorpha meyenianums* with the hair of madmen.

"At the same time," T. Nelson continued, unaware of the droop of his lapel orchid, "the hothouse could be open to the public, as an attraction, of sorts, to overseas visitors and so on."

"How big will this be, this hothouse?" The Minister emitted a short hissing belch of lobster fumes, and patted his stomach. The dredge was disappearing, beneath the William Jolly Bridge.

"Big. Huge. As tall as a thirty-storey building. As my plans show, I hope to build it in the shape of a pyramid. I have been advised that a hothouse as big as this could gather cloud near the apex."

"Cloud, hmm?" the Minister said, turning and leafing through his desk calendar, a damp patch on his shirt revealing itself beneath his deep green floral tie of interlocking fern fronds, moss, lichen.

"On good advice, yes."

The Minister for Local Government and Conservation spun back again to the window.

"If permission was granted, Mr Downs, where would you propose to build this . . . this pyramid?"

"I should imagine the coast would be ideal. It would be good for my plants and . . ."

"The coast?" the Minister said, and looked over his shoulder at T. Nelson for the first time.

"Yes, for the tourists. It would have to be marginally inland, of course, away from the direct salt spray, but . . ."

"Please, no details. I am not a plant expert, Mr Downs."

"There is a lot of activity down there now, sir. I think it would be ideal."

The Minister picked up a pencil and prised the dung from his boots.

"Plants and animals, Mr Downs, have not proved popular there. That old fool near the border, his name escapes me, has had that flora and fauna park for years, many years, and it has failed dismally. He is a hindrance to the progress of the area, between you and I."

The Minister stood with a creak and a second seafood belch, and stuck his pencil into the soil of a small African violet.

"I understand you furnished our Parliament House with your rented plants."

"That's true, yes," T. Nelson said.

"Is that yours, that rubber tree in the corner?"

"It is, yes. I know all my plants."

"It's a very good rubber tree, Downs," the Minister said, raising a single eyebrow. T. Nelson had seen this trick before, on television, and captured exactly in newspaper caricatures of the good Minister.

"Thank you, thank you very much." T. Nelson pulled the front flaps of his coat closer together. "If I may say so, it is looking a little dry."

T. Nelson, on entering the spacious office, had noticed coffee grounds, cigarette and cigar butts, and rusted paper clips at its base. Three leaves had fallen to the carpet, small canoes on the worn Persian.

"And the ferns, along the walkway to the car park? Yours too?"

"Mine, yes," T. Nelson said.

"My wife," the Minister said, retrieving the pencil and pointing its soiled end to a framed photograph on his desk, "she loves ferns."

"They are many people's favourite."

"She cannot find enough of them," he said with a snort. "She would run nude through King George Square for a good healthy fern, my wife."

"They are like orchids," T. Nelson said, noticing with alarm the drab state of his buttonhole Cooktown, adjusting it, nudging the petals while the Minister had his back turned. "The plant hunters emerge when a species becomes popular. They stop at nothing to maintain supply. Whole colonies have been wiped out by these bogus botanists."

"I didn't know the situation was so grim."

"Every day I am offered dozens of protected species on the black market."

"A black market in plants? Come now, Downs."

"It's true. It pushes the prices up, astronomically. The Japanese will pay thousands for a single rare orchid. It's like the Stock Exchange, in a way."

T. Nelson attempted a laugh, but stifled it as the Minister stooped down and poked at the roots of the rented rubber tree.

"I must inform my wife," he said. "She will be most interested. The Japanese, you said?"

"Big buyers."

"Money no object?"

"None at all."

"Interesting," said the Minister, prodding deposits of Vittoria and Earl Grey, lifting rotted Darjeeling and English Breakfast tea bags. "I am encouraged by your enterprise, Downs. It is an unusual idea, this pyramid business of yours. By the way, would you like some tea?"

"No thank you."

The Minister stood. "I shall consider this proposition of yours, but I'll be straight with you. I would not be too hopeful." He walked to the desk and looked briefly at T. Nelson's sketches.

"We have big plans for the coast, between you and I," the

Minister said. "Buildings tall enough for clouds, Downs, you'll be pleased to know."

T. Nelson attempted another chortle, the frond of a bird's nest fern imprinted on the edge of his thumb.

"If you know how to make money from mangroves, let me know. Useless things. Difficult to extract." The Minister returned to his seat and formed a canopy with his fingertips. "But I'll tell you what, Downs. I have a friend down at Burleigh that I would like you to meet. Councillor Wilson. Have you met him?"

"I have known him for some years, yes."

"Good, good. Go and see him. I'll arrange it for you. If the biggest hothouse in the Southern Hemisphere does not get off the ground, we may have other projects we could work on together."

"Yes, thank you."

"I like your balls, Downs, I really do."

"Thank you."

"The Premier, he was very happy with the plants around here. I thought I'd pass that on."

"I appreciate that."

"Thousands, for just one orchid?"

"Tens of thousands."

The Minister looked at the rubber tree. Several of its leaves were already yellowing.

"They are good people, the Japanese. We like them here."

"Yes."

"We like their money here, right?" the Minister said, laughing again and standing.

T. Nelson folded his sketches. "I appreciate your time, sir."

"A pleasure," the Minister said, moving around the desk and shaking hands. T. Nelson noticed his government insignia tiepin for the first time. Small, but solid gold, piercing the succulent heart of a staghorn just above the centre of the tie.

"There *is* one thing," the Minister said, walking T. Nelson to the door. "My wife, she is having difficulty with a largish fern in the lounge room. Tried everything, the poor thing."

"Is it in direct sunlight?"

"No, no."

"What is it near?"

"Near?" the Minister said. "Well, it's next to a Grecian vase. Picked it up on holidays last year. Genuine."

"Then put other plants near this fern of yours. Move the urn. It's congenial for them, with other plants around."

"Is that right?" the Minister said in a surprised tone, touched almost by this mysterious image of the camaraderie of plants. "I'll be damned. That naked discus thrower may have been too much for it, eh Downs?" He roared with laughter, slapped T. Nelson on the back, and wiped grains of soil onto his visitor's jacket.

Let me tell you a quick story.

One day, in the former brothel that was my home, the kitchen sink overflowed. I peered into its old mouth with a torch. Nothing. It was too dark for me to see anything, not that I would have known what to look for.

I called a plumber, and went out.

When I came home I found a seven-metre root, like a giant eel covered in slime, stretched out on the footpath in front of my house, all the way to Charlie's delicatessen on the corner.

The plumber had wrestled this root from my pipes. He said it had wound its way from the rear drain, beneath my house and up into the sink pipe, and was only centimetres from the plughole.

This was how I saw my father. A shoot that had worked its way, so effortlessly, into the complex pipe system of that government of ours. Pushing through those dark funnels, unseen, oblivious to the chaos ahead.

I was hoping to bring you back a fossil, Father. Perhaps the tongued leaves of a Florida tree fern, or one of your favourites, that *Anemia mexicana*, encased in ancient mud. There had to be whole forests of them, surely, deep down in the Carlsbad Caverns. But the caves were so poorly lit, with their winding paths of neat bitumen through the ventricles of this hollow underground heart, as I saw it, that even the most cursory archæological scratchings were impossible.

I was told there was little down there but bat guano. Our elevator was a sack of its moist stench, even at ground level. I walked into it, behind Gunter, turned, and saw a mannequin of a woman, circa 1910, standing in a huge steel bucket, her hair swept up, her dress full of petticoat, her rings false. She looked so much like Andrea, Father, that I was startled for a moment. You would have jumped yourself, seeing her suddenly in New Mexico, of all places, let alone in a guano bucket. My heart raced; really.

I understood then, plummeting deep into the earth, that I was not only fleeing the probability of your death, but Andrea, a woman you said was good for me, that I would find no better. Andrea, who could always elicit from you a greeting or farewell kiss, a squeeze of the elbow, despite your blushing. You saw imaginary grandchildren when she was around, tumbling from your knees or taking your hand.

"You'll never find another like that," you said every time you saw her. Every time. But I had looked, hadn't I, for another? And suddenly there she was, through the elevator door, still smiling as it closed.

"They change the elevator operators here every twenty minutes," our own white-faced elevator captain told us. He said the pressure of constantly dropping almost a kilometre and back up again was too much for the human ear.

When we arrived at the bottom I expected to walk out into an eerie world of illuminated stalagmites and stalactites, of bats and echoes, but the doors parted and we entered an underground department store. There was a cafeteria to the left, with rows of wooden benches that disappeared into the darkness, and in front, racks of clothes, drink machines, and a one-hour photograph processing booth.

Once we were all gathered Gunter said, "You may wish to take a Talkstick with you. At various stages of the walk through the caverns it will give you a history of the place, describe things for you. Please hand them in at the end of your walk. And don't forget, 4 p.m. back on the bus."

132

I took a Talkstick, slender and grey with "Property of the United States" stamped into its side, and stood at the first point of the walk. The torch-sized piece of plastic crackled to life.

"Welcome to the Carlsbad Caverns," the Talkstick said with, to my surprise, a heavy southern American accent and what I suspected was a speech impediment. "More than eighteen thousand years worth of bat guano had collected in the caves before it was discovered at the beginning of this century by explorer Jim White."

I thought I heard bats but, looking up, could see nothing. I imagined them winging through this mesh of commentary, and wondered if the Talkstick's lisp disrupted their sonar and sent them crashing into wet walls. Perhaps they knew this man intimately by now, and could anticipate his inflexions and hisses that surged through the caverns day and night.

"Few believed White's fantastic tales of a giant underground wilderness. It took photographs of the incredible formations to convince the skeptics of the day."

A few hundred metres from our starting point I looked back at the small carnival of the cafeteria, so vivid in this blackness, with tourists scuttling in and out of shadow; our fragile age, so small compared to the dark immensity that surrounded it, the calcified guano as big in some places as office blocks, with countless offshoot caverns still unexplored.

"Jim White immediately set to work and proceeded to take more than a hundred thousand tons of guano from the caves. It was then transported to southern California where it was used as fertiliser on the many orange groves there. It was to make Jim White an extremely rich man."

The Talkstick went static at this point. Perhaps I was walking too fast. I was disappointed. I wanted to find out how much a man could make out of shit at the turn of the century. I walked back, but my Talkstick refused to pick up the lisping airwaves again. But Father, can you imagine how welcome Jim White would have been back in our home State? What ingenuity. What genius, to carry the guano by horse and cart for miles to the orange groves. What resourcefulness. They would have made him a Minister, without doubt. Maybe given him a knighthood for his cunning.

I doubt, however, that Sir James White ever saw the beauty of this place. Just guano and dollars.

The park ranger whispered, even though the three men stood on a thin dirt path thirty minutes' walk from the road, beneath the canopy of rainforest, quiet except for the occasional rustle of undergrowth and the knife-sharp call of a whipperwhil.

"Mr Downs? Pleased to meet you," the ranger said. He had two brilliant yellow mallee fowls stitched onto his shirt sleeves. "How are you, Bart? Long time no see."

"Fine, Max, been a while, eh?" Councillor Wilson said, picking burrs from his golf socks. "Shall we go down to the arch? Bit cooler down there."

T. Nelson was overdressed for the meeting, the purpose of which he still knew nothing. He had expected to attend the chambers of his old friend Councillor Wilson, public figure as well as successful produce vendor and orange juice king. Wilson owned giant perspex oranges in shopping malls all over the coast. These oranges, sliced in half, opened on a huge hinge. Inside were numerous juicing machines, cash registers and stools. Occasionally Wilson himself stepped inside one of his many orange booths and served the public with his own hands.

"I do like to keep in touch," he had told T. Nelson as they drove in a council four-wheel-drive through the volcanic plugs and hills of the Hinterland. "Some others took me on. A juice war the papers called it. But my oranges are still around. The business is growing every day."

He told of a rival juiceman who had started with perspex lemons, then a strawberry, then an apple complete with stalk and leaves, and had a celery stick in production when Councillor Wilson sent in his team of health inspectors.

"It had to be done," he explained, turning off the road into the Natural Arch National Park. "He claimed I used my clout as a council official, you know, conflict of interest thing, whatever they call it, but it simply wasn't true. I have to think of the

134

tourists, right? That's what we're here for. And this man was, plain and simple, an unhygienic juicer.''

T. Nelson tore the thin leather sides of his shoes clambering down to the cave beneath the arch. His tweed jacket was covered with black cobbler's pegs. The ranger burned a leech from his ankle and the blood soaked into his sock.

As it was a weekday, the gangs of youths, motorcyclists and lifesavers were absent from the arch, a three-metre wide tunnel through rock that opened into a pool, once thought bottomless, and a slice of cave that depleted to a tight crevice at the back, not unlike the hinge of one of Wilson's oranges.

''They still come here, to test their manhood, you know,'' the Councillor said, squatting at the edge of the pool and peering up through the funnel. ''Initiations. Rites. It's madness.''

''Three deaths last year,'' Max said. ''I've put mesh across the top but they still rip it off.'' T. Nelson clicked his tongue to register his empathy with the diligent ranger.

It was cool at the edge of the pool and T. Nelson swatted mosquitoes on the back of his neck and his arms.

''Did you know, Nelson,'' Wilson said, ''we measured this pool last year and for the first time ever, ever, we touched bottom? This year it's at five metres. Can you believe that? Why is it suddenly filling up? No one can explain it, can they, Max?''

''No, sir.''

''Yet these young fools still jump. If and when it fills up completely, I think they'll keep on jumping.''

''Extraordinary,'' T. Nelson said, tossing a pebble into the water.

''Indeed,'' Wilson said, clapping his hands. ''Now to business.''

The councillor, his silver hair a dull globe in the sunlight through the rock funnel, questioned the ranger about the plant thieves of the region. Yes, they came at night, fully equipped with rubber-soled boots, spades, plastic bags and pencil-thin torches.

Yes, they knew what they were after: specific species deficient in the marketplace or suddenly popular amongst the world's amateur botanists, paraded at dinner parties, presented gently in cupped hands like precious antiques. Some were not experts, taking away bundles of weeds, lantana and grasses. But the professionals, particularly the wild orchid hunters, covered their tracks as would contract killers, disguising empty spaces, fresh uprooted soil and wounds in the forest's lower canopy. Clues that only a trained eye could detect.

T. Nelson, for an instant, wondered how his meeting with the Minister had led him to the edge of the pool. There was no mention of the biggest hothouse in the Southern Hemisphere, its finely dovetailed network of natural wood walkways, ponds, fountains.

"The fact is," Wilson said, "and it pains me to say this but it is reality, right, it is the real world that we live in, no escaping it, that some of our finer species are being lost forever to these thieves, these poachers, these, you would agree Max, these rapists of our natural heritage, our greatest asset, this wonderful plant life, this extraordinary flora we have here.

"Just look at it will you, just *look* at it."

Max the ranger nodded ruefully, and brushed down his moustache with thumb and forefinger.

"Right, Nelson? Are you with me on this? It's like everything that has ever mattered to this country of ours, I'm not kidding, it's something I have always worried over, truly worried. The tragedy is that you have to protect what you have. Protect it against these . . . these poachers, these unprincipled elements. To do that, sadly, you have to take measures, you have to move in and take a stand. You with me so far, Nelson?"

"I think so."

"Good. That's good. Let me put it this way, Nelson, and this will only be an experiment, an official government experiment and in prototype stage, I might stress, so it would be appreciated if none of this was leaked to the press people, you understand."

He whispered here, although the cave still amplified a hissing version of his speech.

"The Minister wishes, Nelson, that you, in an official capacity, as a representative of the department, you understand, cull some of the more endangered species here."

"Cull?"

"Correct. To deny these thieves, and that's all they are, thieves, simple as that, their livelihood. Their *illegal* livelihood, let me stress that."

"I'm not sure I understand."

Max scratched his upper right arm, jiggling the golden mallee fowl.

"You'll get your nursery, Nelson," the councillor said, "not as big as you envisaged, not at the start anyway, first things first, but you shall be charged with nurturing these precious assets, proliferating the species, so that they shall be available for generations, for our children."

"Oh."

"Let me remind you that the Minister will take a personal interest in this experiment. He's a hands-on Minister, no penpusher. He'll get his hands dirty, no question. In fact it is his wish that we begin this project with ferns, as many different varieties as you can find, and Max will help you with this. And if all goes well, with the breeding that is, we can then send our successes into the public domain, where of course it rightfully belongs. We will have the coast and Brisbane looking like Eden in no time."

They all laughed this time, their echoes guttural and deep like the growls of dogs.

"One question," T. Nelson said, holding up his forefinger although neither of them was looking at him. "Is there any limit to this culling?"

"You see, Nelson," the councillor said, sweeping his hand across the framed forest of the cave entrance, "the greener we can eventually make the streets, the footpaths, building foyers, river banks, the better it is for the department and for the Minister. The greenness is his public profile. The public don't have to see him, not at all, but if they see green they know he's doing his job. Simple as that. He has very big plans for this area, Nelson, very big."

"I only have a small truck," T. Nelson said.

"No problem. Max has a truck and you can use any council vehicles you need. Just a phone call and they're yours. After

137

all," Wilson said, slapping T. Nelson Downs on the back, "you sold me all the damned things, right?"

They walked back up through the rainforest and were all breathing heavily when they reached the car park.

"Thank you, Maxwell," Wilson said, lightly punching one of the mallee fowls. "We shall be in touch. And Nelson?" They shook hands. "I think we'll have a successful venture here. If it takes off, touch wood, I may very well branch out with fern booths." He laughed explosively, brushing sweat from his forehead.

"How would you make a perspex fern booth?" T. Nelson asked.

Wilson looked up at the tree tops with his hands on his hips.

"That's a very good question, Nelson."

"This spectacular family," the nurseryman told me, staring at my notebook as I recorded his words, "is being torn apart."

I loved that phrase, this spectacular family. How gently he treated his orchids, with the fat white fingers of a dentist or doctor. The family of orchids, possibly the largest network of flowering plants on earth.

How often I had pinned these delicate creatures to the breast of Andrea, for them to be lost beneath the relentless feet of dancers at the City Hall, or in the back seat of a taxi on the way home, not knowing that even our State symbol, the Cooktown orchid, was itself close to extinction. I remember seeing buckets full of them in town, along Queen or George Street, or on the footpath outside delicatessens, so common they were boring despite the beauty they lent to my refrigerator shelves in their perspex capsules.

They were everywhere — on tiepins and ties, baked enamel badges, spoon ends, placemats, tablecloths, tea towels, drink coasters, school notebooks, summer shirts and flags.

I treated the story lightly nevertheless. It was a quiet day, a Sunday, and the Monday edition would be traditionally slender. My brief was general. When was the last time you saw a Cook-

138

town orchid? A topic no doubt discussed over the weekend at the dining table of the editor.

I have gone back though. I have muddied my boots in nurseries from here to the Sunshine Coast. I have telephoned Mr Xs and Ms Ys halfway around the world. The details are emerging, strand by strand, and a picture has formed.

I nearly confronted one of the world's most notorious plant hunters in a hotel in Dayboro, of all places. The smoke of his cheroot was still heavy in the room when I opened the door. That's how close I was.

The trade in jungle grown species, I was told, was worth millions. There were even allegations of murder over a *Paphiopedilum armeniacum*, the Golden Slipper of Yuman. I was offered a Rothschild's slipper, delivered within days if I wished to pay extra for a courier. How it made its way from its habitat, a national park on Mount Kinabalu in Sabah, I have yet to ascertain. I doubt, Father, you are surprised.

One source confirmed that these big hunters, and there are only a few, travel the world in search of these plants, mounting expensive expeditions, on safari as such, and remove a single species completely to thwart their competitors. The moss and lichen on the plants are vital as proof of their originality.

These unprincipled botanists insert misleading information in journals and trade magazines to put other hunters off the scent of exotic varieties. There is sabotage, espionage, years of research and planning. A single phrase dropped in the back lanes of a hothouse can be vital. Clues. Clues.

They smuggle shoots in and out of a dozen countries, in their underpants, socks, brassieres, hats, in contact lens cases, thermos flasks, toothpaste tubes and pill containers. They secrete seeds in their ears.

But you knew nothing of this. That is what I am hoping, anyway. It was against everything you believed. Against removing the object from its source. As ugly as Sid's opal-gutted jewellery. A betrayal.

Tell me of your innocence. Of your blindness. Tell me.

* *

139

It was sensual in those caverns. We did not talk about it but you could feel that a warmth, a reverence, had fallen over the group as we walked along those bitumen paths so black you could not see them. It was like strolling through space, untethered, all of us Great Waldos, holding hands. I saw couples kissing in grottoes.

Near the end of the walk I noticed a stalactite dripping white fluid onto a circular mound, at least five metres in diameter, that reminded me of one of Andrea's breasts. That of a dancer, a swimmer, with a slight nipple. I kept looking back at it and un-wittingly walked into another Talkstick zone.

"It is such a time-consuming process that the formations you have viewed today will remain unchanged to the naked eye by the time your great-grandchildren visit the Carlsbad Caverns."

I took it away from my ear and looked back through the caves, the people moving through this cathedral in silent groups along its looping pathways, slowly, as if the air was thicker down here.

The Talkstick crackled and went dead, but there was a voice, the only other sound I had heard aside from the dripping, the miniscule shift of calcium, the air moved by a leathery wing, dur-ing my walk. It may have been a child, a man or woman, it was so faint. It may have come from the Talkstick; a human voice miraculously caught in its electronic waves and squeezed out through the tiny grey grille.

"Do you love me?" the voice said.

8

My father first heard of the pyramid of the God of Mu whilst wiping custard from the chin of an old man.

T. Nelson was sitting on a small brown suitcase filled with antique photographs of steamships, berthed near the old iron bridge at the top end of Queen Street, their pastel hulls rendered spotless in the studio of G.N.Wilson and Co. Photographers, and at rest in clouds of vivid mangrove.

There were other pictures: a man in a pith helmet balanced atop a barrow of pineapples, his partner holding one up with both hands, as a priest would raise a chalice, before a field of scissoring spines; a portion of the Great Barrier Reef, the coral formations so bright and exaggerated by the same carnival colours of G.N.Wilson's fine hairbrush, that the aqua water that arced across the frame appeared not only as a tear in the reef, but a window into infinity.

T. Nelson had yet to produce his pictures, the cane trains puffing grit towards his substantial buttock, the Brisbane electric trams creaking under the weight of his pinstripe trousers, when the old man asked for his apple and custard.

Judging by the skin over the pudding it had been sitting in the nursing home kitchen for some time. T. Nelson delicately removed the film and placed it on the chrome arm of the old man's wheelchair then began spoonfeeding.

It was his second week on the nursing home circuit and it had proved disappointing. A few days earlier, in a red brick home of identical design on the north side of the city, another old man had taken one of his photographs, placed it on his lap and urinated. T. Nelson watched, shocked still at the capability of the human body to repulse, as a tiny deep sea diver in the picture vanished amongst the reeds, enveloped by the fluid that absorbed rapidly across the ancient cardboard.

It had initially seemed like a good idea when it had come to him as he browsed one evening through a copy of the *Worldwide Geography Reader*, Volume Six, Australasia edition. He had picked up the book years before from a barber shop in Roma, attracted by the cover of an English boy in striped blazer, trousers and cap, leaning on a cricket bat, and a girl with ringlets delightedly spinning a globe of the world.

He skipped over the chapters on Strange Animals, The Blacks, The Land of the Frizzly Haired, and paused on A Queenly Colony.

There was Brisbane at the turn of the century, and Mount Coot-tha, its shape unmistakable, a backdrop to the city. Presented with a clean sheet of graph paper, T. Nelson believed he could draw its unremarkable dips and taperings with his eyes shut, and the placement of its pyramidal steel television towers, the red lights at their points constantly blinking. To the millimetre. The lights, his son Samuel had thought, were Sacred Hearts, protecting Brisbane at night.

"Queensland offers excellent opportunities to small capitalists — to men with a little money," the chapter read. T. Nelson sniggered. He thought of the 371 unsold pepper grinders that his father could never offload, passed on to him now, stacked in boxes beneath the verandah where he sat. A second generation of unsaleable City Hall grinders, which T. Nelson concluded did not have a market, even if the pepper granules gathered like drunken dancers in the miniature ballroom.

"Capitalists and labourers in large numbers are sadly needed. Both parties must be men of strong will, energetic, and not afraid of work or possible defeat."

Grinning nostalgically, he came upon Chapter 44, beneath a black and white photograph of sheep drinking from an artesian well.

"Three of the principal lines of steamers involved in the coasting trade of Australia carry invalids and tourists on The Great Queensland Pleasure Trip."

He leant back in his chair and put his new R.M.Williams boots on the verandah rail. The television lights were irregular behind the waves of evening bats across the sky, heading into the suburbs to feast on backyard fruits. He lit a fresh cigar.

142

He did not get his hair permed, or take to exotic bracelets and medallions, or purchase suits with padded shoulders, but my father did enter that phase of middle-age rejuvenation, that grasping, that final sprint.

Notice the boots. And the cigars; no longer Wee Willems, the small stuff, but monsters that came in capsules with screw-off lids. He took to drinking specific brands of imported gin and scotch and boutique beers. He had a special single-bottle leather carrier that he took to dinners and sporting events, slung over his shoulder on a long strap.

To be accurate, the metamorphosis followed his invitation to the Minister for Conservation's Christmas party, at which a backyard fernery, stuffed to bursting with some of T. Nelson's culled species, was unveiled as a gift to the Minister's wife. She was so thrilled she broke into tears.

They placed gold and jewels at the feet of my father that day. He was given the biggest serving of barbecued reef fish and octopus. It was he who was given the honour of officially turning on the fernery watering system, to a generous round of applause and a further mad shriek from the Minister's wife. They toasted him with official party wine, the labels bearing the head of the Premier.

Later, in the Minister's own wood-lined study, he was promised the coup of his career: providing all foliage, all plant life, all landscape design for the World Exposition due in two years' time. He returned home invincible. He was *in* there. He could hatch any crazy idea, any venture, and they would back him. And he would be on show to the world.

All that for a few ferns.

At the NASA space centre in Houston, they showed us replicas of gold records of Chuck Berry's "Johnny B. Goode", and of groaning jungles and squawking toucans that they sent up to God.

They packed twelve of the records on board the Voyager space craft which we had seen occasionally, you remember, Father, on our television screens, spinning through space and sending back images of planets and moons through a light signal. The signal was so weak, we were told, that it would barely rattle the filament of a forty-watt bulb, let alone illuminate it.

I asked them, for you, why they did not send Frank Sinatra up into the universe on these gold discs that are supposed to portray the story of man and, indeed, the whole world, in the event that alien life happened to open the Voyager's special compartment, sit down, if they had legs, and play each of these discs. The guide only gave me a weak smile.

But I found these sample records riveting. They were called ''The Sounds of the Earth'', and we all stood around listening to them until most of the group got bored with the chattering of monkeys and bamboo creaking. Not I though. I must have stood there a full half-hour.

Later we inspected the Apollo craft, this seared and scorched insect of a machine, so flimsy up close and small from what I remembered of it as a child, huddled around a television set in the classroom, herded tightly together by white-cloaked nuns. They continued to dynamite the quarry at the back of our school that day, even though there were men up there, hopping on the moon.

A man in a wheelchair cruised around and around the Apollo, taking photographs and staring into it.

He was still there after our brief tour of mission control.

''Ladies and gentlemen, you will notice there are two clocks ahead of you.''

The clocks were on either side of a giant blue light map of the world.

''One is Greenwich Mean Time, and the other is local time.''

I squinted at the map and wondered where you would be, Father — swinging under the Horn, heading for Tahiti?

''According to the experts,'' our guide continued, ''these clocks lose less than one second every three hundred thousand years.''

Was this the perfect point of time we were witnessing, sitting in our small group behind glass, where millions had come before us, looking down into the control room?

I put up my hand and asked how they could possibly know the percentage of time lost over the centuries. My guess was that the clocks had been on the walls of mission control for twenty years at the most. There was some laughter at this question, and a smug snort from Gunter who stood beside the NASA guide, comfortable in the way most guides are in each other's company.

"I don't know exactly, but here at NASA we trust the experts, let me tell you."

I returned to the gold discs on the way out to the bus, and listened to a Japanese conversation, then the predictable waterdrip Oriental music. It was still on side one.

Was it possible to put sounds of the whole world on twelve gold records? Who was the editor of the selection? Had men and women from NASA been sent out to all territories of the earth to collect sounds: the gurgle of a famous river, thunder cracking, conversations, the amplified padding of an insect across a leaf, lions, a didgeridoo?

They loaded pictures, too, aboard the Voyager, that were intended to depict the progress of our civilisation: the Great Wall of China, the San Francisco Bridge, the Sydney Opera House, mothers with children, old men, a freeway heavy with traffic, a human skeleton, a close-up of a fanned hand and a pretty gymnast in midflight on the horizontal bars, her body shaped like a star.

"Did you send a stereo into space?" I asked the NASA guide on the way out.

"A stereo?"

"For the aliens. To play the gold records."

The guide had become annoyed. "I can check on that for you."

If they had never seen such objects, I wanted to ask, how could they have played them in sequence? What if they jumbled the chronology, or played the whole set backwards?

I know they would have looked down at us affectionately, then, at this world that had once produced Chuck Berry, giant cities and spacecraft, but had, somewhere along the line, got it horribly wrong and been stripped back to the point where Earth was just a glittering globe of small fires.

"I was good friends with Tommy McIlwraith, you know," the old man said, the apple and custard just past his tongue. T. Nelson noticed that the blood in his veins was almost black beneath wide sun spots.

"He was a clever bugger. Mad I suppose, Tommy was."

The old man, still in his blue pyjamas, had a cascade of hair from his giant left ear. T. Nelson wondered why the ears of old men became so large, so disproportionate to their shrinking bodies, as they approached death; if the failing ear enlarged itself to compensate for its weakening state, and if he would wake up one day with ears like the speakers of a Victrola.

The old man sucked on the tin spoon, its surface dull from the passage of innumerable tongues.

"You know what they called old Tommy? Before he became the big boss, the Premier? The refrigerator king." The old man laughed and squeezed the arms of the wheelchair. "Crazy Mister Meat Man, too."

T. Nelson knew nothing of Thomas McIlwraith, visionary and Queensland's first businessman politician, of his dream of establishing a direct shipping route from Queensland to Britain to supply the Mother Country with refrigerated meat.

One of McIlwraith's first central Queensland freezing works caught fire, the old man continued. (This interested T. Nelson, and he held the spoon still for a moment.) The fire started in the engine room, spread quickly, exploded through the cold rooms and roasted the hanging carcasses, then incinerated them. For a brief period the entire town was shrouded with the sweet smell of pork, lamb, beef.

"The dogs went mad," the old man laughed, showing his pink gums.

Another of McIlwraith's plants failed and the manager committed suicide. He was found dead, lying alongside his slaughtered beasts, his shoes comically loose on his frozen blue feet.

Finally, the first shipment was launched, but the vessel, still dripping wine from its bow, sailed into a cyclone an hour out of port and was tossed back onto the mainland. Ox tongues, legs, pig heads and trotters were washed up on the sand for days.

"Oh, there were all sorts of troubles," the big-eared old man said. "All sorts of scandals. Used his power to make money, they said of old Tommy. Ha! He feathered his nest all right, did old Tom. Wanted to build a railway line from Brisbane right across the country. Mad. Made his bundle though and went back to England. Not that silly after all, was he?"

T. Nelson wheeled the old man to his favourite position beside the front doors, already crowded with other patients who gathered at the entrance like eager patrons in the front row of a cinema. It was better to look at the traffic than each other. T. Nelson put his suitcase on the floor and flicked open the catches.

"Old Tommy, eh."

"Yes?" T. Nelson said, sorting his photographs, shuffling them into a loose geographical order — Brisbane to Bundaberg to Townsville to Mackay to Cairns and on, to the Cape York Space Base, even though it had yet to be built.

T. Nelson, too, would call his new enterprise the Great Queensland Pleasure Trip. A journey from the State's birthplace, in Brisbane, by steamer or converted ferry, whatever he could find at a reasonable price, and right up the coast to the space base and, as he reasoned, the future of Queensland, and the nation.

He could see it; anchoring off the coast, his white-suited staff arranging the elderly passengers in wheelchairs or on walking frames, on the front deck, tucking shawls across their knees or around their shoulders in preparation for the latest rocket launch.

Imagine their joy, T. Nelson had explained to Lola, on the last great trip of their lives, witnessing a space craft rising from the mangroves of Cape York. Imagine the burners glowing molten red through the lush tropical growth, illuminating the entire Cape as would an enormous flash bulb, catching the gasping faces of the passengers, their bony hands luminescent, gripping chair arms and handles with the thrill of it all.

T. Nelson's use of the old photographs was intentional. He planned to tap into the youth of his potential customers. To spark recognition, memories, and plumb happier times.

There was little doubt that some would die on the Great

Queensland Pleasure Trip. It was inescapable. But what was wrong with that? T. Nelson argued. Better to die having seen a rocket pierce the universe, than for your last image to be the side of a passing delivery van or motor scooter. A small morgue would have to be fitted on the bottom deck.

"If they knew what Tommy was into they wouldn't have let him become Premier, I'll tell you that much."

"What I want to offer you," T. Nelson said, raising his voice and holding out the photographs, "is the absolute chance of a lifetime . . ."

"Pyramids," the old man said, the roar of a New Farm bus failing to interrupt him. "He was nuts about them. Reckoned Egypt was nothing, junk, compared to the other ones. Saw the Egypt ones in the war. Didn't think much of them either."

"The trip is a while off yet," T. Nelson continued, "but it'll start from where John Oxley discovered Brisbane, where the monument is near the William Jolly Bridge, and go up the coast to Cape York. Have you heard about the space base?"

The old man spat into a handkerchief. "What?"

"The *space* base."

"He reckoned there were three pyramids, ten times older than the Egypt ones, hundred maybe, can't remember, spread around the world, and they were all linked up to each other. Believe that? One in Scotland where he was born, I think. One in South America, somewhere down there, and one here. Somewhere around here. Old Tommy, eh?"

The old man laughed and his eyes watered. T. Nelson shuffled the pictures.

"No passengers under seventy years old. Fully trained nurses at the ring of a bell. The works."

"Down south a way I think he said. The pyramids of Mu, or Moo, they were, something like that. That's why he was interested in cattle we reckoned."

T. Nelson started packing away his pictures. He knew of another nursing home over at West End, by the river.

"Another frozen offering for the Moo God, Mr Premier? We used to stick it up him something shocking."

"What?"

"The pyramids."

"What are you talking about?"

The last time I spoke to the Premier of our State he was walking
with four bodyguards to make his final appearance as a witness
at the public inquiry.

He shuffled along the cobblestones outside the Law Courts,
the men forming a horseshoe around him. He passed the bronze
statue of the woman holding sword and scales, and waved to people in the street, as he had done in the old days. Some pedestrians
shouted abuse at him but he still smiled the same way he had
during his decades as our leader.

"Are you happy that it's nearly all over, sir?" I asked, walking behind his guardians.

The Premier didn't bother to look at me, but said, barely au-
dibly, "Probably as much as you are."

The bodyguards laughed at this, as the Premier always had
the ability to make people laugh, even over the most serious of is-
sues. Then he put his hand into his suit trouser pocket and took
out one of his famous sweets, slipping it into his old mouth so
quickly it was almost an illusion.

In the witness box he sat uncomfortably on the edge of the
padded chair with his legs crossed. His left hand, illuminated by
a concealed ceiling light, appeared gloved. The hand in question
fiddled with the microphone cord. Later, as he left the court, I
realised it was not a white glove at all, but fragments of icing
sugar from his sweets pocket.

It was not until later, much later, that I realised how the white
hand had been a part of our lives. I remembered seeing it on the
government's half-hour television program every Sunday night.

I had asked my father: "Why is his hand white?"

You had craned towards the screen to take a closer look at the
hand. Its whiteness was clearer when he pointed to a background
colour slide of a dam under construction, or a new bridge, or hotels.

"Is it the television lights?" my mother asked.

"Not at all," you said, settling back into your chair. "He is a

149

magician and has left one glove on to remind us that even though he's the Premier, the big wig, he's still a magician.''

"Like you, Father?'' I asked. ''With billiard balls? With rabbits and doves and things?''

"No, no, no. A much better magician than that. Bigger tricks.''

"With elephants?''

"Sometimes,'' you said, ''and hippos. But even bigger things than that.''

"Whales?''

"Bigger!'' you shouted, and we all laughed.

My father was right about the Premier, who had a whole range of tricks. He could make entire buildings, mountains and forests disappear.

"You know it was me, don't you, who introduced our good Premier to magic?'' you told me.

I thought this was another of your jokes, but it was true. When the Premier was a very young man, in charge of the State's education, he visited my father's school. It had been prearranged that my father would perform a trick for the pleasure of the young politician. With the entire school lined up in the playground, my father stepped forward on cue, and requested the watch from the great man's arm.

"And what do you plan to do with it, young man?'' he asked, handing it over to my father. ''Will you turn it into gold for me?'' His officials and the principal laughed at this, for the watch was only stainless steel with a yellowing face. The leather band was stained with sweat.

"No, sir,'' the young magician said. ''Do you also have a handkerchief? I will wrap your watch in the handkerchief, throw it into the air and make it vanish.''

"I see. If you can do that then you must be as good as Houdini.''

"Who?''

My father then enveloped the watch in green Country Party silk and tossed it high into the air. The watch carried the handkerchief, like a comet, for some distance before smashing on the roof of the library. The handkerchief floated pathetically earthward.

There was a long silence before the future Premier turned to my father.

"You must practise more," he said, smiling, handing him a sweet. "You will look foolish if you do not practise."

I spoke to the Premier again while covering the official opening of a new government office. He unveiled a plaque and a statue of Queen Elizabeth II, and spoke of the office, erected on the site of an historical building that his men had torn down one night. There had been protests before the demolition, and arrests, but his solution was always the same. If you made the object of protest vanish, then the dissent would stop. In his speech he never mentioned the old building by name, but just referred to it as "that place".

"Why is it that you never named the old building?" I asked him as he walked back to Parliament House.

He stopped this time and turned to me: "If you didn't know what I was referring to then you are foolish." Then he stormed off.

The last time I ever saw him was at the launch of his autobiography, many years later, standing between two palm fronds at a lectern in one of the city's most salubrious hotels.

He was getting along fine, he told us, after the circus that was the inquiry. He had started a new business. He was a commodity broker. He handled everything from jumbo jets to sacks of wheat. Perfume to rabbit skins. He took orders from around the world. His crowd of supporters stood and cheered, begged to buy shares in his company, although it was not listed on the Stock Exchange, and offered up a prayer for his good health. He had become a salesman of everything, and his market was the world.

Going down in the lift with him and his assistants, I realised, Father, that it would have taken no effort, the quiet entry of a knife between his old ribs, to destroy him once and for all. To throw myself into history.

He walked out and an elderly woman turned to me and said: "He's the saviour. The saviour."

Watching him disappear into the back of a limousine, I

wondered if he would remember that day you tossed his watch into the sky.

It took a long time for me to see it, let me tell you. I had to go away. A long way away. It was as if I had been suspended high up and, looking downward, could see the pattern that had been there all along, but indecipherable at ground level. Like a map maker, studying aerial photographs of streets, suburbs, parkland. Or even higher — the satellite pictures that define the folds of the earth.

Even at the time the government was collapsing, when it must have known its survival was beyond hope, it had continued to promote the space base. We were to believe that this would, above all else, mark us as something special. As people to be reckoned with.

It was their last chance. If they had begun construction, felled the forests and razed the mangroves, sunk wooden marker pegs into the soil and unleashed the yellow graders from their enclosures, they might have been saved.

It was not revealed until months after their demise, in a small paragraph in the *Moreton Bay Courier* that attracted little attention, that only a matter of weeks before the end of it all, amidst the rubble that surrounded them, it was rumoured they had falsified the environmental impact report into the space base.

I remember seeing a Minister, his rubber boots sunken in the mudflats due to his considerable weight, stretching his arms wide, inspecting the pad from which craft would be propelled into space. He had the impact study in his right hand, and used it to brush away the giant northern mosquitoes that had taken a fancy to him. The Minister would later be carried across the mud by two black men to the government helicopter. The photograph of the moment, on the front page of the *Courier* and other newspapers throughout the State, showed the carriers smiling as they locked hands beneath his buttocks.

I have checked the original negatives. The strain on the faces of the black men had been removed and their teeth had been whitened and enlarged to simulate a smile. Even at this late stage, perhaps out of habit, the men had been assaulted with an airbrush to prevent them from appearing strained under the enormous weight of the Minister. To minimise offence to the public official.

The government not only talked about rockets, satellites and shuttles but, because of the nature of our country, its relative silence and its skies less bothered by tangled airwaves, the Cape would also be used as a centre for listening into deep space for signs of alien life.

"We will be at the very centre," the Premier said on the party's television program, "of the hunt for extraterrestrial life in the cosmos.

"Put simply, my fellow Queenslanders, if there is life out there, we will be the first people in the history of mankind to find out."

T. Nelson Downs' flagship for the Great Queensland Pleasure Trip ended up as a hamburger diner just off the Pacific Highway, between Brisbane and the coast, its hollowed-out hull littered with burnt onion rings and lettuce spines.

He travelled to Sydney and stayed in the same hotel at King's Cross as when he had been in search of the miniature horse. He did not contact his sister or the spectacles salesman.

He even went to the Blue Pacific Lounge, which had changed its name to the Bombay Striparama, but only stood at the door for nostalgic reasons. A young woman in a schoolgirl uniform spread her legs in welcome, and he left.

Through his numerous contacts, T. Nelson had heard of an old ferry near Glebe Island, out of service and rotting on the water. He went over its decks, checked its seating, still in place but buckled from the weight of millions of commuters, its windows encrusted with harbour salt. He found some old ferry tickets in the life raft compartment, and put them in his pocket.

By ferry standards it was small; it had only covered the Darling Street to Circular Quay route. But it was fat-bodied, sat like a pelican, and could, he thought, be easily converted into a pleasure craft.

She was taken north on the deck of a container ship, within sight of Newcastle, Port Macquarie, even the canefields south of Brisbane, and into Moreton Bay. He berthed her near the abattoirs, and came home late every evening, his overalls putrid with the scent of boiled sheep bone.

No matter how much work he put into it, he could not transform it into a holiday boat. It remained a ferry, despite the bare-breasted mermaid he had had fitted to the bow. He attached lanterns to the upper deck, a ship's wheel and a belt of coloured party globes around its polished wooden railings. At night he switched the lights on and sat with the boatmen, discussing changes, modifications, additions to the monstrosity that looked worse the more he worked on it.

Then he ran out of money. He returned to the yard a month later and discovered that the craft had been stripped. T. Nelson did not cry but came close to it, imagining the thieves like ants on a carcass, tearing off timber strips, or joking in the wheelhouse that looked out over the mangroves of the reach.

He sold it to a scrapper for five hundred dollars.

Much later, when he drove back and forth to his inquisition he noticed the old ferry one day on the side of the highway, as if it had been dropped from the sky.

He went in only once for a meal.

"What'll it be?" the girl behind the counter asked him.

"I'm sorry?" he said. He thought he felt the boat move.

"What do you want?"

"Just a hamburger thanks."

He noticed the chef in a stained singlet up in the wheelhouse, and could hear meat sizzling on a hot plate.

"Bob, hamburger with the lot."

I never told you father, but the man who lived in the brothel before me was a musician and acoustics expert. We met briefly when he came to collect his mail shortly after I moved in. He said he was hoping to work at Cape York, when it was completed, to join the search for aliens. He told me that if we ever did pick up a signal from another civilisation, it would take the radio waves nine years to return a message.

"What would you ask an alien anyway?" I inquired.

"I would ask if energy fusion research should be continued," was his reply. "It would save governments tens of billions of dollars."

I asked the same question to the English physics teacher on the bus as we left NASA.

"I don't know," he said, rubbing his chin. "Television frequencies have been leaving the earth since the 1930s. They should have picked up plenty of those by now if they're out there." He laughed at this.

"Maybe Jackie Gleason scared them away for good, hey?"

Can you picture that, Father? Can you imagine the only sound from Earth, searing through the universe and picked up by extraterrestrials, being fat old Jackie screaming "Alicccccce!"

9

When the World Exposition left our town people continued to line up outside the site's locked main gates, laden with hampers of food and drink, blankets, decks of cards and straw hats. By late afternoon they disappeared and returned at the same time the next day. They refused to believe, despite the frenzied grading and dismantling, the folding and loading, that it was all over.

This continued for some time, right up to the eventual lowering of the giant canvas sails that shaded the site. A priest formed a post-Exposition stress group to convince some of the people of my town that there were other things in their lives, and that they had to go on.

My town embraced the World Exposition and hoped it would go on forever, blind to the impermanence of the event's prefabricated buildings and attractions that, like a child's play set, could be dismantled with tools in a matter of days.

In the beginning there were daily reports on the progress of the site. The entire population focused on the transformation of the drab dockland into a mini-city. From hundreds of vantage points around Brisbane you could catch a glimpse of the site, on your way to work, during lunch, from office windows, verandahs, church steps, buses and over backyard fences. It was like watching the construction of a beautiful ship, its rigging rising above red tin roofs and purple jacaranda. The whole world was coming to us; collecting on those few precious hectares of earth.

So we brushed up our town. The airport was completely rebuilt, its spidery catwalks and endless conveyor belts big enough for a city ten times the size. New restaurants, cafes, bars and nightclubs appeared. Motels were refurbished. Residents were encouraged to neaten their homes, or at least their front yards, by planting trees, adding a single coat of paint to old timber and keeping their lawns well trimmed. We had to look good for the world.

As for the Exposition, we were tantalised with the promise of foods from exotic nations, dancing and acrobatics, and technology that would be commonplace in the next century. We were to receive a glimpse into the future, and it would be worth our while to buy season tickets, as the future could not be grasped in a single visit.

A rush on hairdressing salons and cornerstore barbers preceded the official opening, the truckloads of hair dumped outside the city, as it was likely the local greengrocer, police sergeant or paperboy, a neighbour, relative or even ourselves, could be spotted by a foreign news crew while strolling beneath the Exposition's magical sails, and beamed via satellite into television sets in Britain or the United States.

My father was the official supplier of plants to the site. Although he had just leased the Universe-Cine-by-the-Sea from the Burleigh Council, having miraculously pipped several developers who wished to see the old movie house demolished, he accepted the Exposition contract as a matter of pride and honour. In the early stages he could be seen striding around the site in a hard hat, applauding wildly when the sails were hoisted and, he admitted to me, privately shedding a tear beneath the monstrous tent pole-like struts. It would be the nearest he would come, he said, to the realisation of his dream of the biggest hothouse in the southern hemisphere. Sometimes in life, he added, it was enough to stand at the edge of your dreams, rather than never see them at all.

Initially, the requirements of the job as plant supplier overwhelmed him.

He strode around the cinema under renovation, talking to himself, shouting the species names of orchids, ferns, palms, and roses into the dank air, repeating them over and over to get the pronunciations exact. He went through a dozen cigar cannisters, discarded on the floorboards like spent shotgun cartridges. He was quick to anger, and spat out orders at the electricians installing his imitation constellation in the cinema's roof, impulsively ordering meteors and shooting stars that they all knew would be impossible to create with fixed bulbs.

It would be required, the Minister for Conservation told him during an extensive briefing, that he create the atmosphere of dozens of different countries within the context of the Exposition. These included a Polynesian village, a Japanese garden, the well-tended yard of an atypical Italian villa, a slice of California and on and on.

Secondly, the Queensland display was to be a priority. It had to suggest the lushness of the State, its unbounded subtropical nature, as well as its rural expanses. Simultaneously it had to contain a subtext, as the Minister phrased it, that revealed a government dogged and vigilant on the preservation of the environment for future generations. An example to our world visitors.

While the display was not to be flippant, it had to ooze a "leisurely, intelligent beauty".

T. Nelson Downs initially resorted to his card system from his antiquities period, and his theory of plants in relation to human emotion. He then telephoned experts all over the world, from his mobile tin office on the site, scratching research notes from broken conversations with gardeners in Fiji, rosebush experts in Tombstone, Arizona, lodge managers in Banff and even Srinagar houseboat captains.

His research was so extensive he began to doodle leaves, trunks and waterlilies without realising it.

Using his network of contacts, he approached local carpenters, bobcat operators, imitation logmakers, fountain builders, bark chip manufacturers and drainage professionals.

He calculated that he would have to employ every nursery within a 250-kilometre radius of Brisbane merely to maintain a daily supply of fresh flowers. He would bring in the hardier plants from an outer circle of nurseries in refrigerated trucks. The vehicles had to be sanitised thoroughly to prevent the fusion of the natural perfumes with that of slaughtered animals.

Some of the plants were seeded eighteen months ahead, nurtured under hothouse lights and inspected by the usher at regular intervals. He knew where to locate exotic varieties, orchids, roses

158

and ferns unseen in our country, but perhaps familiar to the planeloads of guests that would be arriving for the Exposition.

The hybrids excited him, as they had always done. He ordered orchids the colours of Queensland and Australia, or combinations so strange, so dizzying, that they appeared to be from another planet.

"My aim," he later told his inquisitors, "was to give the people something they would never forget. I wanted it to be a magnificent living museum."

On this tour of ours, Pop, where we barely touched the real world, only the asphalt of Texan car parks, the overhead rails of trolley cars, pool cue ends, paper-wrapped hotel glasses and the hands of welcoming committees, I began to tire of the razors of the famous.

I saw dozens, bone-handled, in glass cabinets across America. There were several more at the Alamo, shrine to American spirit and courage. All were opened at the same angle. I asked Jack if there were officials who checked all the razors of the famous in museums and shrines across the world to ensure the continuity of the angles. His Marlboro lifted in the corner of his mouth before a gold-buttoned guard requested him to smoke outside. He crushed the butt beneath his boot.

Davy Crockett had his own cabinet. It contained the fragment of a vest or coat, bricks from his house, and his razor.

My theory was the razors were deliberately left in battle, in prominent positions after death, to ensure their discovery. This most intimate item of man, central to that ordinary daily ritual of removing facial hair which in itself stretched backward and forward in time, helped us relate to the myth. You, father, would have been more interested in the scum of stubble, the actual whiskers, scraped from the rim of a basin. That's what you would have gone after.

In one section of the Alamo, where we were encouraged to whisper, they had battles displayed under glass. Miniature landscapes and men with rifles and knives. The guns that had just been fired had a plastic sliver of smoke rising from the muzzle.

159

The river which wound its way through these scenes of death was clear and solid. The odd air bubble was trapped beneath the surface.

It was not unlike the War Museum in Canberra, where we once went on holidays, with its dim displays portraying the majestic history of our countrymen in battle, reduced to glue and lead soldiers with identical faces.

Jack joined me at the cabinets.

"The ones fallen over, they're supposed to be dead, are they?" he said with tobacco on his breath.

"That's the idea."

"No jungle. Got jungle you got problems."

We walked on to the barracks museum and inspected more artefacts, including a carpenter's plane once used to shape coffins. There was a bean on a red velvet cloth.

"The Spanish dictator ordered that the captured American people pick a bean," a guide in the room told us. "If it was white, they were allowed to live. If it was black they were executed.

"You will see here a letter written by a young man to his mother. He explains that he is to be executed by firing squad. Next to the letter you will see the bean that sent this man to his death."

When the group had moved on I went to the cabinet and studied the photograph of the young man, full-bearded and in uniform. Below his picture was a bean, crazed like old porcelain.

Over a century of being sent through the post, handled by the grieving, by ancestors of the grieving, returned to the curator of the Alamo museum and placed carefully inside the cabinet, the wizened kidney shape, the death sentence bean, had turned creamy white.

Later, at the bar of our hotel, Jack said: "I was thirty-four months as a machine-gunner in a helicopter. A kill squad. We popped 'em. That was our job, all right, and we popped 'em."

He held a Michelob just off the surface of the table.

"Our unit was pinned in and we radioed for help. The VC fired rockets and mortars down on us. A bullet got me in the

160

back, just missed my spine. And a bullet here, through the wrist, and here, on my cheek. Had to learn to walk again.''

On the television suspended from the ceiling at the end of the bar, Jack Nicholson was striking a door with an axe, a full over-the-shoulder swing that was splintering pine. His wife was screaming behind the door, backing into the corner, holding up a giant carving knife.

''I could've swore that old lady had a gun,'' Jack said, turning his empty bottle. ''She was raking in the rice field and I took her head clean off. Blew her fucking head into a million pieces.''

Nicholson was chasing his small son through a maze of hedges. They ran through deep snow and blue light, and the crazed father was dragging an axe. ''Dannnnnnneeeeeee!''

''Jesus,'' Jack said, watching from below his peak cap. ''Does the kid get away? Will the kid be all right? Tell me what happens, quick. I hate scary movies. I get nightmares from this sort of thing. What the fuck happens to the kid?''

When we left the bar Nicholson was frozen to death, his mouth slightly open. An ice statue of pure madness.

After an evening session, T. Nelson Downs invited his old friend Bart Wilson for a drink inside the closed movie house to celebrate the councillor's recent elevation to mayor of Burleigh Heads.

T. Nelson loosened the buttons of his tight-fitting usher's jacket, unclipped his torch, and produced two capsuled Havanas and Chivas Regal in thick tumblers.

''Cheers and congratulations,'' the usher said as they clinked glasses. The mayor nodded and strolled up and down the side walkways of the cinema, inspecting T. Nelson's artefact cabinets. The usher had just started work on an insect display, the arthropods poached from the Burleigh headland's small rainforest, gassed in jars and pinned, their wings and legs opened out and untwisted soon after death.

''Impressive, Nelson,'' the mayor said, the sulphur of a match and the cigar smoke rising to the galaxy of the roof. ''But honestly, tell me honestly, Nelson, we've known each other a long time now, a long time. Are people interested in all of this stuff? Do they pause to look at this incredible collection of yours?''

The mayor checked his hair in the glass surface of a cabinet, his pocked and jowled face dissected by the bootlaces of Ludwig Leichhardt, one ear an open fob watch.

''Are they really bothered?'' the mayor reiterated. T. Nelson instinctively grasped for his usher's torch, but grabbed at air.

''I would like to think so,'' he replied, looking at the tiny emerald in the mayor's Cartier watch as he put the cigar to his mouth.

''You know what I think, Nelson?'' Puff. ''I would say they are wasted here. You have your magnificent roof, splendid, it is the talk of the chamber, has been for a long time, which is, I'll say it outright, ruined, in my opinion, by these cabinets of things.''

''They are items of great significance,'' T. Nelson said. ''From my days on the road. I couldn't part with them.''

''Settle down, Nelson. I wasn't asking that at all. It's just that they should be displayed properly if, as you say, they have such historical significance. A museum, perhaps.''

''They are an important part of what I'm trying to do here, Bart, with respect,'' the usher said, his eyes down.

''Which is?'' The mayor raised his eyebrow, and the usher tried to remember where he had seen it done before.

''I have the past here in my cabinets.''

''Yes.''

''And the present, the world, on the screen.''

''I see. And your roof, let me guess, is the future.''

''Well, yes.''

The mayor laughed and his belly shook. He took a long, long draw on the cigar.

''Nelson, Nelson, really. From one of our pioneer businessmen on the coast and, let's face it, you were a pioneer, no modesty, I am incredulous. Incredulous, is that the word? How long have we known each other?'' The mayor swirled his scotch. ''Say, for argument's sake, you were to leave the cinema, and at your age, let's face it, we're not getting any younger. You have

162

all these stairs, up and down. You work late hours. You can't do that forever."

"I know that."

"So what will become of these cabinets of yours? What I'm saying to you, Nelson, if you were ever to relinquish the lease of this place, we could set you up, somehow. A little museum. Done properly. You could charge admission."

The mayor looked into his glass and noticed, for the first time, that the ice cubes were coarsely shaped like human limbs. He had the remains of a leg and an arm spinning around in the bottom of the glass.

"I'm finished with business, Bart. I lose money here but I don't care. I enjoy it here. Lola and I are happy."

"Pardon? Sorry?"

"I've always wanted to do this."

"Think about it, Nelson. Think about it, please."

The mayor did not finish his scotch and placed the tumbler on a cabinet of toiletries, camel hair and Indian cigarette butts labelled "Burke and Wills Expedition, 1860".

"Another drink?"

"No, no thank you, Nelson," the mayor said, stubbing out his cigar in the base of a fern pot between the cabinets. "Give my regards to Lole, won't you?"

T. Nelson followed him through the thick velvet curtains and the foyer to the front stairs of the cinema.

"It's *Tickle Me* next week!" he shouted to Mayor Wilson who was crossing the street. "Elvis is a rodeo star. Finds a hidden treasure. Classic."

The usher sucked an ice foot before crunching it between his back teeth.

I wondered about the bruised wood around the handle of my bathroom door. Locking it, I had a strange feeling about the white-tiled room. On further investigation I found a spray of what appeared to be blood under the sink. What had happened here? Was it really blood?

I ran a bath and sank into it up to my neck, exhausted from

the day's walk around Graceland, the incessant Elvis Presley music emitted from tin speakers, the roundabouts named in his honour that whirled all over Memphis like the black holes in guitars. I wanted to float above it all to see if my suspicion was correct: the topography of the town shaped by interlocking images of The King — guitars, boots, coats of jewels unwittingly formed by the yards, driveways, street patterns and buildings of the locals.

"Do you ever go a single day without thinking of Elvis?" I asked the girl in the souvenir store opposite Graceland.

"Of course not," she whined.

At his famous statue I asked Peter the video man if he had noticed, through his eyepiece, that there was not a single splash of pigeon shit on Elvis.

"They wouldn't dare," his wife said. "I feel all frisky when I see him, I really do."

"Do you think he's electrified?" Peter asked, lowering the camera. "To keep the birds off?"

"Maybe," I said.

"They did that to Winston Churchill, you know."

"Is that right?"

"That statue near Big Ben. There's still shit all over it."

I noticed that not a single fringe on Elvis' bronze coat was missing. I walked up to the statue and touched the legend's left flare. There was no shock.

"Nothing," I said to them. "Not a thing." Peter filmed me.

"Time to go, folks," Gunter said, clapping his hands. "Back on the bus, please."

As we passed the Pomeroy Hotel, Gunter told us the story of the ducks.

For years, maybe decades, or at least as long as anyone could remember, a small number of ducks walked into the foyer of the Pomeroy at the same time every afternoon. They followed the same path behind the lobby desk, through the manager's office, a storage room, then out a door and across the staff car park to the river. The manager of the hotel swore that it was the same family of ducks. Locals had confirmed that before the Pomeroy was constructed, several ducks were regularly sighted walking across the land to the river.

"To these ducks," Gunter said, "it is as though the hotel does not exist."

I closed my eyes as we headed for Cherokee, weary from two weeks on the road, and immediately saw the coloured tents and annexes of the Oceanic, even the texture of the canvas, and the dark, creaking head of Burleigh bluff, always alive with bird chatter and wind tunes through the foliage.

It flickered before me, in this strange cinema of mine: the time my mother sliced open her thumb on the broken gas light, the hair suddenly beneath my arms, watching the rows of men shaving before speckled mirrors in the shower block, the pines flinging off their cones with the approach of the cyclones.

Father, do you remember going to the Universe, before you became its head usher, seeing that movie about an American Indian and his romance with a young white woman? Remember? Surely.

I can see a struggle, the images blurred now, between the woman and a ferocious wild bear. Teeth, coarse fur, a white blouse torn, and for a second, a millisecond, the nipple of the woman exposed, pink, before the Indian plunges a knife into the bear's throat.

You grabbed me by the arm and stormed out with Mother following. You demanded to see the manager, and abused him for not displaying a suitable warning, that the film was not suitable for children. That at some stage, on that everchanging canvas, a nipple would fly through the projector light and present itself, larger than a man's head. What did you think? That the pink disc would destroy my innocence? That it would derail my carefully plotted passage to adulthood?

You thought I'd forgotten that, hadn't you? I have a surprise for you. Whenever I visited you at the Universe, did you notice I always went up to that stuffed bear you had, its stance intentionally violent, frozen by the taxidermist a moment before attack? That big black Rocky Mountains bear next to Julius Caesar.

I studied its teeth, yellowing and set in black tar, and always thought of that nipple, pink and glorious and enormous. And it made me ache for you.

The World Exposition, our government told us, was a great success. We were given extraordinary profit margins and attendance figures. One elderly man appeared in the newspaper, tending his small backyard vegetable patch, wearing a tatty cane sun hat. He had been to the Exposition nearly every day, almost two hundred times. His life was empty now, he was quoted as saying. He had nothing to do but till his concrete-edged square of soil. The Exposition had become his friend, and now he had lost it. There was a follow-up story, of gifts sent to the man by concerned readers — an exercise bicycle, colour television set, board games, new garden tools and oil painting kits. But in the second picture of the old man, surrounded by his presents, he still struggled to smile.

The government, perhaps concerned for the old man and others like him across our town, left the giant sails standing for some time after the Exposition was over. The white stretches of canvas became filthy and streaked with black marks, the sail cleaners with their scrubbing brushes on poles long since retired.

But it did not matter to my people. It was the shape that was important, the disjointed sheets curving identically into the tips of the poles. They had became a part of the skyline, and it was impossible to imagine what had been on the bank of the river before they were hoisted to the sounds of the West End school band.

"They should keep them there," a woman said on television. "It's a lovely memory. A monument, you know? They could make a big park underneath where families could go for picnics on the weekend."

A man in a singlet added: "It's a great idea. You could have circuses under there. Or big open air movies in summer, like in the old days."

A year later, in the quiet of a Sunday morning, the rigging did come down. In the stunned calm and then the anger on the realisation that the Exposition had finally abandoned us, the debate over what to do with the land continued. It would be impossible, the public argued, to return the site to its previous ramshackle array of boatyards, dry docks, hotels of ill-repute and factory sheds. This land had become, in a way, the city's future. This corridor of red earth would test our vision.

Architects and developers put forward a bewildering selection of options, from ice skating rinks and casinos, linked by underwater tunnel to the city centre, to sporting fields, prestige car yards complete with children's playground and restaurant, and even an amusement park comprised of giant perspex fruits and animals, so popular not only in my State, but the whole nation.

As to be expected, the amusement park attracted considerable interest; the enormous fibreglass cattle, koalas, frill-necked lizards, emus and whales along with mangoes, avocadoes, pineapples and bananas, they said, would be framed by the ridge of Mount Coot-tha. The proposal could, if executed with taste, engender the same excitement, the same mardi gras carefree ambience, as that generated by the Exposition.

The idea was taken so seriously that a scale model was made and displayed in the City Hall for the public's perusal. The animals and fruits clearly showed stairways, not unlike those wheeled to the doorways of aircraft, leading into the bellies of steers and piebald dairy cows, and a viewing platform behind the fanned frill of a lizard. The avocado had a spiral staircase up to its stalk, while the banana resembled a giant slippery slide, with model children shrieking down its skin.

The model of animals and fruits eventually disappeared from City Hall and no replacement was offered. Occasionally, two council workers slashed weeds on the Exposition site with motorised grass cutters, sweeping slowly as if searching for mines. After a while they failed to return.

10

You see what is happening don't you?

From the start it was working towards this. Everything was aligning — the moon, the tides, the breezes, the degree of wear on the soles of his usher's shoes. Hurtling towards their bullseye.

I think he started to get an inkling, and began worrying not for himself, as if the explosion was inevitable, but for me. You know how I felt? I began to think you thought I was you, at an earlier stage along the great line, and that your mistakes could be eclipsed if my life progressed perfectly.

You summoned Andrea. Don't think I didn't know. I can see both of you, watching *The Little Mermaid*, usher and future daughter-in-law, before the serious talk.

And then there was the pyramid business. The first time you went out on your own. Hit or miss. The big one. No one to blame but yourself. A fool only to the trees and the mallee fowl if you were wrong. But it didn't quite turn out that way.

It took T. Nelson Downs eleven days to haul his small drilling rig, piece by piece, to the top of Burleigh Heads bluff. The greatest obstacle was the density of the vegetation near the summit, the vines as thick as a man's arm over the egg-shaped boulders, the entire canopy covered in a thinner veil of shoots and webs. He avoided cutting a path through, unwilling to damage the delicate ecosystem of the coast's last pouch of seafront rainforest, and ducked and weaved his way to the top as best he could.

The portable rig was no problem. At night, after the last session at the Universe, he carried the light aluminium struts back and forth. Each strut took him twenty-one minutes to take to the summit, and it took seventeen minutes for him to return to the Universe. On the walk down he could see the chandelier light of the foyer. He took four struts up each night, for seven nights, and stacked them side by side in a clearing not far from the dirt walking track that ribboned the bluff.

The two-metre drilling shafts, of which he had ten, were also manageable. It was the diesel-run motor that caused the most trouble. He had purchased it from the manager of the Oceanic Baths Caravan Park for a negligible sum. It had been a reserve generator for the park's shower block, in the event of power failure. For some unexplained reason, the council had recently ordered that the whole park be rewired. New cables were laid. There was enough power now for a luxury resort.

T. Nelson received no extra kilowatts, but they had tunnelled under the Universe and laid their coils and wires in the soil. It was necessary, they said, to reach the power junction near the main road. It had caused some inconvenience. Their late-night shovelling was heard beneath the first ten rows during some sessions.

T. Nelson had had to lie to the manager, whom he had known as a boy. He was the son of the last manager, and they had swum together in the baths. It had hurt T. Nelson to lie to his old friend.

"Spare one for the cinema, is she?"

"Yes. The old one's about had it. That last storm we had? She nearly died on me, let me tell you. Movie was almost in slow motion."

"That's right," Roy said, scratching his chin. "*Giant*, wasn't it?"

"You've got a good memory," T. Nelson lied.

"Take a lot of 'lectricity to keep that beauty up on the screen."

"You're right there, Roy."

"And them lights on the roof. Lot of power needed there."

"Exactly."

"Hell of a lot. Bit of surging and you could blow hundreds."

"A constant worry."

T. Nelson imagined his galaxy waning, the stars increasing in intensity until they were white hot, fusing together in the brilliance, exploding and sending fine glass shards down onto the audience. Screaming, cut scalps and hair-thin slices on exposed arms.

"Should see you right for a while, this old girl," said Roy, his cowlick still as strong as ever, the hair straight up above his left eyebrow.

T. Nelson could not look his old friend in the eyes. With the help of two caravan park permanents, they lifted the motor onto the back of T. Nelson's F100, and shared a beer on the grass beside the manager's office.

"How's your boy anyway, Nelson?"

"Sam? Good, Roy, good. Down in the big smoke now."

"Good on him. They have all the opportunities now, the young people, don't they?"

"Sure do."

"Not like in our day, eh?"

"And how's Josie?" T. Nelson asked, blowing the froth off his beer.

"You haven't heard?"

"What?"

"Took off to Greece. Couple of weeks back."

"Holiday?"

"Wants to marry some bloke over there. Haven't even met him."

"No."

"No bull. Her mother spoke to her on the phone. Said she doesn't want to know us. Nothin'. Never coming back. Spoke in some wog language, mother couldn't understand half what she was saying. Like she was on drugs or something, you know, Fran said."

"I'm sorry."

"Broken her mother's heart it has. But what can you do, eh? It's like she's dead, Fran reckons. As good as dead."

On the other side of the bluff, near the Tallebudgera Bridge, was an abandoned nursery. It had been built into a cutting off the highway, like a takeaway burger outlet, which T. Nelson suspected was the reason for its demise. It was too close to the road

170

and, as T. Nelson expected when he visited the nursery in its final days, the plants were grimy and choking on exhaust filth and dust. He rescued as many as he could afford. Its green wire fences were now sagging, and even the palms at its entrance were ragged and wind-torn.

T. Nelson was shocked at how rapidly the neglected plants of the nursery, the forgotten seeds, had taken root and enveloped the small imitation log cabin office. The adjoining pergola was also collapsing under the weight of vine. The plants, long since abandoned by the gloved hands of attendants, had developed tough leaves. T. Nelson theorised they may have ingested the lawless growth of the bluff's vegetation, and that the whole place was being reclaimed by the small mountain with its own climates and animal colonies.

The usher had once supplied ferns to the bankrupt nursery, and had seriously considered purchasing it. These were the days when his giant hothouse may still have become a reality, despite his self-perceived failure over the official government culling operation. He had seen no evidence of the greening of Brisbane and the coast, despite the truckloads of vitally healthy ferns and flowers that he had waved off so often outside the nursery in the Hinterland. No evidence at all.

In the early hours one Sunday morning, T. Nelson cut the wire fencing at one side of the abandoned nursery's bolted gate, peeled it back and drove his utility up the dirt track that led a short distance into the rainforest. He lowered his motor off the back of the truck with a refrigerator carrier, then, stopping every ten metres or so, hauled it up a bushwalker's path and into the scrub where he had hidden his scaffolding. It took him more than an hour to reach the fallen pine, since turned to stone, where he had concealed the rigging. He wrapped the motor first in plastic, then the thick but delicate leaves of a plumed sword fern, a cluster of which he had discovered between two nearby boulders.

Exhausted, he perched himself on a tightly bunched crop of basalt that extended out from the upper canopy towards the sea, and smoked a cigar. As he did when he was a child, he looked to the horizon and imagined, if he sailed out directly, that he would strike South America. Back then he found he could not relate to the flat double-page maps in his school atlas, the earth's surface peeled and laid out in dirty browns, yellows and blues. He had preferred to study his blow-up globe, which was the envy of his classmates, its clear plastic air nozzle at the North Pole.

His world, as big as a soccer ball, had brightly painted continents and if he put his eye right up to it, perhaps off the coast of Brisbane or into the Great Australian Bight, he could see through the globe, filled with his warm breath scented, more often than not, with apple, cheese and bread, to the backs of other continents. It did, however, develop a slow leak. Countries sagged beneath his fingers. His father suggested he dip it into water, which he did one night in the bath, filled to its curved white lip.

He squeezed the immersed globe and a stream of fine bubbles poured out below New Delhi, in orange India. He patched it, as he did his bicycle tubes, but it continued to deflate. He last saw his world being booted around the backyard by his brothers before it disappeared for good.

Finishing his cigar, T. Nelson stubbed it on the rock, already scorched with what appeared to be large burns ingrained in its surface.

South America for sure, he thought, stretching his legs. A village, protected by the most impenetrable of jungle, a tangled wall of growth as old as man, older, right up to the water's edge. And at the back of the village, in streamers of sunlight, the pyramid, secured to the earth by thousands of vine arms.

They would pray before it each day, these villagers, ignoring the play of monkeys, and touch its base stones, worn clean of lichen and smooth from the oil of the fingertips. And in their meditation they would not see the shape of it, its edges and summit, but other things — landscapes of red dirt, dolphins, birds and small animals they had never set eyes on, fires, pastures of shale, snow, tiny quivering flowers, shell and blood.

Later, a bushwalking couple turned their heads to catch a second glimpse of the short, balding man in his suit with gold buttons, trailing a refrigerator trolley along the dirt path.

* *

172

We approached what Gunter described as an authentic American Indian reservation, deep in the woods of South Carolina. Laugh at this if you will, Father, but for a moment I expected the faces of the men and women of Cherokee to look like the couple painted on the side of my boyhood cowboy tent. You wouldn't remember the chief and his squaw, he of the stone face and bright feathers, and she with pigtails and features painted with a lighter hand, by someone over in the sweatshops of Thailand.

It was not as I imagined. The reservation was situated beside a shallow river between two ridges, the pines so dense and tall that they appeared to push in on the settlement. It was cool and dark. Very dark.

Our bus pulled up at the Cherokee township, a small cluster of shops and tourist amusements.

"Get your guns ready, pardners," Gunter said into the microphone. "This here is Injun territory."

We spilled into the car park of the town that, like so many others in this country, appeared to have been built especially for us.

"One hour, everyone, then we'll go to the hotel."

Jack locked the Americruiser and grabbed me by the arm. "Wanna show you something."

Outside the craft store was a long row of painted wooden boxes with glass windows secured by padlocks. Other tourists were laughing, striking the tops of the boxes with their fists and poking faces.

"What the hell is this?" I asked.

In each box there was a live animal — rabbit, hen, rooster, duck. Their names were painted on the inside backs of the cabinets — The Kissing Bunny, The Dancing Chicken, The Drummer Duck, The Try-Your-Luck Bunny, The Piano-Playing Duck, The Basketball Rooster. At the end of the row was another — the Gambling Galar, as they had spelt it. The soft pink and grey bird of my homeland. It was a shock to find it there, backed into the corner of its box. A stolen treasure, so ragged, its tiny heart pumping.

I walked past the row of cabinets when the others had gone. The animals were skittish in the miniature rooms crafted to match their tricks. The decor included a small black baby grand

173

piano with fake keys, a lined basketball court with a single hoop, a balsawood guitar leaning against a chair, a drumkit with tin cymbals, a jukebox and a lamp with a yellow shade.

"Watch this," Jack said, putting a quarter into the Drummer Duck cabinet. Scratchy music began to play and the white and brown bird went immediately to the kit and pecked at the cymbals. When the music ended the duck scampered to a metal dish at the back of the cabinet and waited for a small portion of seed and bread to slide into it through a chute.

"Christ."

"Good, hey?"

A few of the hens were pecking furiously at the glass as I walked past their cabinets, demanding the drop of the quarter. The Kissing Bunny was trying to tear open its food hatch.

Jack pumped the coin return buttons, hoping to fool the animals into performing their grotesque tricks. He laughed uncontrollably, shaking the boxes with both hands, going from one to the other. I felt sick and went again to the Gambling Galar, in the same position behind a plastic roulette wheel. Some seed husks had fallen into it.

"Try your luck," Jack said from behind me. "Go on, give it a go."

The bird moved its head gently from side to side, its eyes like black beads.

"Pop a quarter in, boy. Make that bird give that 'ole wheel a big spin."

He went for the coin return button and I grabbed his wrist.

"Leave it, Jack."

"Come on."

"Fucking leave it."

"Hey, it's just a bit of fun. Shit."

I sat by the river, beside a broken down merry-go-round of rotting wooden horses, and waited for Gunter's clapping.

It was a short drive to the hotel. Every few hundred metres, off the roadside beside abandoned gas stations, a cluster of egg-shaped river rocks and general stores were black bears in cages.

174

Peter managed to film all of them. Most of the bears had a name — Blackie, Grizzly, Daisy — written on a placard outside the cage, and a price if you wished to have your photograph taken in front of them, but there were others simply held in their iron cubes amongst weeds.

From the driveway of the hotel I spotted one bear walking back and forth in its blue flaking cage, no bigger than a hatbox in the distance. It swiped at a cone of insects, illuminated by the afternoon sun.

"Beautiful place here, don't you think?" Gunter said, his hands on his hips. "Love it here. Just about one of the most peaceful places on earth."

"Why do they have the bears everywhere?" I asked. "Look at that one. Middle of nowhere. It's ridiculous."

"They're for us, for you."

"Tame as pussy cats," Jack said, unloading the luggage. "They just want to make the place a bit authentic, you know? Make it a bit wild."

"That's ridiculous."

"That one down there?" Jack said, pointing. "Been here a dozen times and all it ever does is go back and forth, all day, all night. Never seen it sitting still. Not once."

"Like a metronome," Gunter said, walking inside.

"Yeah. Nonstop. Hey," Jack said, grabbing my elbow, "you want some booze tonight?"

"I thought it was illegal on the reservations."

"Sure, but I got connections, see. These good old boys'll get me anything I want. Waddya say?"

After dinner, and a display of American Indian dancing, I strolled out to the front of the hotel and looked for the bear again. I could hear the river, and vaguely make out the cube, but the bear had vanished, diffused in the darkness.

I wanted to think he had escaped, and set free the other bears of Cherokee, as well as the Piano-Playing Duck, the Kissing Bunny, the Gambling Galar. That they were loping or winging to freedom, together, through the woods of this valley of cages. It was I, and the anticipation of my arrival in our silver-ribbed coach, my greenbacks exchanged over a counter in Sydney, Australia, that held them in captivity.

It was strangely beautiful here, though, as Gunter had said, when the cages vanished with the nightfall, on the edge of this great darkness.

In order to remain as inconspicuous as possible, T. Nelson Downs only worked with his usher's torch at the summit of the bluff. He could have used a gas camping lantern but suspected it may have lit up the canopy as it would a green canvas tent, and been visible from the Nautilus and Dolphin high-rise apartments nearby. He could see the shell-shaped aqua lamps and television sets in their upper floors and penthouses through the foliage.

He constructed the drilling frame as easily as he had the meccano bridges, stadiums and ocean liners he had built with his son, years ago, on their front verandah. As he tightened bolts he thought back to them lying on their stomachs, head to head, dismantling and rebuilding over and over, until one or the other fell asleep.

T. Nelson pulled up the silver rig with a rope lashed over the bough of a eucalypt, and walked around it for a while, a job well done, inspecting the joints with short bursts from the torch. A miniature version of the Brisbane television towers, he thought. Father, Son and Holy Ghost.

It was the noise of the motor that concerned him most. He had tested it behind the Universe and it was a clanker. It belched blue smoke. And the canopy was so quiet that, to him, it appeared to amplify every snap of a twig, every quick breath of his, like a huge tin megaphone on the edge of the sea. He spent several nights worrying about the motor.

"Are you ill?" Lola asked over breakfast.

"I'm fine. Fine."

"You look dreadful. You sure you're okay?"

"Never better."

But he had had many late nights. Many, up on the bluff, calculating the number of shafts he had to couple before he hit the ancient stone of the pyramid, the sample bags of soil he would secrete in the folds of his usher's jacket to be sent away for testing. Dreaming of the moment of discovery that would place the entire history of his nation in perspective. It was only weeks away now. Only weeks.

"How did you get oil stains on your jacket cuffs?" Lola asked one evening.

"Pardon?"

"And dirt. In the hems of your trousers."

"Dirt?"

"Red dirt. And the oil. It's all over the braid."

He flicked the television channels with the remote control.

"The projector. Must have been the projector," he said. "Been playing up a bit."

"It was all right last night."

"It's been fading in and out. Surging. You haven't noticed? The bulb's about to go, I think."

"Oh," she said, and poured herself another cup of tea from her favourite pot, shaped like an Italian villa, the lid a haphazard cluster of enamelled roof tiles.

"When De Niro was fishing, fishing on the rocks, remember? The whole lot, him, the river, just about whited out."

"I must have missed that."

"When they were fishing. Dreadful. It's bad on the eyes, the surging."

"And the dirt?"

"What dirt?"

"In your cuffs."

"Oh," he hesitated, noticing grains of it under his fingernails. He bunched his hands, then the telephone rang.

"It's for you," Lola said. "Bart Wilson."

On our last night in Cherokee I sat with a retired British engineer and his wife. He spoke for half an hour about their time in the Middle East, and his position as chief engineer for British Petroleum.

177

"And the scorpions," he said. "Unbelievable. We used to pour a ring of petrol around them and light it. Do you know what they do, scorpions, when in that predicament? They curl their tails over and sting themselves."

"It's true," his wife said.

"Sting themselves. Commit suicide. Now what other creature on earth would do that, hmm? Apart from man, of course." They both looked at me, amused, then resumed eating their ice-cream.

Suddenly there was an urgency about T. Nelson's search for the pyramid. He could no longer afford the luxury of drilling in bursts, waiting for the passing of overhead jets or waves crashing onto the basalt to cloak his clandestine work.

It was warm, and he folded his usher's suit neatly over the bulb of a bush cherry shrub. He tired easily in the humidity, sweated heavily, drenched his white silk boxer shorts. His arms were bruised from steadying the jiggling rig. Sometimes it kicked so violently that it lifted his 110 kilograms off the ground.

After a metre of drilling the single shaft began to jump wildly. He cut the motor, perplexed. He couldn't have been so lucky. Not this soon. He knelt down and collected the pale soil from around the hole he had punched into the head of the bluff. Then he lifted the shaft and scraped the soil from the teeth of its bit with a wooden spoon he had stolen from Lola's kitchen drawer.

He turned the soil over in his hands, sifted it with his thumbs as one would in search of gold, and placed it in his small specimen bags. He found himself running down the bushwalker's path, oblivious to the scratchy tendrils of lantana and fresh spider web. Once free of the bluff's rainforest and onto the boulevard he sprinted, as best he could in his chunky black usher's shoes, to the Universe.

Surely not so soon, he whispered to himself, the words riding out and in with his quick breaths. Not the tip of it, the very point. Only one metre!

A light sleeper in Nautilus had woken to the sound of boots, carried up to the open bedroom doors of her tenth storey apartment, and went out to the railing. She thought of reporting to the police the semi-naked man she saw streaking down the road in the early morning haze, holding an arm out in front of him, carrying what appeared to be a purse, but instead went back to bed.

Lying in bed awake, the river chortling not far off, I thought of the British engineer's scrapbook of his journey. He had retrieved it during coffee the night before, moved his chair next to mine, and carefully turned the pages as if they were surfaced with gold leaf.

"You see, we started here."

The scrapbook contained every possible detail of the tour in a fine, tight hand. The exact kilometre distances between stops. Receipts for coffee and doughnuts. Sketches of fellow passengers.

110 East. 115 North. Las Vegas. 415km.

A blade of grass pulled from outside the *Psycho* house at Universal Studios. A petal from the Largest Rose Bush in the World at Tombstone.

State Route 93 East to Hoover Dam.
Lunch.
140 East. To Williams.
SR 64 North. To Grand Canyon.

Pamphlets, leaflets. A facsimile copy of a pay cheque to W.L. Budd, Hoover Dam construction worker, fifty cents due. A pebble from the edge of the Mississippi River, encased in sticky tape in the centre of the page.

SR 64 South. State Line.
140 East.
Alternate Route 89 South through Oak Creek Canyon.
SR 179 South. 110 East to Tucson.

The spine of a cactus. A ball of green fluff, collected from the corner of a crap table in Caesar's Palace. A fleck of paint from the western side of Graceland.

"It's nice to look back on," he told me, dropping a sugar cube into his coffee. "It really is. And for the grandchildren."

179

With my head against the face of an Indian warrior, painted into the surface of my Cherokee pillow case, I wondered, Father, what record of you had been left for me. I knew you did not have scrapbooks like the British engineer. So what does father pass on to son in the absence of a scrapbook so fat it is impossible to close? What, when all the bits and pieces have rotted, or been lost, or grown into junk? What, apart from my memory of you? Apart from the stories I could tell?

It was as if T. Nelson understood but did not understand the results of his precious soil tests. They were there in front of him, no question about that, printed neatly on computer paper. Precise margins. No spelling errors. Signed by the laboratory assistant himself. But it was perplexing that it had come to this. It was not the answer he had wanted.

"Contents: Fragments of *Hibiscus tiliaceus* bark, carbon, bird and fish bone (.75 per cent), oyster shell predominant; fragments and in powder form."

A personal postscript had been written in hand: "Mr Downs, my guess is that your sample has been taken from a large midden (Yakka Darla). Cheers."

I was half-asleep in my usual seat in the Americruiser, its engines warming for the final leg to New York City. The window glass was cold against my forehead. The engineer leaned over my seat and placed his scrapbook in my lap.

"Look at this," he said, his face ruddy and freshly shaved.

In the centre of a page, his most recent, was a tuft of black bear hair, gathered in at the centre with a thin strip of leather, the globules of glue still moist and barely holding his prize specimen to the paper.

11

He that is without sin among you, let him cast the first stone is what I always say.

How could the poor bastard have known? The tiny hairpin that he was, in the monster machine they had created, so huge, out of control, one half not knowing what the other was doing.

You can argue that he could've followed the trucks from the government's secret nursery in the Hinterland, sniffed out the trail, worn dark glasses, blackened his number plates and loitered at street corners, watching, fitting the pieces together, solving the mystery.

He could've seen how tenderly they handled his lovingly nurtured jungle-grown orchids and ferns, and installed them in luxury hotel rooms, convention centres and government tourist offices up and down the coast. How they placed them with delicacy next to gold faucets in marble bathrooms, on silk pillow slips, on monogrammed stationery next to Mont Blanc pens, at each corner of slate spa baths with a view of the Pacific Ocean. No doubt they used your little Forest Hire manifesto as a guide, Pop. Ah, like bees to honey.

Disguised as a television repairman, or a porter, he could have witnessed the delight on the faces of the Japanese dignitaries, businessmen, tourists, who were the target of his anonymous expertise. With his inside contacts he may have seen further along the trail, to the part he had played in the future of our great country.

He had done the groundwork, opened the doors for business. By the time they set out to extinguish him, the ball had been set in motion and was gathering speed, much to their delight. We know now this is how they always worked.

They had built such a beautiful pyramid, encrusted with jewels and ivory and pearl, with blossoming jacaranda, and the wonderful afternoon light peculiar to our town, with big airy houses and the meandering Brisbane River and warm rain and the beaches and prosperity and high-rolling millionaires and space rockets and moons and stars and hopes for the future. It glittered, the whole thing, its zenith so tall we had to take their word that it was there. If they told us it had a beacon on top, a light so powerful that it was making the rest of the world squint, we would have believed them. We did believe them.

They didn't tell us the whole fucking thing was built on air, did they? They didn't tell us that one sudden movement, as small as you like, as insignificant as a voice crying out in the night, the blowing of a bulb, the rattling of a drilling rig, could've brought the whole thing down.

They didn't mention anything about that, now did they?

Sitting on an upturned oil drum in the Garage Bar, New York City, drinking gin and watermelon juice, I was asked by a huge Egyptian if I liked opera and women.

"I haven't seen much opera, no," I confessed.

"Ah," he said. I could hear his drum creaking, and noticed three seeds in his ice. "I love opera. I travel the world on trains going to the major operas. That is what I have decided to do with my life."

"Sounds great."

He had a straw carry-bag at his feet, which were sandalled, his toes just visible beneath a kaftan studded with dozens of brilliant macaw parrots, their beaks alternately bending in opposite directions.

He touched my wrist again.

"From Brisbane, you say? I have seen your opera house there. Very beautiful. Very beautiful indeed."

"Our opera house? You don't mean the Sydney Opera House?"

"No, no, no. The big red building with the silver dome."

"Oh, the old museum. It's empty now."

"Is that true?" he said, his eyebrows lowered with concern, spinning his ice around. "A shame. It was the museum when I was there, but I knew it had been an opera house. I know of every opera house in the world. I could describe each of them to you. That was a beautiful one, that one of yours.''

He described the German tank in the grounds of the old building. The fibreglass dinosaurs. The rows and rows of polished wood cabinets inside.

''Do you like New York?''

''I've only been here a few hours.''

''For me, the Met is New York. There is nothing else. And this place. This place I adore. It's so chic, don't you think?''

I stumbled across the Garage Bar, Father, looking for the cafe where Robert De Niro drank his coffee between shifts in *Taxi Driver*. For a while I browsed through the sidewalk stalls — the lampshades, bongo drums, old magazines, ashtrays and lacquered spare teeth of dead celebrities all placed neatly on cardboard and blankets — and the Garage Bar just appeared. I felt it had opened its doors especially for me. I thought there would be a drink waiting for me on the bar. That's how comfortable it felt.

It used to be a white concrete gas station, by the looks, in the centre of a gravel yard, the bowsers long since uprooted. There was no reason not to believe that the huge air-filled petrol tanks were still down below.

The entire bar and its yard were covered by a welded metal dome, like an upturned dish. With drink in hand I inspected the canopy and discovered it was, remarkably, a single piece made of thousands of objects: spanners, chainsaws, bolts, typewriters, toasters, frying pans, knives, saucepans, tin cups, filing cabinets, fan blades, car doors, exhaust pipes, hubcaps, parking meters, motors and even big paper clips. Spotlights outside the dome threw shadows of all this on our arms and legs. At my oil drum I had an axe head across my face and the frill of a saw blade across my thigh.

''What's so funny?'' the Egyptian asked, nudging me again.

''My father and I,'' I said. ''We're both hopeless with tools.''

Inside the bar were a number of sculptures. One, on a large wooden base, showed two pink plastic dolls wearing lipstick and eye shadow. One was crawling on all fours and was being fucked from behind by a man made of bolts, his head a large silver polished nut. The plastic was burned where the bolt entered the doll's body. The other was on her back, her swivel arms upright, embracing her metal lover.

The Egyptian screamed something in Arabic at the pieces of art, then turned to me.

"I can speak twelve languages." He tried to twist the head off one of the bolt men with his thick fingers. "I have a trick. Shall I tell you?"

"Go ahead."

"Okay. I go to the Met, or any opera house in the world for that matter, and dress in rags. Real rags. If I speak in a French accent, the rich always ask me to sit in their private boxes or the front stalls with them. Every time, it works."

He ran a varnished fingernail along the threaded penis, picking at each ridge in the bolt.

"I can even fool them in my own country. I can have them running around after me, taking my luggage, serving me anything I want, if I choose the right accent. Isn't that hilarious? I can be anyone I like with all my languages."

He finished his drink, chewing on the seeds.

"You like women?"

"Yes," I said.

"You have a girl?"

"Sort of."

"She is not here with you?"

"No, I'm here on private business."

"Ah," he said, ordering two more drinks. "Yes, private business. You will marry this girl?" He fiddled with the glass eyes of his toucans.

"You have to be grown up to get married, don't you?"

"You look grown up to me. Ha! But sometimes, maybe, it is best not to grow up. Look what happened to me." He slapped his stomach with both hands. "But serious, sometimes it is better not to know too much, you know?"

"Yes."

"Like the opera. It is best just to close the eyes and listen to the voice. The voice is all that matters."

"I must go to the opera."

"When you go, take this girl of yours."

"I might do that."

"Myself, I like men."

"I see."

"Except your Joan Sutherland. She has a cute voice. A very cute voice."

On the day T. Nelson Downs was to receive the subpoena he had risen early, about 5.30 a.m., and while dusting his tomatoes in the backyard hothouse, had decided to tell Lola about the rig. About everything.

He knew she would not be surprised by the silvery aluminium tower attached to the generator which rocked on the fossilised log. It had been this way with him since the night of the miniature horse. He was the dreamer. The man who was hopeless at changing fuses, keeping accounts, remembering birthdays and first names. The mechanics of daily life orbited him. She had known this only too well.

No, the drilling rig would not be unexpected. To her, he thought, it would seem that its flimsiness had always been there beneath the great canopy. As unremarkable as the mermaid weathervane on the roof of the Universe or the alleged long johns of Captain James Cook, which he occasionally removed from the cabinet opposite Row FF, and wore to bed.

A week earlier, T. Nelson had checked the excavation site and noticed a young couple, naked, on a blanket near his rickety tower. They had just walked up from the beach, the woman's hair still stringy and damp. They had stepped lightly around the aluminium frame and shaken one of its legs, then stretched out a blanket and made love, their passion disturbed only by the fall of a bush cherry on the young man's buttocks, and the startled scurrying of a mallee fowl.

He had no way of knowing then, averting his eyes from the couple, that the subpoena was being prepared on a manual typewriter in a room behind the Brisbane Supreme Court, the flap of the pale green government envelope sealed by the tongue of a teenage clerk. That within days it would arrive in the foyer of the Universe and be handed to him beneath the chandeliers.

185

Listening to the gentle lovemaking, the fragile cries of the girl, while he sat there with his arms around his knees, camouflaged, a part of the bush, he could not have known that his life would soon change so dramatically, so conclusively, that he would feel he was another person. That he had dreamt his entire previous existence. Patrons would see him differently. They would notice the vanity of the comb in the rear pocket of his usher's suit, the soil beneath his nails, the ugliness of the strands of eyebrow hair that curled away from the grain of the rest, and recognise his voice as that of a desperate fire extinguisher salesman. They would look at his oily hair and the crookedness of his part, and not his eyes. They would pull their head back at the smell of his breath.

After the couple had finished making love, picking twigs and burrs from their work clothes, and walked off dressed and ready for an afternoon behind the teller counter or a computer, he sat again on the outcrop and thought of Mayor Bartholomew Wilson.

He imagined his old friend, since elected president of Rotary, leading a group of men to the edge of the bluff. Bart, dressed in his full ceremonial robe with its necklace of chains and gold coins, instructing the party to throw T. Nelson's museum cabinets into the ocean. He could see the boxes, buoyant for a while with their pockets of stale air, before sinking. The whole idea made him laugh. He told Lola about it.

He was exploding corn kernels in the popcorn machine for the evening session when the two suited men walked into his Universe.

On arriving at New York's Park Central Hotel they had no record of my name.

"Could you spell it, please?" said a woman with gold epaulettes on her burgundy jacket.

"S-a-m-u-e-l D-o-w-n-s."

"I'm sorry, sir, nothing under that name."

"I'm with the tour group."

"Which tour group, sir?"

186

"Gunter's group."

"Let me check again." She tapped the computer keys. "Nothing, sir."

Jack had moved all the luggage into the foyer. Three bellboys stood and watched him go in and out the revolving doors.

"Just fit me in anywhere," I said. "I don't mind."

"It is the long weekend, sir. We're virtually booked out, but I'll try again for you."

To my surprise they managed a huge two-room suite overlooking a green slither of Central Park. I tossed my bags on the bed and slumped into a sofa when the phone rang. It was the lobby.

"I apologise, sir, but we've given you the wrong room."

They gave me another key at the desk.

"Enjoy your stay."

"Thank you."

My new room was on a lower storey, but I didn't mind. I was exhausted. I opened the door and the bedside lamp was already on. A cigarette smouldered in an ashtray.

A naked man walked out of the bathroom.

He froze. "It's in the side drawer," he said, pointing, covering his genitals with his other hand. He had an anchor tattooed between his nipples.

"Sorry?"

"Money. The traveller's cheques. Just take them. I never saw you. Honest."

I was finally given a room on Gunter's intervention.

"He'll expect a bonus," Jack said, wearing again his cap with the bamboo strips and dragon eyes.

"Bullshit."

"I'm telling you, kid, he records everything he does for you. Everything extra."

"Get out of here, Jack."

"Before we have our farewell drinks tomorrow he'll remind you of everything he did for you on the tour."

"Like giving me a headache with that weird voice of his, you mean."

"Photographs he took of you. Cups of coffee he bought. The works."

"You're joking, right?"

Jack touched his chest with his fingertips. "Hey, this is me who's talking to you. This is the seventh trip I've done with this asshole. He's one of the smoothest operators in the business. He loves the oldies the best. He'll go up to their rooms tonight, right, tuck 'em in, say hope you had a lovely trip, say beddy-byes to them, nighty night, and bang, hundred buck tip in the back pocket."

"Let him try it on me," I said.

"He's already done it, buddy boy. He's been picking it up the whole way along. Slingbacks from day one."

"Go on."

"That crummy joint outside Phoenix? Boss lady gave him a payoff. The leather shop in Mexico, the flight over the Canyon, that dump outside Houston. The place wasn't even finished, remember?"

"All the way along?"

"That Cajun restaurant outside New Orleans, with the big welcoming sign for us? The San Antonio tour. Even the goddam sodas in the cooler at the front of the bus. He charged you what, a buck fifty? Bought 'em for a couple of bits each."

"No."

"He tell you he was born in San Francisco?"

"San Diego," I said.

"San Diego this time. Man, the guy's a fucking illegal immigrant on the run from West Germany or something. I can't say nothing about it. He could get me the sack. One word from him to the company and I'm history. I'd love to whip his ass, just once."

We finished our coffee and looked out at Fifth Avenue.

"I called you last night. What you get up to?"

"Went looking for Robert De Niro's cafe."

"Yeah? Which one's that?"

"In *Taxi Driver*."

"Yeah? Find it?"

"Nope."

"I love that De Niro guy. Up in the mountains, shootin' that deer? Remember that? That was fucking beautiful, that was." Jack slapped me on the shoulder. "It's just the movies though, eh? I know a great oyster bar on Seventh Avenue. Let's go there tonight, our last night. Waddya say?"

"Sure."

Lola Downs said nothing as she read the court order in the empty cinema in the light of the wholesale Woolworths cosmos. She went through it several times, turned it over, noted the small black map of Australia in the corner, and the government insignia in the centre.

The usher waited by the rear curtain, flicking his torch on and off. He then walked casually down the left aisle, his hands behind his back, shining the torch inside his cabinets and picking up his own smudged fingertips on the glass, or cards filled with his own crabbed handwriting.

He sat down in the row behind Lola and, as they always had, her earlobes, the light furrows on the back of her neck and the wisps of grey hair saddened him. He wondered if she had noticed the gradual re-angling of his own hair. The way he was combing it now, diverting it forward, a degree or so per month, concealing his thinning hairline. She had said nothing.

He could hear her folding the letter, and a moth striking a cluster of bulbs on the ceiling, above Caesar and the Bear.

"Honestly, Lole, I've done nothing wrong. I'm as surprised as you are."

She looked into the white screen, the envelope in her lap.

"I don't know what the fuss is about. Really. I just looked after a few plants for them. No big deal. I'll just tell them everything I know. That's all they want me to do."

He had once enquired about the moths, and whether the life of a cinema moth was affected in any way by the constant state of near-darkness. The absence of the rhythm of day and night. Could the insects adapt, he asked an entomologist, to the man-made deception within the cinema? Could it shorten their lifespan? Prolong it? They were well fed, he said, on red velvet curtain. The experts never got back to him with the answers.

"They were just ferns and stuff," he said. "They asked me to do it, Lole. They came to me."

There were two moths now, bombarding the same constellation. Could it have been the violent self-destruction of the moths that had weakened his filaments over the years? Had they the strength to black out so many, to shake so many vacuums, considering their meagre bodyweight?

"For Christ's sake, Lole, it was only a few plants."

She said nothing as he led her by the hand to the rig, after a late screening of *Manhattan*. He guided her with his torch across the moss-covered roots and stones on the forest floor.

"Careful," he said. "A step here."

They thought they could smell a fire, but it was nothing. After a while Lola gathered her cardigan together and said, "I don't need to see any more, can we go back?"

"Lole, please," he whispered. "I want to show you how it works. I want to show you everything." He pulled the dead fern leaves off the generator. She stood back and could only see the torch, suspended in the darkness, darting around the motor, its pipes and wires an odd heart that floated too as she could not see the stone log it rested on.

"Nelson, you'll wake people with that thing."

"I don't care," he said, "now that you're here. I know it's here, Lole. It's like I've always known, since I was a kid."

She jumped slightly as the motor screamed to life.

"Stand back," he shouted, and suddenly he was beside her, leading her away from the rig to the crescent of an ancient boulder. Squatting behind the rock, he trained the torchlight onto the shaft, where it entered the bluff.

"It's here, I know it," he said. "Beyond the damned shells."

Lola put her hands over her ears, looked up and saw the grainy white-flecked soil emerge from the hole in waves, rolling in on itself like a live thing, flowing upward and outward. Then the soil stopped coming and the canopy shook with a metallic

190

shrieking. T. Nelson dropped the torch which rolled into the leaves. Even though he could see nothing he felt the vibration of the shaft, struggling to pull itself from the earth.

The piercing cry stopped and they both looked up. Grabbing the torch they watched as the skeletal rig began to shake, then sway gently, its legs rocking rhythmically like those of a woman lifted inches from a dance floor.

"What's happening?" Lola yelled, her hands still over her ears.

Nelson put his arms around her and looked up in time to see the rig shaking insanely. He felt the whole cap of the bluff was moving, and that the roof of vines would untangle and collapse on them like a heavy net.

Then without warning he dived on top of her, pressing her face into the dead leaves and moss and mulch, and the entire rig lifted up on the rising shaft. The aluminium pyramid, driven by the smoking motor, was thrown effortlessly into the scrub bringing down lantana and a few saplings, with some of its bolt heads popping into the darkness.

They heard the crashing sound and after a while looked up over the crescent of the boulder, just in time to catch the old Oceanic Baths generator explode in a shower of golden sparks.

We were asked to wear our national dress at the farewell cocktail party held in our honour in the Park Central's restaurant. It had been a stipulation on the tour brochure that we had all read, presumedly in our own countries before arriving in America, that costumes be brought for this "special gala event". I, of course, had not seen the brochure, let alone the clause.

Jack had warned me about it the night before in the Famous Oyster Bar Restaurant, and I had pondered this. I had seen on television a month before a major international sporting event in which the national dress worn by one of my country's athletes, in a parade seen by millions, was a high-cut swimming costume. Jack liked the sound of this. I tried to think of other alternatives: a horseman's outfit, or a T-shirt and shorts. I had nothing to wear.

191

At the party I was asked about my costume. Where was it? Where was my kangaroo suit, the West Germans asked? Where was my stockman's hat and were they really made of compressed rabbit skins?

"What about your emu?" the hotel manager asked me. "We have emu farms here in the States. The oil, you know, is for medicinal purposes. And the toes make excellent jewellery." I did not dare ask who was behind the scheme, in case Uncle Sid was mentioned. "I read that each bird produces up to five litres of oil."

Later, on my seventh or eighth Rolls Royce cocktail, I listened numbfaced to the British engineer who was dressed as a Beefeater.

"But the greatest crime would have to be the secrecy surrounding the dead sea scrolls," he said enthusiastically. "Only a few scholars have access to them. A handful, really."

"Tragedy."

"That's putting it mildly, don't you think? Did you know the scrolls are in fact thousands of coin-sized pieces? Not as you would imagine, like rolled up newspapers. They were eaten by moths, you see. Do you think that ironic?"

"Terribly."

"That these most extraordinary documents be gobbled up by the common old moth?"

"God in their bellies."

"Well, exactly," he roared.

Later, Jack and I tried to toss olives into each other's glasses across the room. The greyhound patch on his shirt was soaked with martini.

"Your attention please, ladies and gentlemen, please," Gunter said, tapping his glass with the end of a pen. He was dressed as a Californian, or so he said, in board shorts, a shirt of palm trees and black-lensed sunglasses.

"Keep it down," he joked, resting the glasses on his forehead. "As you know, this is the end of our tour, which I think you will all agree has been wonderful."

Hoots and rounds of applause.

"Before I bid you farewell, you will find in your rooms some forms to fill out about the trip and so on and so forth, what you liked and didn't like, to help us with future trips. But I think you'll share my opinion that this was one of the smoothest trips we've had. Like clockwork, really.''

Another shout of approval.

''On behalf of Jack and myself, I would have to say, without a word of a lie, that this has probably been the friendliest group of people we've ever had the pleasure of working for.

''Before we all go our separate ways, however, I am at your disposal to help you fill out your forms, and to assist you in any further travel arrangements. So let's enjoy ourselves, and thank you again.''

By the end of the evening I found myself standing next to Gunter, the Californian. He took a Vesuvius from a passing drinks tray.

''Why, Samuel,'' he said, taking a sip, ''but where is that kangaroo suit of yours?''

Jack wrote some time later to tell me that the immigration authorities had finally caught up with Gunter on his very next trip, a ten-day excursion with a group of German architects and their wives into Yellowstone. He swears he did not know who tipped them off.

After a brief chase the armed men found Gunter curled up at the base of a giant red cedar, whimpering, so thin and pathetic amongst the dead leaves that had just begun to drop. The bruise on his right eye had gone from purple to yellow, much like the leaves, from the night I shattered his Californian sunglasses.

Jack claimed that a bellboy had had to use a step ladder to clean the dripping orange alcohol off the Park Central's only chandelier.

12

Call me paranoid, I don't care what anyone thinks any more, but when they destroyed the Cloudland Ballroom in Brisbane, that pink and white plaster chunk of cumulo-nimbus on a hillock, nucleus of the city's courtship rites and scene of unspoken conceptions, I suspected they had begun erasing all evidence of my father's existence.

Let's not underestimate the significance of the site, and the government's need for its obliteration. Cloudland was romance, you see, the apex of love. A Brisbane generation was borne out of its cosy, flaking shell. If the dining room sideboards of the city were simultaneously burgled, and the contents placed in a cairn, it would contain tens of thousands of framed photographs of post-war couples standing before the same white drapes, the same plaster pillars, of a single corner of the Cloudland Ballroom.

To look at Cloudland, visible from most points of the city, was to look at love, pleasure, dreams. Things could come true at Cloudland.

Even you, old boy, completed your courtship there, asking Mother to marry you beneath the half-dome of plaster that captured whispers and threw them out over the city. On a still evening, you said, the cloud even picked up the rattle of trams coming down through Fortitude Valley, car horns, dogs barking and the chime of the City Hall clock, and took them into its foundations.

Of course they had to get rid of it. They had to tear it down in the middle of the night. Not cut the giant cloud respectfully into manageable pieces, or remove it whole, but smash it with balls and chains. They had to show they were in control, obliterating something so dull, so dated, yet so extraordinary to the people of our town. They were shaping the future, so why not reshape the past to suit themselves? There was no other way.

Was it deliberate that the place where you had asked to share your life with my mother, former exotic dancer, collector of Venus de Milo statuettes, occasional usherette and candy bar captain without parallel, was the scene of your disgrace? That your confessions to their kangaroo court would join those words of love in the salmon-coloured surface of the cloud? Oh no, not at all. Not in the least. If they were delicious at anything, it was irony.

You were the final performance in that ballroom. The star of the sham of the century. You must have wondered why they had conducted their bogus inquiry into the theft and sale of protected flora there, of all places, and not in the courts of law down in George Street. Why you were never charged with a single offence, but summonsed as the accused to the Fern Inquiry, as it has since become known. Why it was an inquiry closed to the press. You, on a small metal chair, in the middle of the empty ballroom. Did you recall the rustle of mother's full petticoats, or the sweet smell of bathwater on her neck, while facing your inquisitors?

Maybe the whole thing would have been easier if you had been murdered. I could have devoted my life to assembling the facts surrounding the moment of your death. I could have drawn charts of possible scenarios, of suspects. I could have been the dogged son seeking justice for his father, and on solving the crime, raised my fist in the air and shouted: "That was for you, Pa! That was for you!"

You made it hard for your boy, let me tell you, simply slipping on a saddle of moss and disappearing. Bloody hard. But rest easy, I've been working. I've been chipping away for you.

For I have the transcripts of the inquiry. That was their big mistake. They hadn't accounted for me, spinning towards them like a bullet that was born for its target. Their pathetic transcript, recording every laugh at you, every quip, every fart and belch from those fat frauds, feasting daily on oysters and beer down at the Breakfast Creek Hotel before returning to dissect you a little further. I can hear them recalling your evidence at dinner parties, or in the Parliamentary Annexe over cigars.

They didn't know then, Father, that it was already too late for them. They didn't know that their undertaker had already been born.

"Your full name please?"

"Downs. T. Nelson Downs."

"For the records, Mr Downs, could you tell us what the 'T' stands for?"

"I don't know."

"You don't know?"

"It has no meaning as far as I know. My father, he took the name from a book he was reading at the time."

"The name of the book, Mr Downs?"

"I think it was called *After Dinner Sleights*. A book of amateur magician tricks. Disappearing coins and handkerchiefs and things."

"And the 'T'?"

"A magician in the book, he had the same last name as ours, Downs, so my father just picked it out."

You are accurate here. I have the book before me: *After Dinner Sleights and Pocket Tricks* by C. Lang Neil, author of *The Modern Conjurer*, published by C. Arthur Pearson Ltd, Henrietta Street, London, 1914.

"You are the proprietor of the Universe-Cine-by-the-Sea?"

"Correct. And head usher."

"There is more than one usher?"

"Not really. My wife Lola sometimes helps out."

"I see. Please listen to the questions and answer them as succinctly as you can, Mr Downs."

"Of course, yes."

"Other business interests?"

"None."

"No other forms of income?"

"None."

"Can you cast your mind back, Mr Downs, to the period covered by the terms of reference of this inquiry, at about the same time you took over the Universe?"

"Yes."

"You are aware of the allegations we have received concerning the theft and sale of protected species from the Natural Arch National Park?"

"I am."

"Can I ask you to recount to the best of your knowledge what occurred on the day you allegedly met Councillor Wilson at Natural Arch?"

"I'll try, yes . . ."

"Thank you."

"He called me at about nine-thirty that morning, I think it was, could've been closer to ten. I have known him for years, from when I sold cars to the council . . ."

"Please, Mr Downs, that day?"

"Right. He asked me up to the arch and I thought, you know, why not, it may have helped me with my submission for the hothouse."

"This hothouse you refer to, Mr Downs, for the record, is the walk-in greenery and theme park, as such, you had put forward to the Minister for Conservation, am I correct?"

"Correct, yes."

"Could I please tender the documents pertaining to the hothouse? Thank you."

"Exhibit eleven."

"Continue, Mr Downs."

"So Bart and the ranger . . ."

"The ranger shall be known in these proceedings as Ranger X, if you will, Mr Downs."

"Yes, of course. Ranger X and Bart and I, we went down to the arch to talk about this and that."

"What exactly did you discuss?"

"Well, Bart said there could be a job for me, coming up, with the approval of the Minister . . ."

"The approval of, you said?"

"That's right."

197

"Go on."

"We talked about the plant trade, you know, how it was at the time. I know a bit about the plant . . ."

"How was the trade at the time, Mr Downs?"

"Pretty healthy from what I remember, pretty healthy. A bit of a shortage of good ferns. There'd been a bit of a rush on them."

"A rush?"

"Yes, they were becoming a bit popular again, you know, people take to things now and again and . . ."

"Stick to the questions please, Mr Downs."

"Yes, sorry. I don't remember the exact words, but Bart mentioned a project for the government, and that the Minister wanted some of the more rare species taken from the park . . ."

"Taken?"

"There was a bit of trouble with the poachers, you know, there always is, so the Minister decided . . ."

"You are a good friend of the Minister?"

"An acquaintance, I would say. A good acquaintance. I went to one of his Christmas parties and . . ."

"I see. How did you come to be in that position, Mr Downs?"

Watch it, Father, they're moving in. Are you sweating? You always were a heavy sweater. It would have been warm on that metal chair, middle of summer, humidity around ninety per cent. How often I had wiped your sweat onto my trouser leg after slapping you on the back, trying to get closer, trying to be a friend.

"I had supplied the indoor plants for Parliament House. They knew of my work in there."

"That being the installation of pot plants and other such items on a rental basis."

"That's right, yes."

"Go on, please."

198

"They liked some of my ideas. I had big ideas. They liked that."

"By big ideas, Mr Downs, you mean, as an example for the record, 'The Great Queensland Pleasure Trip'?"

"That was one, yes."

"An abysmal failure, was it not, Mr Downs?"

"There was a problem with . . ."

"A spectacular failure, I dare say, wouldn't you, Mr Downs? Your ferry now a hamburger outlet on the highway? I have tasted their wares, Mr Downs, and must say even they have not made a decent fist of your little ferry."

"That's a matter of opinion."

"But it is not a matter of opinion, is it, Mr Downs, that the scheme behind this big idea of yours was little more than an attempt to defraud incapacitated persons?"

"That's not true. I . . ."

"Then came the biggest hothouse in the southern hemisphere. That, too, could be categorised as another of your big ideas?"

"I thought I could . . ."

"A simple yes or no will suffice, Mr Downs."

"Yes, it was."

"Yet none of your grand plans, Mr Downs, not a single one, was embraced by the government you claimed you had a particularly close rapport with, am I correct?"

"I never claimed I . . ."

"In fact, to put it kindly, Mr Downs, and with respect, you have for many years toyed with several unrealistic business ventures. You have been a sort of Jack-of-all-trades and master of none, haven't you, Mr Downs?"

"They have all been very real to me."

"The stuff of fancy seems to take your fancy, doesn't it, Mr Downs?"

"I don't think that's . . ."

"Have you ever heard of the word pteridomania, Mr Downs?"

"I'm sorry?"

"Pteridomania. It is, as I understand, the description given to one with an obsession, a mania, for ferns."

"Yes, I have heard of that."

"Good. Do you suffer from this, Mr Downs? Would you say you were a pteridomaniac?"

"I think that's hardly fair."

"Then let me put it to you, Mr Downs, that you, suffering from this illness, had operated alone, as a sole agent, in the theft of at least seventeen protected species from that national park. That you, in your desperation for certain varieties, raped public land for your own personal gain."

"I refute that. That is a lie . . ."

"That your motive was to raise sufficient capital to commence renovations and the operation of your cinema in Ocean Boulevard, Burleigh Heads . . ."

"May I speak? You have it all wrong . . ."

"That your covert operations continued until the desired amount of capital, blackmarket capital, tax free, had been obtained . . ."

"Ask Bart, he'll tell you . . ."

"Please, Mr Downs. What exactly happened to the plants in question?"

"The plants?"

"That's correct."

"I have no idea."

"You have no idea."

"They were taken away in trucks, some of them."

"No idea at all. I see. If the commissioner pleases it might be an appropriate time for a break."

"All stand."

She always was a good reporter, my Andrea. A ferret. A true reptile of the press, but a pretty one.

I remember when I first saw her, in her sky blue dress, a pale pink clip holding back her long auburn hair, in the office. I was coming off an early morning shift, my tie abandoned, the cigarette smoke through my clothes, totally beat; the hand of a twelve-year-old boy poking out from beneath a police tarpaulin on the side of the road still clawed behind my eyes.

"You look like you need a drink," she said, smiling.

That night we agreed to meet up at the rotunda, between the television towers on Mount Coot-tha, and drank a bottle of cheap champagne.

Perhaps I knew then that she was my future. But it's all very well knowing, isn't it? All very well. You have to have the courage to face it. To take it.

As I walked along the platform at London's Victoria Station, my small bag so heavy in my left hand, the right one still sore in soiled strapping, she was standing there, beneath the clock, her hands behind her back.

I put my bag down between us, and we just stood. For hours, it seemed. Then she took the bag in both hands.

"I've come to take you home."

"Your evidence will continue under your previous oath, Mr Downs."

"Thank you."

"Mr Downs, firstly, good morning. I would like to commence today with your interest in Burleigh bluff."

"Yes."

"It has been a major part of your life, has it not?"

"Yes, correct, since I was about four or five."

"Your father, let me check, Urban . . . is that correct, Mr Downs, Urban?"

"Yes. Urban."

"Your father, Urban, had a permanent site there at the Oceanic Baths Caravan Park, is that right?"

"Yes."

"Permanent in respect that you would attend the council-run park for a certain period of time each year."

"At Christmas, yes."

"For a week?"

"Two weeks."

"I see. For two weeks of the year you would spend your vacation there."

"That's right. I'm sorry, I don't see what you're getting at."

"And subsequently, upon the death of your father, that site was transferred over to your name."

"Yes."

"Its permanence, that is, was allotted to you."

"I had been taking my family to the Oceanic well before then, when my own parents were unable to use it."

"If we can move on, Mr Downs, without further interruption, thank you, you subsequently showed an interest in the cinema adjacent to the caravan park."

"I did. I had been going there most of my life until it closed down."

"The cinema, according to council records, fell into serious disrepair before you showed some entrepreneurial interest in the complex."

"That's right."

"And the council, subsequently, accorded you their fullest co-operation in terms of the development of this particular site."

"They did. The place was stagnant. It was attracting undesirable elements into the area, and they were more than happy for me to spruce it up."

"Spruce?"

"Yes, to bring the families back into the area."

"Did you, in fact, achieve that result?"

"I did, sir, yes I did. I don't know if you know, but I received a community award from the North Burleigh Rotary Club for my achievements."

"Congratulations, Mr Downs."

"Thank you."

"However, a study of your financial records shows that your turnover at the cinema has hardly been meritorious."

"It is like everything. The business fluctuates with the state of the country."

"The state of the country?"

"When the country is hurting, I am hurting."

"That is your simplistic judgment of the matter?"

"That's the reality, yes."

"There are no other variables?"

"Not that I can see."

"Not that you can see. Not that you can see. Let me put it to you, Mr Downs, that there is another variable, a rather significant variable in this matter, namely the selection of films screened in your cinema."

"It may be so, but I doubt it."

"It may be so indeed, Mr Downs. May I tender several examples of the Universe-Cine-by-the-Sea's programming schedules taken over a period of time?"

"Exhibits twenty-two to twenty-seven . . ."

"Before we examine the exhibits, is it not correct that you gave the council a strict undertaking that you would manage the Universe Cinema to the best of your ability, in compliance with all council ordinations, including upkeep and safety, and abide by the conditions of the lease?"

"Naturally, yes."

"Naturally. The lease was to be held by you for an indefinite period, upon compliance with the regulations."

"Yes."

"Basically, the council could decide whether you were a fit and proper person to be running the Universe."

"That's right."

"Never breached any regulations?"

"Never."

"Yet according to the council minutes of 28 May, the chamber was notified that you had deliberately breached fire and exit regulations pertaining to the building."

"That's news to me."

"Is it news to you that patrons observed the major exits deliberately obstructed with various cabinets of junk, statues, plants and other decorations, including a three-metre stuffed Canadian grizzly bear?"

"American."

"A bear, full-size, nonetheless."

"No one ever complained to me about it."

"Returning to the exhibits, and a chart prepared by my asso-

203

ciate, if I may hold it up, commissioner, for the benefit of the commission . . ."

"Certainly."

"It is self-explanatory, I think — the red line indicating monetary takings and the blue line attendance figures — that both have been in a drastic state of decline for some time."

"We have had a slump, yes, but I don't think . . ."

"The fall directly attributable, I dare say, to the manager, that being you, Mr Downs."

"As I said before, if the country . . ."

"You began, as the exhibits show, screening popular American films upon the opening of the Universe. Blockbusters, as they are referred to in the trade."

"Yes, yes."

"Within five months, according to the exhibits, you began to change the focus of the Universe."

"I don't think focus is the right word."

"You don't? It is patently obvious that you began a steady march backwards in terms of cinematographic history, is it not?"

"I don't see the point."

"The point being within two months you had dispensed with the films of the 1980s and 1970s, dealt with the 1960s in a single month, then began screening, in prime evening time, the matinee films of the 1950s, which you obviously had a predilection for, as the period has extended for several months and is still in evidence as we speak."

"I didn't start out with any plan in mind."

"And according to your future program lists, you have allotted the 1930s and 1940s the Christmas period, whereby you will begin the new year with silent films. Am I correct?"

"There are so many lovely . . ."

"As an example, I can see here that on Christmas Eve you plan to screen a little film titled *Cutting Out Diseased Potatoes from the Warrnambool Herd*."

You should have told them about the *Moth of Moonbi*, Father, you know how much I loved that one, and *The Mystery of a Hansom Cab*. What about *Across Australia with Burke and Wills*? Tell them about the couple who came all the way from the Alice to see that one. From the Alice to the Universe. Go on, tell them.

"Quiet please."

"Thank you, commissioner. Mr Downs, I will ask you again. I put it to you that you, well, there are no other words for it, you thumbed your nose at the council with these antics. A council that had placed so much trust in you, particularly Mayor Wilson, not to mention the families you set out to entertain."

"I have a good public."

"You do indeed, yes. An average of 12.5 per screening as of last week."

"I am not overly concerned about the numbers."

"Could you repeat that again for the commission?"

"I said I'm not overly concerned about the numbers."

"Then what does concern you, Mr Downs? Could you share this with us?"

"I wanted to see how it all fitted together, our place in it."

"You've lost me, Mr Downs, I'm sorry."

"I wanted everyone to see it all."

"See what?"

"Everything on the screen."

"Mr Downs, we're getting nowhere here. Answer me this if you can. How far back were you prepared to go?"

Bet you'd love a cigar now. Reach into your left poocket, to the case I gave you for Christmas one year. It had not been enough for you, had it, just to accept the silver engraved case? It took you several months to trace the name, engraved inside, to the ship merchant in Bremen, and then to the Holocaust, where it had somehow escaped the flames of hell and found its way to me and then to you. These endless loops we find ourselves in.

* *

205

"I will tell you for the tenth time. It was not intentional. If it happened it happened. I was not aware of any pattern until you pointed it out to me."

"To *Soldiers of the Cross*, perhaps, Mr Downs. To the first feature film?"

The martyrdom of saints. The work of the Salvation Army Limelight Department. I know, I know, Father, we have talked about it many times. Of Major Perry and the lantern slides, touring every State in the country, singing to the images they brought to life. Sight and sound for the first time. Then pictures of daily life, of streets and carriages and slums, then the saints and even the Commonwealth inauguration ceremony. What did they say again? That the magic power of light and picture and screen was the creation of God. That the Limelight Department would be the saviour of mankind.

"I think it best to leave it there, Mr Commissioner."

  "Very well."

  "All stand."

"Why do you ask all the time?" I said to her. I poured another wine from the plastic bottle and leant back on one elbow. Men were sweeping up shattered glass down in the Boulevard Saint-Michel.

  "I have to be reassured with you," Andrea said.

  "Why?"

  "I just do."

  "You know how I feel about you."

  "But . . ."

  "But you live in the future all the time. You're always planning everything. How many children. What we'll do. Where we'll live. You plan everything and worry about it so much you don't enjoy the present."

"I can't help it. I've always been like that. I don't see there's anything wrong with that."

"Dad was going back. Did you know that? Further and further back."

"What do you mean?"

"And you're always looking ahead."

"I can't change that."

"I just don't understand it, that's all. I think you're missing out on a lot, thinking ahead all the time."

"No, I think you are."

And on it went, endless, the cinema glass being swept into piles after the explosion. Looking down, I could only smile at the glittering pieces, some of them catching the afternoon light, and remember my beautiful box of glass eyes.

I had wanted to see *The Last Temptation of Christ*. Was looking forward to it. They had banned it back home. The only place in the Western world to ban the film. Now they had blown up a cinema here. Don't mess around with the myths, Father. That's what they were telling you. You start digging and you might find something.

"Your mother's still paying for a search plane," Andrea said.

"How many days has it been?"

"Thirty-nine."

"God."

"She needs you now."

"Yes."

"Minister, thank you for giving the commission your time this morning."

"You're most welcome. Anything I can help you with."

"Thank you. We understand you have other engagements so we'll get to the point."

"Appreciate that."

"Perfectly all right. Mr Minister, can you tell the commission if you know the gentleman second to my left?"

"To your left?"

"That's right."

"I do."

"Could you tell us who this man is?"

"Mr Nelson Downs, I believe."

"T. Nelson Downs?"

"I was unaware of the 'T', but yes, that is he."

"Could you describe briefly your relationship to this man?"

"I met him on a few occasions some years ago, and more recently at the time of the Exposition."

"The World Exposition."

"Correct. Mr Downs was employed by the Government to provide the flora for the site."

"We'll come to that a little later, Minister. When did you meet him on those previous occasions that you mentioned?"

"From memory I met him in my office in the Annexe. He wished to discuss a project with me."

"Is that your customary practice, Mr Minister, to personally meet individuals to discuss such projects?"

"It is not, no, but the Premier had become aware of Mr Downs' expertise in . . ."

"The Premier?"

"That's correct. Downs had furnished Parliament House with his rented plants, from memory, and the Premier had had trouble with a rather large weeping fig in his suite."

"Go on."

"He had called Downs for advice on the matter."

"Was the problem solved?"

"With great success, I am told. The Premier had not allowed for sufficient light and the leaves kept dropping off. All over the place . . ."

"With respect, could you get to the point, Mr Minister?"

"Yes, I apologise. Anyway, Downs had a project in mind and the Premier had referred him to me, as a favour."

"A gesture of goodwill following the fig matter."

"Precisely. There was nothing unusual about the circumstances and anyone who implies as much will face the full brunt of the courts from me, I can tell you."

"There was no implication of that, Mr Minister."

"Well that's good."

"So he came to see you?"

"The Premier?"

"No, Mr Downs."

"Yes, yes he did. That is my job, to speak to my people. After all I am a public servant."

"Of course."

"But his project was, well, with respect, a little ambitious."

"Can you elaborate please?"

"It was a giant hothouse, from what I can recall. On the coast. A massive thing."

"Anything else you remember, sir?"

"Shaped like a pyramid. A huge structure. With my experience, as you can understand, I saw instantly it was not feasible."

"In what way?"

"Too big. Way too big, just for a few plants. We are undertaking substantial growth in the area where Mr Downs wanted his pyramid thing. Substantial. The State under this Government is growing faster than any other in the country, and this Government has, and always will have, a true commitment to . . ."

"You didn't like Mr Downs' idea?"

"You may not be aware but the area in question is growing faster than Sydney and Melbourne combined. It is on target in becoming one of the pre-eminent tourist destinations in the world, and is a priority region for this Government which has always put the interests of the people . . ."

"His project was at odds with this priority?"

"I don't care what they say down South, all the hoo-ha they go on with in Canberra. This area is the future of our State, the future of our children and our great-grandchildren. Tourism. Tourism is what will make our nation great. Tourism is the hub of the great wheel of our progress, and I cannot stress that too much. Bring the world here, planeloads of them, planeloads and planeloads and . . ."

"Am I correct in assuming Mr Downs' idea was at odds with that?"

"You surely must be aware of that damned fool and his . . . I'm sorry, could we retract that word from the transcript?"

"Damned?"

"Yes, if you could."

"Certainly."

"Most appreciated. Yes, that old man with his little animal sanctuary down there, you know the one. People don't want that stuff anymore. We can't get him out. Some land title problems. He's an impediment to all we are trying to do down there."

"You feared Mr Downs could become a similar impediment if his idea had been approved?"

"Possibly, yes."

"A burr in your side?"

"A burr, yes, highly likely."

"The whole idea was a bit foolish?"

"Just let me say that people will not come to this country specifically to see plants."

"Why, in your opinion, do they come?"

"A silly question, sir, if I may say. They come to have fun. To take photographs. I don't have to go on. If they want to see plants they can walk into their backyard."

"How does this opinion, with respect, sit with your position as Minister for Conservation?"

"I'm not the Minister for Conservation."

"You're not?"

"I'm the Minister for Tourism."

"I see."

"As of a month ago."

"Ah. Congratulations."

"Thank you very much."

The biggest living museum on the planet, that's what they were turning us into. Of course. All of us, dressed in identical suits, knife-edge ironed trousers and pleated skirts, starched white shirts and kangaroo skin shoes, our hands to our brows shielding the sun, looking to the horizon for aeroplanes, for glints of light off their metal skins, dropping down to us like jewels from the sky.

* *

210

"In Mr Downs' statement to the Commission, Minister, he said that the ferns and other exotic varieties of plant he acquired illegally from the State-owned forests of the Hinterland, were in fact removed with your consent."

"That is a fabrication."

"That in fact this approval was conveyed through Mayor Bartholomew Wilson."

"I don't even know the man."

"Mayor Wilson?"

"Never heard of him."

"It was further alleged that your wife had a rather keen interest in . . ."

"I don't know what you're implying but I'm saying watch yourself."

"Watch . . ."

"I wouldn't know this Wilson character from a bar of soap, and anyone who suggests otherwise will be taken to the highest court in the land and face the full powers of . . ."

"It is all untrue?"

"I repeat, to the highest court."

"And your wife?"

"She will take identical action."

"Does she have an interest in anything botanical?"

"None at all. We live in an apartment. We have an African violet on the bathroom shelf. That is all."

"Thank you, Minister."

"I did not wish to cause a fuss or call in my officers, but I had asked Mr Downs repeatedly to clear the exitways of his cinema but he refused to do so. I considered it a fire hazard. If his patronage was any higher I would have issued an order."

"Go on, Mayor Wilson."

"It had been a beautiful picture palace, beautiful, but sadly Mr Downs let it fall into disrepair. Especially the roof."

"The roof?"

"At the beginning it was magnificent. Full of stars. You could see entire constellations, the Milky Way even. Superb. Now the galaxies, well, to put it lightly, they are bedraggled.''

"Yes?"

"Dull. Bits and pieces. He has not bothered to replace the broken stars. The bulbs, that is. It's a junkyard up there, really, it is. He seems to have lost interest in the whole thing.''

"Was it deliberate, do you think?"

"I can't comment on that, but the man himself seems to have lost his entrepreneurial pride. That's a bit of a mouthful, isn't it? But true, nonetheless.''

"Continue please."

"Well where do I begin? He attended to me in the foyer of the Universe one evening covered in dirt.''

"Dirt?"

"His usher's suit, covered in dirt, filthy. He was not the same man I knew from the Magic Mile.''

"That being the motor vehicle business?"

"Correct. Could have brushed your hair in his shoes back in those days. The whole affair has bemused me, I might say. The whole affair.''

"In what way?"

"I am unsure about how much I can say to the commission at this time, but I will say that the police have been called in to investigate.''

"You may say anything to the commission. It is a closed hearing, sir. All the facts would be appreciated.''

"I don't wish to preempt the police matters, but a large quantity of apparatus has been found on Burleigh Heads bluff which we believe, at this early stage, is connected with the activities of the usher of the Universe.''

"Mr Downs, that is."

"Yes. A drilling operation of some sort. A motor. All on council land.''

"Have you ascertained the reason for the apparatus?"

"It appears that the operator of the rig may have been drilling for oil.''

"Oil? Crude oil?"

"Investigations are continuing, but that is how it appears.''

"That's rather odd, isn't it?"

"Odd? If it's true, I would say it was the work of a madman."

Did you think I would laugh at you about the drilling? Did you? About the God of Mu, linking us to the rest of the world, making us a part of something greater? Tell me, tell me for once, what you were thinking.

"For precious stones, Mr Downs?"

"No."

"Opal, ruby, diamond?"

"No."

"Was it minerals? Copper, bauxite, uranium?"

"No."

"Lead, perhaps? Zinc? Was it gold, Mr Downs?"

"No."

"Treasure?"

"No."

"Fossils? Fern fossils? Was that what you were after?"

"No."

"And definitely not oil?"

"No."

"Commissioner, I am unable to proceed with Mr Downs, as you can see."

"Yes, I see. What do you propose?"

"I suggest, sir, you take into account the recommendations I have drafted for you in terms of your eventual findings."

"Very well. Mr Downs? Do you wish to say anything before the conclusion of the inquiry?"

13

The day we arrived in Delhi a farmer, who had walked from Agra, entered police headquarters with a brown paper bag under his arm. The bag contained the head of his wife.

There was nothing to distinguish the man from any other, dodging the bicycles and motorised trishaws and Ambassadors on his way to the police station. Past the lassa stands, the shoe cleaners, the fruit sellers, the beggars without legs, the bodies in white cloth being carried horizontally through the crowds, with his crinkled brown bag under his arm.

He placed the head on a table and said: "I wish to surrender." A jewel was still fixed to the nose of his wife. "I have killed my wife and I wish to surrender."

The story of the man and his crime was a small one, in the middle of the newspaper. On the same page was the story of the tiger hunters who had taken to wearing masks of a human face on the backs of their heads, to confuse the animals and avoid attack from behind.

Let me tell you now, Father, that I had every hope of finding you here. Cruising in to land, only hundreds of metres above Delhi's ragged lights, I could see cinema screens in the middle of nowhere, teeming with gods and killers, explosions, romantic embraces and aquamarine saris. How could you not be here, in this country of five thousand travelling cinema operators, bringing bits and pieces of the world to millions of villages?

In the street of silver merchants I thought I saw you emerge from a side alley on a jewelled white horse. There you were, the greatest usher of them all, in a brilliant suit of gold epaulettes, braid and buttons, a sword in a silver scabbard touching your horse's perfect flank, the feather in your turban nodding with the gait of the animal. They stopped and looked at you for an instant, parted for you to go through, then went on with their lives.

"Today I saw the greatest usher in the world, on a horse of di-

amonds and emeralds and rubies, and I will never forget him,''
they are saying around their fires.

Within a week, the news of your presence would be known
throughout India, having travelled through the enormous family
networks, from the big cities and out to the smallest villages, as
far away as Jaipur, Trivandrum, Srinagar, where the lines pe-
tered out. This tightly woven net of voices that covered the whole
country.

"The usher is coming," they are saying, then simply
"usher", and await your arrival with each travelling cinema
show. How easy it would be for you to become a god here, in a
country of so many gods.

It was later, when I met Donald T. Nigli, at Fisherman's
Cove, south of Madras, that I became even more hopeful.

We had gone there to relax. There was nothing there but a resort, a beach, a small village and fishing boats on the sand. And
there was a temple, sitting on a finger of sand facing the Bay of
Bengal, its elephants and gold leaf shaved by the wind and salt
air.

The resort lift played "Jingle Bells", day and night, every day
of the year. The tune was so loud we could hear it from the
beach, or the verandah of our waterfront cabin, called Pompa-
dour Eleven, the number on the door poised in the mouth of a
rainbow-coloured fish.

On the afternoon we arrived, we made love on the white
sheets, beneath the ceiling fan, and were constantly interrupted
by a stream of drink waiters, cleaners, beach security guards.

"A drink for you, madame and sir?"

"New towels for you."

"We are on guard twenty-four hour, sir, for your safeness."

"Two Kingfisher beers for you and madame as welcome."

We held each other and giggled uncontrollably, feeling the in-
tense heat through the walls and glass of the cabin.

Later, we strolled down the beach. Fishermen offered to take
us out to sea along with a dozen children, but I did not like the
dangerous curve of their boats. So we sat and looked for you
from shore. Nothing, except for the bobbing heads of large Rus-
sian women floating up and down with the waves.

One morning, sitting alone on the beach except for the armed security guard in his beret and jungle greens, who also doubled as a lifesaver, I saw a man in a grey suit and sandals emerge from behind the temple. He stepped over the fishing nets, the driftwood, the fresh piles of human shit, and stood at the end of my towel, smiling, his hair heavily oiled, carrying a folder under his arm.

"Kind sir, you are the journalist?" he asked.

I sat up, surprised, and said, "I am, yes."

"I am Donald T. Nigli. I have some of my poetry that I would like for you to read and pass a judgment on, if you would be so kind."

There, on my towel of the Australian flag, I leafed through his work, *Kal,* grains of sand sprinkling across the television sets and wardrobes and music machines of his dreams. The death of his wife and child, his mother and father. His carnal exploits with the prostitutes of his village. He stood with his hands behind his back, despite my offer to share the towel, and looked at me with such anticipation that I felt the weight of being his conduit to the rest of the world. After ten minutes of reading he had moved a little closer, his toes curled over the edge of the Union Jack. The Southern Cross remained beneath me.

"They are very good," I said. "You have been to all these places that you write of?" Central Park in winter. The Tower of London and its black ravens. A discotheque in Hamburg.

"At night with my friend, sir, I go into town and we watch the television in the store window. This is where I have seen all these things."

He gave me a photograph of himself, his wife and his child, the little girl on a wooden pot plant stand in a studio somewhere in Madras. He was wearing the same suit, too short in the legs with wide and soiled lapels. His wife was barely half his height.

He continued to stand for an hour, longer, and we talked.

"Let me tell you, sir, your father is not dead, as my wife and baby girl are not dead too. They are with us always. The soul is immortal and the family never-ending, that is what you must believe." He told me he applied make-up daily to a large photo-

216

graph of his wife that he had in his bedroom. He wanted her to always look beautiful.

"My father had a cinema," I told him, for no reason, and then he sat down on the end of the towel.

"Oh, I love the movies," he said, smiling, and told me he went to the cinema at least six times a week, often to see the same film. He loved to sit and watch the billboard artists paint their giant advertisements for the latest blockbuster. It was thrilling, he said, to see the great actors emerging three metres tall, in cowboy outfits, or with their chests crossed with brass bullets, or pointing their guns across the streets.

He hitched a ride on the back of a bullock cart, or borrowed a bicycle, or walked if he had to, to the cinemas of Madras, thirty-seven kilometres away.

"Sometimes when I get home I feel it is time to go back again."

He had just seen the latest hit, *Gone with the Wind*, which he wanted to see at least three more times. Very sad and beautiful. He had clipped his moustache meticulously in the fashion of Rhett Butler.

Everyone, he said, was waiting for *Fantasia*. It was due any day.

I told him I had planned to go to Agra on the way back to Delhi, and he told me that I had to visit the Dayal Bagh Temple.

"It is not far from the Baghwan Cinema," he said. "The Anjana Cinema is there too. Next to the Shah Cinema. It is a very good place for cinema. The Dayal Bagh will be more important for you than the Taj Mahal. That is my advice to you. Make that your last visit in India is what I am saying to you."

"Why?"

"You will see," he said. "Taj Mahal is beautiful, yes, but it is dead. It is a big gravestone. A headstone, is that the right word?"

He stood and took back his sheaf of poems.

"What is *Kal*?" I asked him.

"In English," he said, "it means, I think, yesterday and to-morrow."

* *

217

One couple had taken their caravan to Brisbane and backed it up onto the footpath outside Parliament House, but the protest had little effect.

The woman had time to tie a makeshift clothesline to the wrought-iron colonial fence and hang a few dry clothes but a tow truck had been ordered in shortly after, taking the car and caravan away, firing wooden pegs into the air and leaving a pair of underpants on a Government rose bush.

Down at the Oceanic Baths the permanents held regular strategy meetings and made up placards with their children's paint sets. But when the cyclone fencing was erected around the park and the perimeter of the Universe-Cine-by-the-Sea they appeared to lose heart.

Although a makeshift gate beneath the neon dolphin remained open, they felt the Government, by erecting the fence, had deliberately made them a spectacle, and cut them off from the rest of the community.

"People gawk at us now through this damned fence," one man said. "We are like animals in a zoo. They come and take pictures of us."

The fence had brought attention to them. Marked them out. They could not go to the shower blocks in the afternoon without being whistled and jeered at. They suffered laughter and abuse as they ate their dinners in the annexes.

"We're made to feel poor. Scum of the earth. We never felt poor before," a woman was quoted as saying.

Aldermen, engineers, businessmen and other observers inspected the park several times each week, sketched designs in the air with pointed fingers, took notes, kicked the dust of the laneways, nodded, smiled.

It took little time for the whole organised fabric of the Oceanic to collapse. Soap holders in the shower blocks were snapped off by vandals unknown. Graffiti appeared on the walls of the manager's office, and in some cases, on the sides of tents and vans. Cars were stolen. Washing machines and dryers were sabotaged and looted. The blue neon dolphin exploded spectacularly one evening, pieces of the fish tinkling onto the road. The police did not bother to investigate.

218

"There is no order because we have no future anymore," the manager said.

With only a few permanent residents remaining, the Government erected a billboard at the front of the Oceanic, fashioned by a team of eleven signwriters, three electricians and a supervisor.

It was the most extraordinary billboard anyone had ever seen. It covered two hundred square metres, and consisted of eight separate sections. It was held up by four concrete pylons, large enough to support a small bridge. It displayed 7,120 words of facts, figures and other data. Embedded in its surface were full-size neon tubes, fairy lights and a twenty-four hour digital display that carried the news headlines of the world, all controlled and sequenced by computer. Above it, five steel arms holding yellow mothproof bulbs curved like a wave.

The painting of the future of Burleigh Heads bluff was stunning. The viewpoint for the signwriters was one of considerable altitude, a few hundred metres up, offshore and fairly accurate considering they were working from the scaffold of their imaginations. They captured the beach perfectly, the colour of the sand, the drainage pipes and basalt columns. The grass beneath the pines was perhaps too vibrant, too neat, free of crushed milk cartons, beer cans, the odd condom in the weeds. And their sky was beautifully clear, ideal, fading closer to the top of their work of art.

In the picture, however, the Oceanic Baths did not exist. Where the mermaids had stood, holding up the small building's roof, was a boulevard of zigzag brick, winding its way through hoop pine and palms. Couples in vivid trousers and shirts, lime green bikinis and pink saris, strolled hand in hand, enjoyed drinks above the boulders, and shared an ice-cream and conversation on wooden decking that extended out over the rock pools.

The Universe-Cine-by-the-Sea had also been erased. In its place was a majestic terraced garden, stemming from several marble pillars, spilling down towards the beach, the steps, at least fifteen of them, dense with exotic tropical foliage. Down the centre of the garden were pools dropping into other pools, larger each time, and into a grand pool, bracketed by two escalators protected by clear plastic canopies. In between these, rising half a metre alone on the billboard, was a statue of Neptune, his beard in curling bronze down to his waist, a trident gripped in his right hand.

Neptune's Casino. A five hundred and twelve room, five-star international class hotel. Fifty-three blackjack tables. Twelve roulette wheels. Two two-up rings complete with spectator seating and referee high-chairs. Twenty-four hour licence. Three convention rooms, indoor and outdoor swimming pools, sauna and spa facilities, gymnasium, three astro-turf tennis courts and a squash court. A la carte restaurant, bistro and oceanside eatery, discotheque, thirty-one specialty shops, in-house masseuse, beautician and hairdressing salon.

The billboard showed each beachfront room of the twenty-five storey hotel occupied. The locals who gathered on the sidewalk, some with foldout canvas chairs as it took so long to read the sign's finely printed data, could only imagine what was going on in the well-lit rooms, the small bulbs burning bright then dimming, turning off and on like bedside lamps with minds of their own. These were the rooms of their dreams.

The part of the complex that would house the casino was most alluring. It resembled the pointed canopy of an enormous smoked glass tent, attached to the face of the hotel, draping down and out to the edge of Burleigh beach and only metres from the sand. The electricians had installed the neons on the surface of this canopy, equally spaced and synchronised, switching on and off from top to bottom, surging up and down, so that the pyramid appeared alive and moving. According to the Architect's Note in the left-hand corner of the billboard, the lights were to be a symbol of the never-ending crash and retreat of the ocean's waves against this "island continent of ours".

In the left-hand corner was the all too familiar face of our Premier, his picture floating like a raft on the signwriters' sliver of ocean, above the currents that claimed T. Nelson Downs. The great man's face, tinted and airbrushed to perfection, was ruddy-cheeked from the onshore breezes. But trusting. As trusting as ever.

"My fellow Queenslanders," the note below the raft told us. "We will be the envy of the world. This magnificent achieve-

220

ment will put us at the forefront of international tourism. Yet another step towards making this State great.''

What does the man look like from your side, Father? Can you see behind that crusted paint? That perpetual smile? Why did it take us so long to understand what he was doing to our lives?

In the expansive Agra Ashok Hotel we were introduced to one of India's foremost film producers and his latest screen beauty. They had just returned from filming in the mountains of Gulmarg. He wore Levis and a T-shirt that read, The Met, New York.

"Yes, your father would like it here," he said, sipping thick black coffee then crossing his legs. "To my people, the cinema is a religion. The cinemas, I think, are like the temples."

His ravishing star just smiled at us.

"Because our temples, you understand, are small versions of the whole world. I am not sure if you understand, but we believe that the real world, the earth, is one giant temple of God. So the temples that we have built, so many temples, are all meant to be little worlds. Little wombs of divinity."

He was stroking his star's leg. Some hotel staff had gathered on the other side of the foyer and were pointing at them and whispering. A manager hustled them away.

A Sikh wedding, due to commence any minute, had been delayed as a baby elephant had run amok in the grounds of the hotel. Waiters were chasing it, swinging their coats above their heads. Through the rear glass doors we could see the elephant standing stubbornly in the child's wading pool. Several men were trying to push it out of the water, but it refused to move. Out the front, the rickshaw drivers were rocking back and forth on their pedals, waiting for the groom to appear on his white horse. We could hear the sharp blare of trumpets, heralding his arrival, and the shriek of the defiant baby elephant.

"What a marvellous thing," the director said, looking to the elephant. "Anyway, when a movie star dies in India, the death is mourned as much as that of a prime minister or head of state.

This is true. Everybody mourns the movie star. Nobody can believe such a death.

"But back to the temples. I know foreigners are greatly interested in the temples. The towers are the most important, you see, as they are filled with the gods and men and women and animals and plants of the earth. And they are built to represent the sun and the planets orbiting around the sun.

"So we come back to our cinema, and on our screens we must put in everything, the plants and animals and people. It is what our people want, you see. They want it all in the cinema."

"You must make long films," I said. The elephant was lashing out with its trunk and tail.

"Some are very long. Epics," the director said, lighting a Marlboro. "We will film next at the Taj. The romantic part of our film, because the Taj is the great symbol of immortal love. Do you think so?"

"Definitely, yes."

"That's good," he said, holding up his empty coffee cup which was attended to instantly.

"You have seen Fatehpur Sikri?"

We had been there by bus that morning. The abandoned red stone citadel of the Akbar. I had photographed a group of Indian children diving repeatedly into the Chamber of the Peerless Pool. The water was emerald green.

The groom had arrived now, alighted from his horse, and the men of his family and the bride's formed a circle on the driveway of the hotel. The two crescents of men faced each other and, systematically, one male was paired with another, and they met in the centre of the circle, hugged each other, lifted each other off the ground to the screams of the crowd, and stuffed rupee notes into each other's pockets.

"You would have heard of the pachisi game," the director said, sweeping the hair off his forehead dramatically. "They say that Akbar and his cronies stood in the towers and played this game with naked virgins as their pieces."

We had stood in the chessboard-like courtyard.

"Fatehpur is not as popular with the Indian people as the Taj because the Taj is a monument to love. But Akbar, he had hun-

222

dreds of women. Do you know why they abandoned it? Because of the water. They could not get enough water into the town. This is true.''

"There is a permanent community still there though,'' I said.

"Yes, you're right. They are all relatives of the mystic Shaikh Salim Chishti. He promised Akbar three sons, which was wonderful news for the emperor. He built a shrine for Chishti's family. It is the sixteenth generation that lives there now. They are the only ones.''

"Sixteen.''

"That's correct. I am tantalised to do a film on them.''

A small boy with oiled hair had led me by the hand to the top of the wind tower. He held my forefinger, climbing steps almost too steep for him, and stood panting at the top, his hand extended.

"Many of the children there have twisted limbs,'' I said. The elephant was spraying the waiters now with the pool water. I saw the manager stride quickly through to the pool with a rolled up copy of the *Times of India* and what appeared to be a painted mask in his hand.

"It is the tragedy of India,'' the director said, lighting the cigarette of his star with a Zippo lighter. "Their legs are broken at birth and they live their life as beggars. It is the tragedy of the monuments. In my opinion, the monuments have created the beggars.''

The wedding party had moved into the reception room now, each guest bearing a thumbprint of crushed rose petals on their foreheads.

The baby elephant had vanished. The waiters were dabbing themselves with towels.

The graders and trucks worked day and night in those first few months to beat the cyclone season. The special floodlights were so powerful that dozens of surfers rode the waves off Burleigh bluff into the early hours of the morning.

When the pile drivers began operation, the entire population within a kilometre radius of the site went without decent sleep, suffering lethargy and irritability. It was as if the whole area was dictated by these booming metronomes, rattling time with their monotonous poundings.

Later, apartment blocks less than five years old were demolished with explosives to make way for Neptune's, the plaster and brick folding in on itself, bringing down with it metal cut-out sea horses, starfish, hibiscus flowers and horsemen that presided above the penthouse suites. A pale cloud of dust hung over the bluff, visible from Coolangatta in the south and Surfers Paradise in the north.

It was as if a giant monster, asleep for thousands of years beneath the bluff, had been disturbed and was groaning itself awake.

Our tour guide told us as we approached Dayal Bagh Temple that to the right, between the silversmith and the bicycle store, was the shop of Babu Khan, Hair Dressing Artist, who once, in one of the big hotels in Delhi, cut the hair of President John F. Kennedy from America, as well as the Ministers of India, local screen idols Dilip Kumar and Sunil Dutt, and international celebrity Kirk Douglas.

An American couple wanted to stop and take a photograph of the famous salon, but we drove on to the temple.

"This is it?" one of the Americans said. "This is the rival to the Taj Mahal?"

From the street the temple was not unlike an English cathedral, its grubby and chipped front stairwell fanning down into dirt. Its huge columns of intricately carved white marble and its polished arches were unremarkable. The whole structure sat heavily in a confusion of mud, abandoned tools, weed, rotting rope, cow dung, bits of machinery, shelters and the broken toys of the street sellers. One of our group found a small, filthy red coat with gold cotton trimming that our guide assumed had once belonged to a dancing monkey.

Walking up the front stairs the intricate work of the temple builders became more clear: the black and white onyx, the variegated agate, the red carnelian and yellow chrysolite of the ornamental roses and poppies.

"Attention please," our guide said at the top of the stairs.

"They have been working on this temple for more than two hundred years. As you can see, they still have no roof." She attempted a laugh at this.

The four side walls of the building were virtually complete. There was indeed no roof, but the inside of the temple was choked with hundreds of pieces of cut wood, all about the same thickness and length, all knobbled and dark, lashed together in a web of scaffolding so thick it was difficult to see through. The wood crisscrossed madly a hundred metres up, as if pulling the walls inward and saving them from collapse. Standing beneath it all and looking up, the sky appeared as a blue mosaic of odd-shaped pieces.

Outside, Father, a man was sitting in the mud polishing a piece of marble that would eventually be pulleyed up towards the nonexistent roof. He was crosslegged, and rubbed the marble back and forth, splashed water and rubbed some more, smoothing ridges, the veins in the marble visible, a vein in his head outstanding, running down from his hairline to between his eyebrows and caked in dust like a deep green root. He never stopped working on the piece and he never looked up, despite the click of cameras.

"This piece here," our guide said, standing beside him, "has taken him many months. He still has weeks before it will be finished."

Clearly this, Father, was not the product of the emperor's purse, nor a memorial to a dead wife, to a place in history, to the understanding, even, of the universe, but something for God, wrenched from the earth by the hands of these men, the tenth or eleventh generation from the original architects and workmen, the people of the streets of Agra. Here were lines of family stretching right back, these rhythmic hands crossing the marble pieces without end, through time, onward and upward into the sky.

* *

The company recorded only one death during the construction of Neptune's Casino — a statistic of which they were most proud.

A twenty-seven-year-old concreter had completed trowelling the upper terrace garden beds when he sat down on the rubber wheel of his upturned barrow to enjoy a cigarette. The company confirmed that he had been wearing his canary yellow hard hat at the time.

Somehow a steel-edged plank had dislodged itself from the perfect grid of steel tube scaffolding up near the seventeenth floor, and silently whistled its way to earth. The accident report said the plank, freakily, had struck the concreter directly upright in the centre of the yellow helmet. Investigators postulated that if the concreter had been looking at his cigarette, his head at an angle, the plank may have glanced off, leaving him at most with a broken neck and collar bone. But it hit plumb on, the unsuspecting worker with his head erect, perhaps looking to the beach and the fineness of the weather, or to women. His head was driven down into his body.

When they found the man his split helmet lay in the dirt. His head, according to the autopsy, was where his stomach should have been. Tobacco grains and a piece of cigarette butt were found in his lungs. Thankfully, the newspapers were told, he died instantly.

Apart from the tragedy, construction went ahead without delay. When Neptune was finally lowered into place by crane, management threw a party for the workers. They drank beer and cooked steaks and sausages on portable barbecues around the bare feet of the green god of the sea.

Some of them drank too much, and assaulted the life-sized mermaids that had been fitted on brass pipes throughout the stepped gardens. They pulled their trousers down and pretended to copulate with the concrete women. They kissed and sucked their slight nipples to the laughter and applause of the others.

"You wanna fuck mine now?" one yelled. "She's got bigger tits than yours, mate."

The following morning the tilers had to clear away hundreds

226

of empty beer bottles and broken glass and cans from Neptune's pool and in the gardens surrounding the mermaids.

"Not a bad do, eh?" one worker said, filling garbage bags with refuse.

"Wait till the real opening," his workmate said. "That'll be a fucking beauty. They're getting Harrison Ford out here, and Kim Basinger. Might even be getting Frank Sinatra to sing."

"You're bullshitting me."

"No bull. They're going to cut the ribbon and shit like that."

"Crap."

"It's going to be the biggest fucking piss-up you ever saw. He was a carpenter once, you know."

"Who?"

"Harrison Ford."

"Crap he was."

They have completed the wooden planking, Father, right out over the top of the boulders and our favourite one, the one we used to fish off, and around the bluff to Tallebudgera. You can't see where the waves surge up around the rocks. The foam doesn't fire up any more either. It's all under the boulevard now.

They've cut all the breadfruit trees away, too, and cleared all the brush up the face of the bluff. They've put netting all over it so no rocks come down and hit the walkers on the boulevard.

In ten days, with the help of the council, they will begin razing the top, peeling it back like a scalp, and lay the foundations for the amusement park. It will be linked to the inside of the casino, so they say, by a monorail train.

They are bringing the giant animals and fruits from Brisbane on the backs of semi-trailers. They will be coming with a police escort in a convoy down the Pacific Highway. First will come the beasts — a black and white dairy cow, a kangaroo, a koala, a merino sheep, a cattle dog and a glider possum. Then the fruits — a pineapple, a banana, an avocado, and a mango.

I have seen photographs of the animals and fruits and they are enormous. The eyes of some of the animals are made of glass. Where their intestines should be are stairwells, and their brains

227

are steel viewing platforms big enough for a party of visitors to look through the retinas to the metropolis of Surfers Paradise, the long white beaches or just out to sea. The fruits are mainly for the children, with interesting cavities, climbing ropes and slippery dip rills.

We are told that when they arrive in Burleigh there will be balloons, streamers, and tickertape fired into the air. A free beach party will be held in front of Neptune's and, in the evening, fireworks will be launched above the bluff, lighting up this strange menagerie.

In the centre of it all, where the rainforest used to be, and the ancient logs and ferns and family of mallee fowl, a giant oyster is to be constructed, its twin shell prised open. And in it, the Premier told us on the television last night, will be the finest seafood restaurant on the planet.

14

It is a different type of grieving when there is no body. You don't have the finality of hearing the clod of earth resound on the coffin lid, or the squeaking rollers as the casket disappears into the furnace. Just a memorial service, and bouquets tossed into the waves, onto that moving, uncertain surface.

Still, Mother goes down to Burleigh beach regularly and scatters rose petals. She follows the same routine. We have breakfast in the Charts Bistro, on the ocean side of Neptune's, with its wide panes of glass, and she takes the two fresh roses from the vase on the table, then plucks the petals and folds them in her lavender-edged handkerchief.

We leave the bistro, and the thorned stems, and walk into the foyer of pyramidal glass, splendidly lit by the early morning sun, and pause reverently before the foyer's centrepiece — a glass cabinet containing, on a piece of maroon felt not unlike the old drapes of the Universe, a piece of rock. A printed card tells us that the rock is, in fact, an axe head. It is pink, and reputedly the earliest example of toolmaking in the history of the world. The card says that it was discovered by ''noted local businessman and amateur archaeologist, T. Nelson Downs, on this site'', which in itself is inaccurate.

We laugh now at the word ''archaeologist''. Every time we read it we nudge each other in the ribs, or put an arm around each other.

''Your father would find that funny,'' my mother always says, or words similar. ''He used it to keep his office door open.''

It's true. For years my father used the precious artefact as a doorstop under the canvas screen of the Universe. My mother fractured her small left toe on it and I used to hold it under running water, when bored, to reveal its colours. But to T. Nelson, the great archaeologist, it was just a doorstop. He would not have even bothered with it if he had not found it in the grip of a tree root, a metre off the ground and grown into the trunk. He found it curious that the tree had, perhaps centuries before, picked up the rock and carried it as a footballer would carry his leather kernel. He had to use a chainsaw to cut it free.

My father did not see that on its own, the stone was nothing. But with the tree it became remarkable. When they probed it, X-rayed it, scraped its surface and discovered its significance, it made little difference. By placing it in the cabinet they too had disconnected it from its history, its stories.

At my father's wake, which was held in the foyer of the Universe before it was destroyed by Neptune's people, my mother presented me with his usher's cap. Unattached to my father the cap — which had been so much a part of him, tilted slightly, resting miraculously on the back of his large head, the rim soaked with his hair oil — became the sum of its parts, a felt-covered piece of stiff cardboard.

If the truth be known, the worth of the pink axe was discovered by chance. We were clearing out the Universe, a laborious and often painful task. I had carried out the Rocky Mountain grizzly on my back, up the centre aisle, through the stripped foyer of dangling electrical wires and into the street to the delivery van. I had placed the bear on the grass of the old promenade, the sweat of my back moistening its stiff old underbelly. In the glare of the sun off the sand its ferocious grimace, its forearms stretched straight out, its yellow claws extended towards the sun-baking topless women, were slightly comic. I saw young surfers pointing to the bear on the edge of the sand. Some waved.

It took two of us to bring out Julius Caesar. I cradled his head, my friend Johnny his ankles, and we righted him next to his companion, the carnivore.

We had been advised that we could take all that we wanted from the Universe, and that anything left would revert to the council. I wanted it all, but my mother reasoned with me and in the end we bundled the contents of the cabinets, the forgotten articles of my country's great men and women, into cardboard boxes. I cut a square from the canvas screen and kept it in my wallet.

I also turned the Universe lights on one last time. The galaxies were patchy, I won't lie, with Orion, the Milky Way, the Saucepan, barely recognisable. I'm sure, Father, you would have viewed the dim universe not as deteriorated, but still evolving, swirling into life, just as a sunset can be confused with a sunrise if you are disoriented.

We completely overlooked the doorstop.

When the truck was fully loaded I walked down across the grass at the far end of the beach and onto the thousands of basalt boulders. You would think, being so old, that the rocks would have settled, but even then, when I stepped across them, they wobbled and clicked against each other like ancient skulls. It was necessary to look down constantly to secure a good footing, but after a few minutes of this it was difficult to maintain balance.

I imagine this is what happened to you. That you had made your way through these ruins, deluded by their weight and size and, like myself, found the whole area moving, the pillars alive with their grouting of shells, molluscs, pebbles and sea water and, with the aid of a worn sole, been tipped into the ocean, a giddy usher.

"He left the cinema at about 3.17 p.m. I would say," my mother recalled. "I know it was that time because he had asked me. If it had been 3.16 p.m. or 3.18 p.m. he would not have left. You know what he was like about even numbers. He said he was going for a walk and would be back in time to switch on the Universe and farewell the customers."

"How did he appear to you?"

"He was tired. Yes, plainly tired after everything that had happened. He wasn't sleeping well. Hadn't been for some weeks. He wasn't himself."

"In what way?"

"You know what your father was like. The eternal optimist. Those silly jokes of his, you remember? Those little facts he remembered and bored us with. I don't know where he picked them up from. One minute he'd be talking about craters on the moon and the next about cannibals in Borneo. Date growing in Egypt. All that rubbish. I don't need to tell you.

"Remember the fence posts out west that he went on about? How they'd been so fanatic in the early days about clearing and fencing the land that they made the posts out of red cedar? Beautiful red cedar to keep the sheep in. He never got over that one.

"And the things he'd pick up," she said. "Remember that monstrosity he bought over on Fraser Island? It gave me the willies."

"The famous orange-haired mermaid. Whatever happened to that?"

"It was the most revolting thing I'd ever seen. It had things living in it."

"A fish with a spider monkey's head sewn onto it."

"Don't remind me. He kept asking for it. 'Where's the mermaid, Lole? You seen that mermaid of mine?' He never found out what I did with it."

"What were his last words to you?" I asked.

"You know I wish I could remember. I wish more than anything I could remember but I can't. It just . . . it just doesn't occur to you that someone will never come back. Does it?"

"The usher? I remember that day, yes."

"You were swimming . . ."

The old man leaned forward in his canvas chair. His wife came out with a pot of tea on a tray. The lips of the cups were circled with glazed roses.

"You remember him, don't you, Gladys? We swim the same time every day. There were a lot of jellyfish that day if I remember correctly. Is that right, Mum? Lots of jellyfish?"

"Lots of them, yes. Milk?"

"We were coming in, that's right, and we saw the fellow over on the rocks."

"You actually saw him?"

"Sugar, dear?"

"Yes, I remember clearly he was wearing a suit and I thought he was a bit odd, you know, to be wearing a suit down on the beach. We thought it was a bit strange, didn't we Mum?"

"It was a bit strange."

232

"Are you sure you saw him? He would've been hard to see amongst the basalt I would imagine."

"No, no, no. He stood out like a sore thumb. We swam for a little while and didn't think anything of it. It was rough that day, very rough. The red flag was up, you know, that's how bad it was, but we like our swim. We swim every day, you know. It was the jellyfish, though . . ."

"A good friend of ours . . ."

"...died after he got stung by one of those bluebottle things. Had a heart attack. Terrible it was, big red welts across his chest. Anyway, we remember him every time we see the jellyfish."

"Just dropped dead on the beach. A biscuit?"

"We saw this fella, your dad's, hat on the beach, like, when we were drying off. We didn't put the two together, see. Not until later. We sat there for a while, you know, like we always do, and we couldn't see the man, the one in the suit. Thought he might have gone around the point or something. Then it clicked, see, and we thought we'd better tell someone."

"The lifesaver was still there, wasn't he, Roy, so we told him."

It was late and I could hear the creak of the rainforest behind their house, at the edge of the Burleigh reserve.

"The army used to train there, just down there, for the war," the old man said. "Long time back. They used to drag the cannons along the beach and fight each other in the dunes. You could hear them screaming and mucking around. Bit silly when you think about it." He stood and put his hands on the verandah railing. "Be a shame to leave. Been here fifty-six years. But they gave us a good offer."

"An offer?"

"Real good offer. You have to think of your grandchildren, don't you?"

"Neptune's?"

"How much did we pay for this joint, Mum? Ninety pounds? One million dollars they're giving us. One million dollars."

"That's a lot of money."

"And life membership to the casino. Not bad, eh? Fancy a couple of silly old buggers like us being millionaires, eh?"

233

They both laughed. I noticed their saggy rubber bathing caps on the hat rack just inside the front door.

"We had all trawlers placed on alert, yes," the station sergeant said. He lit my cigarette with a bone-handled pistol lighter.

"Got it for Christmas."

"Very nice," I said. "That was after the helicopter sweeps, was it?"

"Correct. The police helicopter covered a grid of roughly three square kilometres."

"Just one helicopter?"

"That was all we had available."

"You mean you had others?"

"Correct. Our second was operational in Brisbane."

"Doing?"

"From the best of my recollection, we had to rush a Minister of the Crown to emergency surgery. To Royal Brisbane Hospital."

"That was the incident with the Racing Minister?"

"That's correct. He was rushed from the racecourse with severe abdominal pain."

"Food poisoning was it?"

"Off the record? It was a plate of oyster kilpatrick in the members enclosure."

"The government helicopter was not available?"

"Correct. It was being used to take the Premier home."

"The trawlers came up with nothing?"

"Negative, that's right. A good school of tailor were running, apparently, but nothing else."

"You resumed the search the following morning?"

"At first light. We thought we had a sighting but it was nothing."

"A sighting?"

"Correct. Let me check the report here. Yes. A local boatie reported an object, possibly a body, travelling south at roughly two knots off Tweed bar."

"You found it?"

234

"Yes, we recovered a fully clothed shop dummy."

"I'm sorry?"

"Female, 178 centimetres. Wearing a red evening dress."

"You're kidding."

"I'm not. We were unable to trace the owner so it went to auction."

"That's a bit strange, isn't it?"

"It's a strange world, sir."

The official inquest into T. Nelson Downs lasted exactly ninety-seven minutes.

The finding was that Mr Downs had been the victim of unseasonal king tides, and that his presumed death by drowning would have been aided by the encumbrance of his usher's suit, particularly with the vest buttoned as he was last seen. It was ruled Death by Accident.

The story of the pink axe was told in the Annette Kellermann Memorial Ballroom of Neptune's Casino. It is a remarkable room by any standards, with solid cedar ten-metre high walls and four modern square chandeliers. A sepia picture of Kellermann, our country's first world class swimmer and nick-named the Australian Mermaid, hangs above the ballroom entrance.

The film based on her life, *Neptune's Daughter*, had been viewed by my father dozens of times. He knew Esther Williams' every move, and still roared at Red Skelton each time he saw it. He liked to imagine he was Red, and contorted his face in a similar fashion. I like to think of my father singing "Baby It's Cold Outside" to keep himself warm, treading water out there, missed by the rescue beam of the helicopter by a matter of centimetres each time.

He had once travelled to Sydney for the auction of Kellermann's personal possessions: her eighteen fans made of silk, ivory and mother of pearl, three wine goblets, a porcelain jewellery box, bronze and silver inlaid knives, and gramophone records autographed by Al Jolson and Lucille Ball.

He made a bid for her daring one-piece swimming costume that led to her arrest on a Boston beach in 1907, but lost it to Kellermann's granddaughter who had come to reclaim some of the belongings.

My father did manage to buy one fan, and brought it home in an old trumpet case he had bought especially to keep it safe from the bumps and knocks of train travel.

He took great delight in spreading the fan for the upper stall guests before screening *Neptune's Daughter*. "That's right, folks. The actual fan of Annette Kellermann. No touching please."

Somehow, and we still have no explanation, the pink axe head found its way into the trumpet box along with the fan; the fragile, exquisite workmanship with the rock beside it.

As it turned out, *Neptune's Daughter* was also one of Mayor Wilson's favourite films. He was the only other person, apart from my mother, to handle the fan and expose its mother of pearl in the light of my father's stars.

"Magnificent," he told T. Nelson. "The tail of the mermaid, eh?"

In her grief, and unaware of his betrayal before the Fern Inquiry, my mother had given the trumpet box to the mayor who had to turn away from her and stand by the window of his chambers, so touched was he by the gesture.

"He would have wanted you to have it, Bart," she said, the sullen mayor with the box in his hands, his head down.

He opened it later and, to his surprise, discovered the rock. He thought, he told the congregation in the ballroom, that the rock had belonged to Kellermann, the famous water acrobat. He theorised that she may have used it in her act, as a weight perhaps, to assist in her rehearsals. He also pondered that the rock may have come from that Boston beach where she had shocked fellow bathers with the brevity of her costume.

He kept the smooth-faced rock on his desk as a paperweight, he told the enthralled crowd, when one day a council engineer and amateur geologist had spotted the pink rock and asked of its origins.

"It belonged to the Australian Mermaid," the mayor had told him. The crowd laughed here.

"But as it turned out," he said beneath the giant chandeliers, "that paperweight, that piece of useless rock that broke the toe of the wife of the dear departed, is the oldest known example of a man-made tool in existence."

I can see the axe head in the foyer of Neptune's from my harness, up near the inner peak of the pyramid of glass. It is tiny from this height. But just before 9 a.m., for about thirty seconds, with the tank of window cleaner gurgling on my back and the sponge on a stalk attached by a chain to my belt, I can look down and see the sun hit the cabinet and the quartz in the rock, and it glows like a cartoon heart.

15

He still tells the story — as if I wasn't there sitting before him, sipping a beer — of the afternoon he pulled the groom over the edge of his trawler and onto the deck of prawns and Spanish mackerel and chunks of ice. And of the white carnation still in place in the upper left buttonhole of the groom's suit.

"And you know the first thing you said to me when we'd thawed you out a bit?" he always roared, as he would for the rest of our lives. " 'Are they running today?' Can you believe it? Are they fucking running today!"

"And you said, 'the church is that way, son'," pointing to the emerging lights of Neptune's and the silhouettes of the menagerie on the bluff.

That was the day I met Ted Waterstone, trawlerman. I first saw him and his enormous beard upside down, the prawn whiskers catching on my hired suit, the medallions of ice under my back. His puckered nets were the most beautiful veils swooping down from the ship's rigging. He was nonplussed at his most unusual catch.

"The best sized groom I ever caught," he always joked. "Eighty-five kilograms of pure groom."

That is how I came to be married in a pair of Ted Waterstone's old overalls, faded, frayed at the cuffs, collar and pocket edges, with the faintest perfume of seafood about them.

Ted and his wife Susan, their trawling schedule already ruined, had taken me in to shore and accepted my invitation to the wedding. From the mooring at Tallebudgera Creek we walked back around the bluff to the white church where Andrea was waiting. I could see the tears through her veil, like the water on Ted's nets, and we embraced and held hands.

"Explain later," I whispered to her as the priest prepared the Eucharist and the wine. Then we both broke into laughter and soon the entire congregation was applauding, my suit strung up and drying on the back of Ted's trawler, my hair still wet. It was the happiest day of my life.

Years later our daughter Gabrielle would ask why her father wore a dirty boiler suit to his wedding. Why he looked like a mechanic, a builder, an electrician, a cleaner, a road ganger, or a fisherman, who had just strolled into the official ceremony and taken his place next to the bride. Why were my sleeves rolled up, as if ready to begin a day's labour, looking silly holding a glass of champagne?

"That was my first day at work," I told her.

She would just shake her head at this, touching me in the photographs with her fingertips, searching for the real groom.

"That is really him, Gabby," Andrea would say. "That is your father."

To be honest, I cannot be sure if I slipped, as you did on those rickety boulders, or whether I deliberately joined you in that current that I knew would be there, despite its tip covered by the boulevard of timber. That was one thing they couldn't destroy.

I was hit by a sudden coldness that cut straight through my black coat and trousers, my white ruffled shirt and even the hide of my shoes. I was immediately picked up by the current. It was so strong it smoothed the surface of the sea. It was roughly five metres across, a placid band, a new road, bordered by choppy waves and puffs of spray.

I showed no panic, let me tell you. Not even at the fingers of the current playing with my legs which were already cramping. Not even as I saw the abandoned ice-cream cart on the boardwalk, the snaking of the monorail, a couple walking in the afternoon breeze, get smaller and smaller. Did they see me, the soaking head of the groom, being whisked out to the horizon?

I could have yelled for help but I did not feel helpless. I had never felt more clear-minded in my life. I swear. The whole ocean was embracing me. I was the dear friend of shark and seahorse. The glass cone at the entrance to the casino, too, looked beautiful, the waves of neon so alluring, tempting. I could hear their clicking, even with ears full of sea water.

Objects brushed my legs and arms. But I could not be harmed

here, with you, my arms out to my side, the giant green Neptune looking over me.

I felt protected by the gaze of the bluff animals as well, their glass eyes glowing from the security lights inside their heads. I could see the giant oyster filled with diners, unfolding napkins and sipping wine, toasting me out at sea. You'll be all right, boy.

I felt so close to you. I had broken through that globe that surrounded you, not intended to keep me out, as I suspected until now, but one you had spent your life trying to smash out of.

My hands pruned quickly in the water. I could feel my skin tightening all over, puckering like gathered material. I swallowed water when it should've been champagne. It didn't worry me though. Not at all. I had come to tell you a few things on this day, my big day. To explain matters, but to ask some advice for the first time. Just between you and me. Father and son.

Mayor Bartholomew Wilson, on the eve of his election to State Parliament, his pockmarked face on every light pole, bus shelter, construction site hoarding and roadside tree in the region, had his career obliterated by a new set of golf clubs.

Let me tell you about it. Where it all began. Where it always begins, in those wood-panelled chambers across the nation. The world for that matter. The smallest, most overlooked chambers of power.

After the good mayor evicted you, Father, and erased the old caravan park, the baths, the Universe, it all came down to those silver-headed golf sticks. He was keen on the game, you know that. When he was a councillor, you would both hit balls off the bluff and out to sea, just for practice.

"Down the middle of the fairway!" Wilson shouted after his whistling Red Dot. "Right down the 'ole guts." And the children were out there with diving masks on, bobbing under the waves like starving egrets in search of the balls that they later sold back to you both, to your amusement.

That's how the tendering of the Neptune was sealed, on real grass fairways. The company delegation applauded Wilson's every hack, flying divot, wave of bunker sand and crooked putt.

Find a man's pleasure and you find his weakness. They got him all right. He was the last barrier. The entire machine had been put into place, down to the last doorknob and goldfish faucet. It was Wilson, with the tin chains around his neck, falling asleep beneath the Queen, farting occasionally into his cream vinyl mayor's chair, who was the last hurdle. A set of Arnold Palmer specials and he was theirs.

The Government intended to reward him as well, of course. They had promised him a seat in Parliament. That's how they all got rewarded. Once there, the possibilities were limitless. It was an open cheque. Limousines, chartered aircraft, restaurants, overseas travel. Free golf balls for life. They'd give him his own suite in the Parliamentary Annexe — the Taj Mahal — overlooking the Brisbane River, the site of the World Exposition, the hills and the television towers from which, on occasion, his face would be beamed into tens of thousands of living rooms.

They would not forget how well he handled you, Father. How he dealt with the madman of the coast. You had flown outside their control and were on the brink of discovering the truth about us all. But Wilson had fixed it. Leave it to Wilson.

All it took were a few too many beers in the clubhouse, a bit of bragging, a bit of tomfoolery, and the spark became a flame, became a fire that burned the whole thing down.

When people from other parts of the world ask me how the web of lies, deceit, corruption, theft, blackmail, pay-offs and evil in our police, judiciary, local government and parliament was finally revealed I say this — it all started with a sand wedge. That's all I need to say.

I could see it all from out there. I was warmed by their tiny fires and heard their laughter. They gathered around the flames, telling story after story. The voices went on for so long they were part of the waves rushing up on the sand and gurgling over the rocks.

The dolphins were their trawlers back then. They herded the fish in for them. Ushered them into traps. The men stood in the surf and beat the water with sticks, manoeuvring the dolphins and rewarding them later with some of the catch.

Such beautiful stories.

I undid the buttons of my vest so I could stretch my arms out comfortably and drift, my wedding ruffles wavering like useless gills. I managed a laugh at the thought of my underpants, festooned with small sailors wearing caps, their arms apart just like mine.

What overwhelmed me was the sky. With my head back there was nothing but the constellations, so brilliantly clear but deep, deeper than yours, Father, layer upon layer. It was the deepness that was more frightening than the water I was floating on top of. It got darker as I was carried further away from Neptune's. From the muffled chatter of diners feasting on fresh lobster and fish, pinching thighs under tables, drawing languorously on cigarettes, a short ride away from their fortunes, or the promise of sex on the sand, or high up near the stars, the maids finding gambler's chips in the sheets the next morning.

If I lifted my head slightly I could see the galaxies surrounding me in the water, the pinpoint stars beneath my arms, between my open legs, my fingers, and on my sodden boots. Everywhere.

''Father!'' I screamed out. ''Father?''

At the opening night they all stood beneath the glass canopy at the entrance and watched the fireworks explode offshore. A special pontoon, anchored securely off the beach, was the launching pad for hundreds of skyrockets. Even from inside the foyer you could hear the whistling of the trajectories and then the dull thud of the exploding gunpowder. There were red, green and orange flowers, showers of light, crazy whirligigs, giant spheres of stars. It lit all their faces through the glass, including the Premier and his wife, almost the entire Cabinet, Mayor Wilson in a tuxedo fit for a concert pianist, company officials, television celebrities and countless others.

Later, they all walked to the bluff for the official opening of the fun park.

The animals and fruits remained under canvas covers. Despite a fierce wind that attempted to flick the veils from them, the official party and the public had previously been reassured that the animals, in particular, had been made cyclone proof. Their feet were bolted three metres into solid rock, and their hides made of the same noncorrosive, virtually indestructible material used on the skin of the NASA space shuttles. There had been some concern that the winged possum, faced with excessive winds, could take flight and crash into the casino itself. But no. Even the giant fruits had been secured in a similar fashion. There was no need to worry.

On opening night the wind was strong enough to lift dresses and expose petticoats and, in a few cases, no underwear at all. It blew champagne out of glasses. It was impossible to light cigars.

The Premier himself, standing at a special lectern, did not escape the gusts. His hair rose at odd angles, some strands snaking peculiarly upright, oblivious to the constant sweep of his left hand.

As the photographs later showed, our ageless statesman appeared quite mad. His sameness had been his mainstay. He had what previously appeared to be an invulnerable blandness. But at the lectern, it was impossible not to be absorbed by his hair, by the sudden exposure of the shape of his skull, the chiselled bone around his eyes and the sharpness of the jaw. His minders stood behind him, fearing he would take off, at any minute, like a child's balloon.

"So please, every . . . you tonight, celebrate . . . magnificent achievem . . . a tribute to the people of this . . . and for every man, woman and chil . . . future of our great Sta . . . This is what we've bee . . . not just for Queen . . . but for the nation . . . is our country . . . ur future."

With that a helicopter, on cue, appeared from below the bluff and hovered above the crowd, its blue beam darting from side to side, attempting to build excitement, then striking each covered object individually. Frantic staff unfurled wires from each corner of the canvas covers and attached them to a central cable that dangled from the helicopter.

The Premier had ceased worrying about his hair, his skin translucent and deathly in the television spotlights and that of the

243

helicopter, and gave a stiff wave to the pilot. That same wave he had bestowed on leaders of the world, billionaires and truck drivers, to football crowds and even the organist in his local church. With that the chopper lifted into the air and flicked away the canopies.

It was beautifully done. The trick of a master magician. It was the grandest trick of all.

It began to turn around and ease me to one side, the other, and then in a complete circle. I felt as light as air. And strong. I could've swum to the horizon and back.

They would have begun the hymns now. They would be looking more frequently at the door. I know what they are thinking. He has done it to her again. Afraid of responsibility. How could he do it again? Remember when he just vanished? Went around the world? They are singing "Nearer My God to Thee", the sugarcoated bells limp at the end of each pew.

My mother will go up to Andrea. "Are you all right, dear?" she will whisper. "Would you like to go out the back for a while?"

"No," Andrea will say. "He'll be here soon."

I can see the ushers waiting at the front doors, fidgeting, adjusting their cummerbunds, checking their watches.

Suddenly there was light from behind. I heard nothing, but the light traced over me, warm, catching the gold edges of my three false shirt buttons, the eyehooks in my shoes. The beam turned the water a brilliant jade.

It was the same green in the dream of my death. I am in a desert beside a lake and a military helicopter hovers overhead. A man is screaming into a hand-held megaphone but I can hear nothing above the roar of the blades. Then the chopper banks and disappears. In the distance I see a wave of flame stretching right across the horizon, barrelling in on itself, rolling towards me. It is so far off, yet I can still feel its heat. It is booming across the sand, faster and faster, turning everything in its wake to glass.

I run but keep tripping and falling in the sand. I go as fast as I can but it's pointless. I stop, my heart pounding, and stand with my arms apart, welcoming the wave, and it thunders over me. After that I am floating in jade jelly, and around me tumble the objects of my life: shoes, books, watches, an electric fan, old football trophies, a scout hat, coins, glass eyes, toy soldiers, shirts, photographs.

"Father?" I said.

I was pulled from the beam. Plucked clear out of the ocean. I could only see white for a while, then, shrouded by acres of bunched netting, ready to be unfurled, to drag the currents for trash and treasure, the face of Neptune emerged.

When the inquiry was announced by his deputy, the Premier was in Disneyland, Japan, distributing Neptune leaflets, appearing at press conferences next to a styrofoam statue of the green god, posing for photographs with his arm around it, and generally drumming up business.

He arrived back in the country secretly, and was found by reporters and television crews fishing on the edge of a stream on his property.

From the air, Father, his many acres are denuded of most trees and other flora, as are adjoining properties, except for ten square hectares near his back fence line. It is like a velvet patch in a dull calico quilt. It is his personal paradise, which has been written about often enough.

Surely you've read about it, and seen our leader walking through his own rainforest, a man-made glut of cedar and Moreton Bay fig, jacaranda, vine, fern and just about everything else, installed and cared for by Government gardeners. He even ordered them to build a stream, deep enough for catfish, shallow in parts for trout, with couch rolled to its very edge.

Deer roam his private Eden. Wallaby. Kangaroo. Bilbys. Birds were trucked in from all over the State. Black cockatoos, rosellas and others. Two swans glide through the rock pools at the head of his stream. They say even insects were installed.

The entire forest has been enclosed with electric fences, to keep out unwanted visitors, fanatical fishermen, plant thieves, media people. Not to mention cattle and rabbits.

"I have always been in love with nature," he once said. "I know every bird and animal and plant on my property. Ever since I was a boy I loved nature. This is my own little sanctuary and I deserve it, for everything I have done for this State."

With the entire order of our society on the brink of collapse they took photographs of him threading worms onto hooks, sitting on the edge of the water, dangling his feet. He waved to journalists lined up along the electric fence.

"What do you think of the inquiry?" they shouted.

The Premier smiled and waved.

"Did you know about the corruption?"

He put a finger to his lips, gesturing them to be quiet so as not to disturb the fish.

"Are you going to resign, sir?"

When he finally did appear before the commission of inquiry he said he had no idea what had been happening around him. He was as shocked as everyone else.

The inquiry was set down for thirty days. It ran for over a year, probing every government department and institution, from drivers' licence testing centres to the top wigs of the judiciary. From the base of the societal pyramid to the pinnacle. Even you rated a mention, Father, but merely in a statement tendered to the commissioner. The assassination of the usher was there, nonetheless, in bits and pieces.

It became the biggest show since the World Exposition. For all of us it was both revolting and alluring. It was like watching our own vivisection. Painful and bloody. And humiliating. That was the most hurtful thing.

I sat in the public gallery now and then. I saw a young woman reading the history of the Third Reich during boring evidence. An elderly woman knitted three jumpers, seven sets of babies' booties, and a scarf in the colours of her favourite football team during the entire course of the inquiry. I congratulated her on the achievement.

When the Premier appeared as the final witness he was

laughed at, booed by the tiny gallery, jostled in the elevator. He smiled and waved, even in the witness stand.

"I don't think I have anything I can help you with," he said. "Can I go now?"

Sitting inside the giant oyster restaurant next to my wife, I explained that I had lost my planned speech. That I mislaid it on the way to the church, to which I was given a rousing round of applause.

But I had many other things I wanted to tell them. Many matters that my father, T. Nelson Downs, head usher of the Universe-Cine-by-the-Sea, amateur magician and now famous archaeologist, would have wanted to share with them too if he had been able to make it to the reception.

Later, my wife and I stood at the huge windows that held open the shells of the oyster restaurant, and watched a flotilla of trawlers, following each other like a line of elephants connected by trunk and tail, making their way out to sea.

16

T. Nelson Downs had watched the slow progress of the building
of the boat since he was a boy at the Oceanic Baths. By the time
he had come back and taken possession of the Universe, the boat
was still only a skeleton. Its beams were ashen grey from rain and
salt air. And its shape was old fashioned, even though it was a
long way off being launched.

He instinctively looked to the boat, in the backyard of a house
set back from the road at the rear of Burleigh bluff, whenever he
passed. It seemed it had always been there on its rotting brackets
and shaded by banana trees. He had never seen a man working
on it, although if he were to walk down the side of the house and
inspect the vessel, he would find wood planes and chisels in beds
of old shavings, tins of rusted nails joined in clusters, and
fibreglass, unused, as if the boat builders had not known how to
use the material, or whether it could be successfully grafted onto
their old plans.

One Sunday in April, during the screening of *The Greatest Story
Ever Told*, and knowing he had 225 minutes until the final credits, T. Nelson went to visit the owner of the boat.

He left his usher's cap upturned on the seat of his truck and
approached the front stairs. Without thinking, he walked down
the side of the house to the vessel instead, small nettles catching
on the golden braid of his trousers, and stood beneath its airy
bow. He was surprised at its size. It had looked larger from the
road. But he may have always seen it through the eyes of his boyhood, he thought, as a grand vessel of polished wood decks and
brass.

With the hissing of the banana leaves T. Nelson imagined it
already at sea.

"I'm not selling," came a voice through the glass louvres of
the back verandah. The old man had been sitting there all the
time, watching T. Nelson walk around the boat, touch its keel,

bend down and look at the sky where the decking should have been. The old man assumed T. Nelson was from the Navy, possibly an admiral judging by the epaulettes, and most certainly a collector of boats.

The old man got to his feet with difficulty and opened the back flyscreen. He wanted a closer look at the admiral who had wandered into his back yard.

Embarrassed, T. Nelson said, "I'm sorry, I should've asked first."

They met at the bottom of the stairs and shook hands.

"I'm Billy," the old man said. "Billy Wagtail."

"T. Nelson," the usher said, "from the Universe cinema."

"You're not an admiral then?"

"No, I'm not."

"Thought you'd come to take my boat."

The usher laughed. "I get seasick myself. It's just your boat here. It's been here ever since I was a kid."

"Has it been that long?"

Billy Wagtail inspected the bones of the vessel with his visitor. He slapped the frame weakly. His breathing became rapid, and T. Nelson walked him back over to the stairs. The old man's cheeks puffed in and out, the tough whiskers like silver thread against his black skin.

"Always wanted my own boat," he said with difficulty. "Time got away though. Just got away."

As Jesus was crucified on the canvas of the Universe, T. Nelson sat down with Billy Wagtail and shared a pot of tea. Lola later had to guide the audience from the cinema on her own in the absence of the usher, nodded farewells, touched elbows, and put the story of Christ back in its cans.

According to Billy Wagtail, the Hinterland ranges were formed by the Dingo spirit who was carried there by men of the tribes around Burleigh bluff, and placed on the ground to be buried. The land rose up on that spot, and formed the peaks that T. Nelson could see clearly from the roof of the Universe whenever he conducted repairs, or secured tin sheets in the cyclone season.

249

The people were so sad at the death of the Dingo spirit that their tears formed Tallebudgera Creek, which wound its way from the peaks, beneath the blue steel bridge, around the southern side of the bluff and into the ocean.

"A river of tears," Billy said. "Sounds like a country and western song, eh?"

T. Nelson sipped from his tin cup.

"You seen the shells behind the big pines, Nelson?"

"Near the neon dolphin?"

"Sure. My people would come from all over to eat there. From miles away. It was the top place for food, the headland was. Seafood, birds, roo. They'd light their fires and after eating tell their stories and sleep. Food and stories. Food and stories. Then sleep. Especially in April and May, when the mullet came. I love the mullet. The mullet made me want to fish when I was just a little fella."

"You always wanted to be a fisherman?"

"Yep."

They talked of Cannon Rock on the top of the bluff.

"Javreen, you know Javreen?" Billy asked.

"Never met him."

"You know nothing of where you live, Nelson."

"I know about Swain and the mansion."

"No, no," Billy said. "Back. Long time back. Javreen, he brought the boomerang to show everyone. He threw it, over and over, till it hit a tree.

"There were two girls under the tree, okay? They were collecting wildflowers. They took the magic thing back to Javreen. One girl had only white flowers, the other girl had coloured ones, see?

"He was very happy with this, Javreen was. Very happy. He took the girl with the white flowers, see, and made her the moon. He made the girl with the coloured ones a rainbow."

T. Nelson suddenly remembered *The Greatest Story Ever Told* and looked at his watch. It would be close to the resurrection, he guessed. The boulder at the entrance of the cave slightly open, the stone slab draped with white cloth.

"This Javreen," Billy Wagtail continued, "stood where Can-

250

non Rock is. He swam out to the horizon and back. He was very strong, Javreen. When he got back he was very hungry and found some honey. When he finished eating he was full, he ate so much. He was tired, too, after the swim. It was a big swim, even for Javreen.

"So he went to sleep, and where he slept the land rose up and formed the headland."

"Burleigh bluff?"

"That's right, Nelson. That rock they call Cannon Rock is Javreen's fist. You can see the fingers."

T. Nelson wondered when Billy Wagtail had last seen Javreen's fist, tattooed with symbols of anarchy, expletives and phallic drawings done quickly with a spray can.

"He's still there?"

"Sure he is," Billy said.

"You know a lot about this place."

"We go right back, my family, all the way back. This was our place."

"All of it?"

"The Government people, they come down from Brisbane long time ago and give us this bit of land here, see. They give us this and took the rest. That's when I started building my boat.

"They took my mullet spot down on the rocks, you know? I didn't care about this house or nothing like that. They took my mullet spot. I figured, you know, they couldn't take the sea away from me, right? They can't have the whole sea. I could go anywhere in a boat I figured. Anywhere I want. Javreen look after me."

Billy continued with his stories, stroked his beard, drew maps for T. Nelson — plants, rock formations and inlets on butcher paper. Christ, T. Nelson was sure, would be ascending by now.

"There was a beautiful girl, eh, so beautiful," Billy said, relighting the gas ring. "And this boy, he fell in love with her, right here on the headland.

"They were so in love, this girl and boy. But Javreen, he got jealous. He liked the girl too, see. He killed her so the boy couldn't have her. He drowned that girl, just off the rocks."

T. Nelson listened politely. He did not know how to excuse

251

himself. Bats had begun bombarding the banana trees around the boat, chattering and gorging on unripe fruit. Some hung from the vessel's beams and rocked, tucking their leathery wings close to their bodies.

"The boy was so unhappy that he threw himself off the rocks to be with the girl. That's how much he loved her. Javreen, he felt bad. He made the girl into a beautiful water flower. You have seen the purple flowers?"

"I have actually, yes."

"And the reeds around these flowers?"

"Yes."

"That is the boy. Javreen made him the reeds so that they would always be together."

T. Nelson thought that if he did not leave soon he would be in danger of missing the evening feature.

On his way out he invited Billy Wagtail to the Universe cinema, to come whenever he wanted, but the old man complained of poor eyesight and his worsening asthma. T. Nelson wondered if Spencer Tracy in *The Old Man and the Sea* would lure him to the upper stalls. He'd keep it in mind.

There were so many films and so many stories. T. Nelson often wondered if it would be possible to see all the movies ever made in a single lifetime. If a person, made to live in a cinema for an entire life, watching movies continuously and only diverting their gaze for sleeping and eating, could know as much about the world as anyone outside, just from what flickered on the screen.

Billy was exhausted by the time he walked T. Nelson to the front gate. His eyes were teary with the effort.

"You ever going to finish that boat, Billy?"

The old man smiled. "I got to."

"Why's that?"

"My name, Nelson. Billy Wagtail. The rains came so heavy, long time ago, that Wagtail was swept away, into the waterhole. I have to have my boat ready, eh?"

The usher drove off leaving Billy at the gate. The clouds were heavy and he didn't know what to expect.

* *

252

When they knew Billy Wagtail was dying, a team of more than thirty relatives and friends began work on the boat of his dreams.

With the shell of the old vessel virtually useless, they started on a second one beside it. Within a week the two boats sat side by side behind Billy's house, one anchored to weed, the other to fresh sawdust.

Billy sat on the back steps with a blanket wrapped around his legs. He watched the men crawling over and through the new frame, sawing, hammering, polishing, laughing and shouting reports of their progress to the old man as they worked.

He was glad they had not destroyed his old boat. He had sailed it so often in his sleep, and it had been good to him. He had hauled his biggest catches onto its deck, steered it through the most ferocious storms and taken it out to the horizon and back, just for the fun of it.

Even when Billy went to bed, they continued to work under spotlights clamped to the guttering of the house, sanding and polishing in shifts. Even T. Nelson contributed, donating a crate of parts from a dozen ships which he had bought once at an auction and never used — nameplates, bells, railings, rigging and brackets, all salvaged from shipwrecks.

Billy waved T. Nelson over to his bed, which they had brought out onto the back verandah. "It's too big," the old man wheezed.

"What, Billy?"

"The boat."

"Too big? It's the best fishing boat on the entire coast. Nothing but the best for our Billy."

"They'll never be able to get it out."

By the time the men had completed the hull, the point of the bow jutted into the airspace of the verandah. They had had to remove the louvres. The back of the vessel also hung over the sagging back fence and the flue of a neighbour's brick barbecue.

"Should you tell them?" T. Nelson whispered back, "before they get the fibreglass on?"

Billy Wagtail just smiled and shook his head. He watched them working happily between his naps and mouthfuls of oxygen from a small tank.

"Chart desk done, Captain Wagtail!" they yelled to him from inside the boat. "Kitchen sink in, Captain! Storage hold complete, Captain!"

As it neared completion, the men, hazy in clouds of fibreglass dust, their black faces covered in white masks and their arms and upper torsos and legs glittering with tiny shards, their voices muffled inside the boat, reminded Billy of the story of the three turtle hunters who had paddled out in their canoe and been confronted by the Snake.

"Give me a man to eat, as I am hungry," the Snake had ordered the frightened men. They gave the Snake everything they had — turtle spears, rope, baler shells and finally their paddles. The Snake was still not appeased.

They offered the Snake their canoe, convinced they could swim safely ashore. But the Snake was unhappy, and ate the three of them in the canoe.

Their people waited for them to return, and after a day thought the men had landed ashore elsewhere. After two days the tribe began to worry.

Meanwhile, the Snake had gone to a plain where he heard people at their camp, and surrounded them. After eating many people the Snake vomited up the canoe, as well as rope, spears, baler shells and paddles.

The relatives and friends of the turtle hunters got word of this and went to the plain where the Snake rested, unable to move as it was so full of people. They cut the Snake down the middle, killing it, and the people it had just eaten were alive and well and walked out of its belly. But the turtle hunters had already been digested.

In between deeper sleeps, Billy opened his eyes and saw his old boat, its frame brittle and white, as the canoe that had survived the jaws of the Snake. He felt the rains coming. Relentless rains. Yes, they were on their way.

EPILOGUE

The half-pyramid of Neptune's Casino has 372 separate glass panels. At 3 a.m. each Saturday I go into the storeroom and un-pack my rigging gear. I stretch it out on the concrete floor and carefully extend its vibrant yellow and green tendrils in the man-ner of an experienced parachutist, to ensure there is no tangling.

In the quiet of the morning, the fruit machines alight but largely unworked, the green felt flattened by palm and finger oil and, in places, stained with continents of whiskey and beer, I take the lift to the seventeenth floor of the hotel. At this stage I am already strapped into my harness with the wiring strung over my shoulders.

Directly out of the lift, between two potted figs, is a door that reads FIRE HOSE. There is a coiled hose in there, yes, but it also contains a passageway that narrows to a bolted door, for which I have the key. The door swings inward, and opens be-neath the apex of the pyramid that is webbed to the hotel with white canvas.

From above this doorway, attached to a giant ringbolt, are three cables that stretch to earth, parallel with the geometric struts of the pyramid. These cables are especially for me, the pyr-amid cleaner.

To prepare for the job I was sent on a two-week abseiling course in the Hinterland, where I bounced off the volcanic plugs of Egg Rock and Ship's Stern. Of course we did not begin there. Initial training was carried out on the roadside, and in gullys. I felt foolish in my special boots, helmet and gloves, easing my way down the face of three-metre clay banks, crushing baby ferns to the toot of larrikins.

"There is nothing to fear, ladies and gentlemen," our instruc-tor yelled, "but fear itself." He always came out with those sorts of phrases.

Conquering Egg Rock, however, gave me new confidence. I

felt invincible. People commented on how I had changed. How self-assurance radiated from me.

I took to wearing my abseiling gloves while driving, or taking my daughter for a walk in her stroller. I pushed shopping trolleys in them, weighed avocadoes in their leathery palms at the green-grocer's, and, on more than a few nights, made love to Andrea with them on. I was the daredevil mountaineer, after all.

"Why do I need to start so early?" I asked management. At three o'clock in the morning there were few who could see me in my gloves, my boots, my perspex helmet. Only the losers, the in-curable gamblers, their eyes watery and rolling.

"It is the policy with all Level B cleaners," they told me. "Level B staff are not to be seen, or to be seen as little as possible, particularly window cleaners."

They added that to see a man floating in the apex of the pyra-mid could be unnerving, giddying to some guests, even nauseat-ing.

I must admit I have felt this way myself, rocking constantly, steadying against the glass with my aluminium rod and self-moistening sponge, a fine clear hose leading to a small tank of cleaning solution strapped to my back. The rod, too, is attached to me by a safety chain in case I lose my grip. This has happened once without damage. Several droplets of suds struck the Italian marble foyer unnoticed.

Mine is a delicate art. The small panes near the point are easy, wiped over quickly, an accidental streak undetectable from the ground. As I winch myself to earth the panes become larger and require the constant overlapping of the sponge to avoid streak-ing. This consequently necessitates grander, more bold strokes, which leads to the imbalance of the harness.

I have developed a rhythmic system, however, that allows me to use the rigging to my advantage, and employ gravity to assist in more efficient cleaning.

Not everyone appreciates my expertise. "Explain to us again," they ask my wife, "why he did it. His job was so inter-esting. Always interviewing fascinating people. Celebrities. Travelling around. Writing stories. Why did he drop all of that?"

256

"He's still telling stories," she replies. "Now he can tell the true stories. He doesn't mind that he's had to compromise. The telling is the most important thing now."

"What do you mean?"

"Why don't you ask him?"

But they never do. They never ask about the rhythm of the pyramid cleaner. One that is nonexistent at the apex, where the breaths of gamblers and wheeler dealers and hookers and gamblers and politicians collect. As I inch further down the rocking begins, slight, almost imperceptible, and then, near the base, it becomes wild and unpredictable.

When I finally lower myself down to the marble tiles of the foyer it is difficult to walk. I tremble. My arms are tired, my fingers clawed. I have to sit down in one of the plush leather chairs to settle myself.

There is nothing I can do about this. There is no other way to do the job.

I say it over and over and I will say it again. If you wish to clean a pyramid, to make it sparkle, to allow the clouds or the sun or the stars to be viewed perfectly through it, you must start at the top, that powerful point on which its beauty hinges, and work your way down to the base.

Take it from me, that is the only way.

Without fail, Gabrielle falls asleep in the nets before we even get out past the shark barrier. We go trawling with Ted the first Sunday of each month, and by dawn my little girl is curled up on the netting, her blonde curls brilliant against the folds of green.

We steam along flanked by other identical trawlers, part of a grand navy of working vessels, escorted by ribbons of birds that dive and loop and circle the net rigging.

Ted always says you never know what you might find when you trawl. Every sweep is a surprise.

"Nothing escapes a well cared for net, boyo," Ted says in the wheelhouse. "Remember that. You've got to take good care of them. Check them regularly. They're your most important investment."

He changes when he is at sea. He is authoritative, calm, alert, all those things. He squints and stares straight ahead even when the sun is not in his eyes. Even at night.

"It's just me out here," he says. "Me and an engine and the nets. If you look after your engine and your nets, there's no excuse is there? Pure and simple."

"Black and white."

"You got it."

"The truth, the whole truth and nothing but the truth."

"So help me God."

"Ever found a mermaid, Ted?"

"Not yet," he says. "Found plenty else. Chairs. Sandshoe with a foot still in it. Books. A fireman's helmet. Women's underwear. You name it."

"Would it be possible to find an usher out here?"

"Found a groom, didn't I? I would say it was entirely possible."

I have the keys to all the bellies of the beasts on the bluff. I asked for them, and with some reluctance they gave them to me.

"Why do you need to get into the animals? We only want you to clean their outsides."

"Maintenance," I said. "Things will go wrong. They'll require maintenance."

"You are experienced at maintaining animals?"

"Absolutely," I said. They appreciated my enthusiasm. I became the keeper of the bluff. That's how simple it was.

To be honest, it does not take much skill to upkeep a giant cow, merino sheep, koala, kangaroo, sundry fruits. It is a simple matter of blasting them with a high-powered hose and lifting off the salt which automatically returns their natural sheen. As for the windows of their eyes, it is nothing compared to the pyramid. I can buff them from the viewing platform in no time at all. Easy. Takes me an hour, even allowing for excessive human oil from noses or palms. Then I vacuum the carpet that lines their insides, the merino the most time-consuming due to the deep pile. Then

258

I check the bulbs of the concealed lights and my job is virtually done.

But I am more than just the keeper. Oh yes, much more.

The tourists that come to Neptune's, our most valuable asset as the management continually stress, arrive in the bullet-headed monorail shortly after breakfast with their cameras and their accents and their wonder.

While it is not required of me, officially, I greet them at the small rail station, introduce myself, shake hands, and they take me into their confidence. Some still have egg in the corners of their mouths, or toast crumbs, even jam seeds between their teeth, but I welcome them all just the same.

I lead elderly ladies by the crook of their powdered arms, or children by the hand, up the spiral staircases and into the cool carcasses. We stand together on the viewing platforms and look left, up the coast, straight out to the horizon, and right, to the eerie plugs of the Hinterland.

Some have come from the other side of the world to stand in the head of my sheep or cow. From every part of the globe. The locals drop in too.

It makes no difference to me. All that matters is I have them here. It doesn't bother me if they wander off, take photographs, or just stare out through the massive retinas as I talk, ignoring my hand gestures, or the green head and gold cotton beard of Neptune on my sleeves. They're mine. For a brief moment, they're mine.

". . . and after his long swim to the horizon, where the spirit people are wedged, just out there, yes, there, Javreen came back and rested right on this spot. The land then rose up and there used to be, just to your lower right, his bunched fist in the rock . . ."

When it is just Gabrielle and I, early in the morning, sometimes at night, whenever she asks, really, I point things out to her. The car park, yes, that is where the old Oceanic used to be. Where the boomgate attendant's box is, that's right, sweetheart, that's where my daddy and his daddy came for holidays. And where the ice-cream seller is, correct, that's where the mermaids

259

used to be. One day I will just have to point, and she will understand it all on her own.

This is my real job now. My responsibility. I cannot let it drift away from the source. If I have to shout it I'll shout it. The acoustics inside the animals are good, very good. If I have to stand on top of the merino, which is best, the curled horns providing safe footing, then I will. I'll scream if I have to. I'll scream the whole damned obituary of my father.

"His name was T. Nelson Downs and he was the usher of the Universe . . ."

And if they leave? I can hear you asking. If they walk away? I'm not too worried. There'll always be others. And some will listen.